What readers are saying about *I, W*...

'**Cracking thriller** and a ... ing, smoking, rock-music lovin... **My kind of woman**' C... *Ian*

'I was swept away by this **punchy, pacy thriller** . . . I **devoured** it in a single day'

Helen Callaghan, author of *Dear Amy*

'Tough and uncompromising, *I, Witness* had me **totally gripped**. I'm looking forward to hearing more from PI Madison Attallee' Alex Lake, author of *Killing Kate*

'Cutting-edge **gripping**' Sam King, author of *The Choice*

'An **absolutely gripping thriller** founded on the horror of familial abuse and a great, flawed, female PI'

Dame Jenni Murray

'Totally engaging, **fast-paced** and **edgy** . . . completely captivating. *I, Witness* **kept me guessing till the very end**'

Elle Croft, author of *The Guilty Wife*

'**I couldn't put *I, Witness* down**. A hugely accomplished novel with a dark, sad story at its heart . . . A **2018 must-read**'

Phoebe Morgan, author of *The Doll House*

'**Had me hooked within two pages**, it has every bit as much appeal as some of the bestsellers of the last few years, like ***Girl on the Train***'

Robert Scragg, author of *What Falls Between the Cracks*

Niki Mackay studied Performing Arts at the BRIT School, where it turned out she wasn't very good at acting but quite liked writing scripts. She holds a BA (Hons) in English Literature and Drama, and won a full scholarship for her MA in Journalism. *I, Witness* is the debut novel in the Madison Attallee series.

To find out more follow Niki on Twitter @NikiMackayBooks or visit her website nikimackay.com

I,
Witness

NIKI MACKAY

ORION

An Orion paperback

First published in Great Britain in 2018
by Orion
This paperback edition published in 2018
by Orion Books,
an imprint of The Orion Publishing Group Ltd
Carmelite House, 50 Victoria Embankment
London EC4Y 0DZ

An Hachette UK Company

1 3 5 7 9 10 8 6 4 2

A CIP catalogue record for this book is
available from the British Library.

ISBN 978 1 4091 7461 5

Typeset by Input Data Services Ltd, Somerset

Printed and bound in Great Britain
by Clays Ltd, Elcograf S.p.A.

www.orionbooks.co.uk

To Andrew, for telling me I could

Prologue

2005

I am a terrible mother. I wasn't even good at being pregnant. I spent each trimester in a state of shock. I saw other mums-to-be, smugly patting their burgeoning bellies whilst I was horrified by every new swollen millimetre. It is an awful thing to be scared of your own children. When they arrived, they overwhelmed me, exhausted me. I was never sure I wanted them but there they were anyway. An accompaniment to a husband I desperately needed. Always more his achievement than mine. My gift to the man who had rescued me. The offering of life for the one he had saved. It's all I had to give him.

The first nanny was a naturally maternal girl. Young and full of life, robust and energetic. I found her in our bed. I didn't blame him. Poor James was sadder than I was. She was gone the next day. I could have replaced her. I could even have kept her. I didn't resent either of them, not for the affair anyway.

It was the looks she gave me, half-pity, half-disgust. Her head in my husband's lap was just an excuse. She was too present, too near. She noticed when the children touched me and I flinched. They ran to her instead of me, her arms were wide open waiting to gather them up in hugs and kisses. She saw my relief. She knew.

I am sitting, sweating. My back pressed to the wall, knees

raised. Tense eyes, so like my own, are watching me, waiting. I vomit. It's uncontrollable. Hot acid spilling everywhere on my open legs, seeping through my nightgown into my already wet knickers. My bowels open, the smell is disgusting. I cough, heave, retch. I'm losing consciousness. Soon I will choke. I can't fight, I was never in with a chance. I'll be found here, not dressed, drenched in my own bodily expulsions. The pills and vodka are on the table. Only one conclusion will be drawn. So obvious. I was almost born for suicide. All the signs were there after all. Someone like me: fragile, breakable, a victim.

I sentenced myself to this. I am drifting and then something brings me back. It's my child's hand on my shoulder, pulling me up, pinning me to the wall. I don't flinch this time, I don't have the strength. I meet clear, bright eyes. We lock, just for a moment. I see a face filled with curiosity. The mouth turns up at the corners. A smile that chills me and I am held there in time, inanimate, frozen. An intimate moment for all the wrong reasons. My eyes shut for the last time.

I hear singing. A lullaby I used to sing, when I had the energy, to the very person humming it now, watching while the life drains out of me. Lots of things are running through my mind. The outcomes of different choices, ones I hadn't made. I made the wrong ones. This is the price of my weakness, so very, very high. I think I am sick again. I think my body shakes, my back slides down, my head hits the ground, a cold slap against my cheek. I hear a voice say 'Goodbye, Mummy' and then everything is black.

The Surrey Comet

Mother's distress as her child's killer moves back to the Borough

Teenage killer, Kate Reynolds, 24, has moved back to Kingston after serving six years of a twelve-year sentence for voluntary manslaughter.

Ms Reynolds was just 18 when she pleaded guilty to stabbing Naomi Andrews in 2010. It was a crime that shook the nation, not just because of its brutality, but also due to the tender age of the victim, 17, and her killer.

Despite a petition led by the victim's mother, Anthea Andrews, the convicted killer is 'allowed to live where she chooses' according to Judge Marstam who set out the rules of her release.

Mrs Andrews said: 'I am disgusted to think that I might bump into Naomi's murderer at any time. It's bad enough that my daughter is dead. I am saddened and outraged by the court's decision.'

Naomi Andrews was stabbed 13 times whilst attending a party at the Reynolds' family home. Ms Reynolds pleaded guilty to voluntary manslaughter and was given the maximum sentence.

A toxicology report showed both girls had consumed large quantities of pharmaceutical amphetamines and alcohol. Mrs Andrews said, 'The sentence should have been longer'.

We will be looking back over the case online this week and would like your views. Email us at editor@surreycomet.com.

1.

Madison Attallee

Emma says my name softly. The same way she says everything. When I look up she is standing, holding out a coffee for me. I grunt and signal for her to put it on my desk. Then I realise there really isn't enough space. I sweep a pile of papers to the other side. I scowl and she walks off, head down. I congratulate myself on failing yet again to be pleasant. It's weird having a PA. She always seems to be everywhere all at once. Being efficient and useful. I can't complain; she does all the shit I'm useless at, and then some. I'll nip out soon and when I come back my desk will be clear and ordered. Little neat stacks topped with Post-it notes so I know what's what. I'll hunt for a specific piece of paper and she'll know exactly where it is. Better still, she'll have put it into digital format and filed it electronically as well. I sigh again. The sigh of an ungrateful bitch.

'Going for a smoke.'

'Righty-ho.'

Who fucking says that? Righty-ho. Outside I light up and inhale. Relief floods my body as the craving is satisfied, I feel my shoulders drop. I look back at my odd little office. It's a large brick hut. I like it more than I care to admit and it's minutes away from my shit flat. But it's not what I'm used to and, God help me, I miss the station. I miss the bustle, the

5

people, the status. Fuck, maybe I miss the status most of all.

I used to laugh at private investigators. We all did. The rogue wannabes, either not good enough, or too old to do the real job. Yet here I am. In my sixth month, on my fourth marriage-wrecking case. I should be glad of the work. I get told this endlessly. *Aren't you lucky? You can pick your own hours, no boss and none of the nasty stuff, eh.* All correct, but the real truth is the company's almost broke, before it's even got started. And I miss it. The boss, the long hours, the team. I miss the nasty stuff, and I miss the feeling of being at home somewhere in the world. I feel rudderless here, in my breeze-block office with efficient Emma and my hysterical clients. Desperate housewives.

In all of my cases so far I've advised them they probably don't need my services. 'You're mad, talking yourself out of money,' I was told by a well-meaning friend. But I also tell them, if you think something's wrong, it probably is. In one instance it wasn't an affair though. Her husband had been sneaking around all right, but his ladylove was the race tracks and casinos. I'm not sure which is worse. At least the spouses of the cheaters will get some cash. This poor woman had none left to get. She was relieved nonetheless. I don't think she realised gambling would probably be stiffer competition than another woman. He's in rehab now, the husband. There's rehab for fucking everything these days. I don't think about it. I flick my fag and head back in.

I'm bored, which I hate. I hover over Emma pointlessly; she is tapping away at her keyboard. I ask how her weekend was and she offers me a pleasant smile. Apparently it was good. She went for a lovely walk and a pub lunch with her partner. She asks how mine was and I mumble that it was okay and skulk back to my own desk. I don't tell her I was here for most of it. She probably knows. My case notes are up-to-date. She's likely transcribing them now. I think of other weekends, ones filled with Molly and Rob. The temporary bit of my life when I was almost happy. Almost.

I slurp at my coffee and spit it back into the mug. It's cold. Emma's there in seconds with a fresh cup, removing the old one. For fuck's sake. I smile thanks and open emails. I have a news alert from the *Comet*. Kate Reynolds. Jeez, there's a blast from the past. I skim the article and then go back over some of the historical pieces in a bit more detail. One of my first cases. I was a rookie then. Just out of uniform, new to murder. In my trial period and desperate to be taken onto the team.

I was sent along to secure the scene, as I happened to be close by. I nearly threw up when I walked in. I'd never seen so much blood in my life. It wasn't my first dead body, not by a long shot. But there is a difference between the accidental deaths you find on the road, or the oldies in their beds, and what I saw that day. This was rage. Human nature at its most disgusting.

There was a girl in the middle of the floor. She was the one bleeding. But that day she managed not to be the main event. Not for me, anyway. Kate Reynolds was the star. Half smiling at me as I walked in, her hands gripped into the other girl's dead flesh, the knife grazing her knee as she rocked back and forth. She was gibbering. Whispering. My colleague and I, another newbie who was not quite lucky enough to hold his lunch down, watched for what must have been a full minute before we did anything. And then I woke up and knew I had to move the girl, the living one, away. I knelt down and spoke to her.

Her glazed eyes turned on me. She was still chattering but making no sense. Soaked in blood and that half-smile. She told me it was the wrong face. When I asked what she meant she held the dead chin and angled it towards me. I resisted the urge to smack her hand away. 'It's not her, it just looks like her.'

Shock had her in its confused grip, muddied further by being high. Eventually I prised her off and got her out. The Scene of Crime officers came in and started their business. I walked the bloody girl through the now cleared house. There were teenagers littering the lawn, by this time pushed back behind yellow police tape. They whispered amongst themselves as they watched, a gruesome sight.

She was treated for shock, albeit briefly. Taken in for questioning, and then she was charged. I was surprised when she was sent down for voluntary manslaughter. There was a madness on her that day that was as far away from a sound mind as you could get. She was confused, and had dissociated herself from reality and certainly from her dead friend, muttering over and over, 'It just looks like her.' As though it must all be some kind of dreadful mistake. But the case stuck. I've followed it over the past five years. Articles debating evil often reference it. I don't believe in evil people as such. I don't think it's born, which means it must be created. Something that makes the hand and the mind warp. The outcome being scenes like that.

It was my first nasty. There would be plenty more. Not now though. Now I am part of the home-wrecking network. Part of the universal paranoia. All the worse because it is justified. Hurrah for the digital age.

I wonder why Kate has moved back to Kingston. Had she headed anywhere else, changed her name, she could have started afresh. As I recall she came from wealthy stock. Maybe she'd been cut off. Although it seems unlikely probation would have housed her here. Maybe she doesn't know where else to go. Maybe she's just plain stupid. It's a funny place, this town. A large borough that straddles both London and Surrey. It has a reasonably big population but it's close-knit nonetheless. The *Surrey Comet* is one of the few local papers in the city that is

8

still widely read. Kate will get shit for this. There isn't a recent photo accompanying the article. Just the same one from 2010, of an angel-faced blonde child. It was that image that stayed on the front pages for months, contrasted next to Naomi Andrews. Equally stunning but dark haired, dark eyed.

It was the story that had it all. Drugs, murder, a wealthy party lifestyle, and at its very heart two beautiful young girls. The public loved it. And now it was resurrected. Stupid she must be, plain dumb-ass stupid.

I wake up before my alarm goes off. When I get outside it's drizzling. I get soaked on my way to the car which gives me the hump before I even arrive. I make notes, email them to Emma. I file a couple of invoices. There's nobody to spy on right now. Surveillance is the highlight of my working day. The bit where I'm not tied to my shitty desk doing mundane tasks. Emma smiles and waves goodbye promptly at five thirty p.m., to go I don't know where. I should know that by now, for God's sake. I don't know if she lives alone, with friends, parents. She talks about a partner, maybe with them? I don't know if that's a boyfriend or a girlfriend. I assume she has a social life. She can't be more than thirty, though she has the air of someone far older and wiser. Fuck. I make a mental note to try harder. I wouldn't want to lose her. She's actually very good. She's also not put off by me, which is a bonus.

I should be out of here in about half an hour. I've pretty much spent the day trying to figure out how other PIs make a living and if I can handle a life of fraud investigations and divorces. If the alternative is security I guess I'll have to at least give being a PI a try; I worked bloody hard to get out of uniform and I'm in no hurry to put one back on. These thoughts are depressing me and I'm gasping for a cigarette but its dark outside and starting to rain again. I slip off my shoes and climb onto my desk in stockinged feet. It's now actually illegal to smoke on a work premises. For fuck's sake. I sweep the window open as wide as it will go and lean out. Fucking stupid smoking laws. I light up and relief hits all the good places. I'm halfway through when I hear the door click open followed by an 'Oh'.

I drop the fag out of the window and turn, frown in place, expecting Emma, but it's not. The woman standing in the doorway is petite, dirty-blonde hair, probably mid-twenties, poorly dressed in some sort of hideous sportswear. Her outfit seems at odds with the rest of her. Neat hair. Neat small features. I'm now squatting on my desk, no shoes, exhaling a puff of smoke. I wish Emma was here. I'm still scowling as I climb down. My shoes are on the other side of the desk. I try to look business-like nonetheless.

'Can I help you?'

She asks, 'Are you Detective Inspector Attallee?'

'I'm Madison Attallee. This is my private investigation company. I'm no longer with the police.'

She frowns but it makes her look nervous rather than cross. 'Yes, well, I knew that.'

'Can I help you?' I glance at my watch. Six forty-five.

'Oh well, I don't know. Sorry to come so late.' She's familiar, though I can't pinpoint it. I wait.

She goes on, 'You don't remember me?'

'No, I don't think I do.'

'Kate Reynolds.' She says it quietly with just the right amount of shame injected into the words. Then I see it. She's still waiflike, too skinny even, not that I can talk. Her hair is darker, shorter. She looks older. Of course she does. She was a child last time I saw her. A blood-covered child.

'Right, and how can I help you?'

'You're not scared?'

I shrug and resist laughing. 'I'm more worried about getting a smoking fine, to be honest.' I reckon I have a few pounds on her.

She smiles and I see that she is still pretty underneath the premature worry lines.

'What do you want?' I ask.

'I want help.'

'Don't do bodyguard services if that's what you're after.'

She's frowning now. 'No, that hadn't occurred to me. Gosh.'

Gosh. Six years in prison hasn't removed all the plummy-ness, though her voice is definitely rougher, less refined. I remember her clipped tones. Her startled confusion.

'Then what is it?' I look at my watch again, openly this time. I might have all kinds of places to be. She doesn't know any different.

'I . . . I'd like to hire you.' Her voice is low, her eyes are carefully trained on the floor.

I nearly laugh, but she looks serious, so I don't. 'What the hell for?'

'I think I'm innocent.'

2.

Kate Reynolds

She's just staring at me, with piercing, bright blue eyes. I think I might have made a mistake. This whole thing is probably a mistake. My brother Marcus called me earlier. His overly concerned voice: Am I okay? Had I seen the paper? All code for 'What the hell are you doing here?' and 'Please do us a favour and go away again.' Maybe that's exactly what I should be doing. I could go somewhere, anywhere. A nondescript little town. Not another country. My licence won't allow for that. Somewhere near the sea. I used to like water. I'm about to turn around and go when she stands, walking around the desk and stepping into impossible-looking stilettos. I try not to flinch as she passes me. She runs a hand through an already wild mane of bleached hair and gestures at me. I think she means for me to take a seat and I do. She slumps back behind her desk, frowns and pulls out a pad and pen.

She's waiting for me to start, but now I have no idea what to say. I sit dumb and silent.

'What's changed?' she asks.

I take a deep breath and say it aloud: 'Nothing.'

She leans back, arms folded, eyes narrowed. She's quite pretty in a sharp, cross sort of a way. She's model thin, not scrawny like me. My memory is of someone softer. Kinder.

Another deep breath. The truth will set you free. I've read that somewhere. It's been running amok in my brain for months. Lying in a cell, on a metal-framed prison bed dreaming of being free. But what if you don't know the truth? How will you find freedom then? I made it here. I'm asking for help; I so want to be free.

I tell her, 'I remember coming into the room.'

Her shoulders sag a little. She looks disappointed. It doesn't sound like much. 'Okay, well I'm sure it's great that you're starting to get your memory back,' she says, 'but I can't see how this in any way equals your innocence.'

'She was already there. Lying on the floor. I remember not knowing that . . . that she was there, if you see what I mean. Then I knelt down and held her.' I can almost feel the weight of her body on my knees as I describe it. The sickly wet feel of her blood, spilling and still warm. I remember looking at her face and wondering what was wrong with her. So much of Naomi had been tied up in her expressions. A raised eyebrow, a puckered mouth, haughty and disapproving. She had looked almost kind that night, relaxed and benevolent. Covered in blood. I shut my eyes, inhale, exhale. When I open them again Madison is staring at me. Her mouth is set, a deep line runs between her eyebrows while she takes me in.

We are silent. A minute passes, maybe two, or maybe just seconds. I meet her gaze, unwavering, but my heart is pounding.

Her eyes narrow. 'She was already dead?'

'Yes.'

'How do you know it's not fake? Something your memory made up. I'm sure you'd like it to be true.'

'I don't.'

She runs a hand through her hair. She's still looking at me suspiciously. 'Don't what?'

'I don't know. Not for sure. Everything was a blur from

13

getting arrested to the end of the trial. I think I was . . .' I search for the words, 'not thinking properly.' I feel tears prick at the back of my eyes. I blink them away.

'You confessed.'

I nod. 'I know.'

'Why?'

'I thought I must be guilty. The evidence said I was guilty, I was still drunk when I was arrested, my memory was hazy at best and . . .' I pause, I have to say it. 'I wanted her to be dead.'

'Best mates, eh?' She's half smiling and it takes a bit of the hardness out of her face. I don't smile back. She says, 'Shrink said you weren't fit to stand trial?'

'Yes, he's been very supportive.' This is an understatement. Without Dean I don't think I would have survived the past six years. He's been more than a therapist, more than a friend. Like family. How family should be.

'You've brought this up with your lawyer?'

'I did, a few months into my sentence. She said we could appeal but we'd be unlikely to win. My father refused to pay her anymore so it became irrelevant anyway.'

'Wow, tough call from Dad. Why didn't you go to the police?'

'Why? It's not hard evidence. I'm not stupid. I know it's not enough to reopen the case or I'd have tried harder. I'm telling you.' I hear a pleading edge creep into my voice.

'So I can investigate?'

'Yes.'

'What if I don't believe you?'

'I'm not asking you to. I'll pay you either way. Whether I'm right or wrong.'

'Why on earth would I want to work with a criminal I helped lock up?'

'Maybe you need the money?' I've done my research. I've

followed this woman's career. The ridiculous high, rising through the ranks in record time. The humiliating series of lows that ended it. I remember her opening my fingers, standing me up, walking me from my house, her arm around my shoulders, talking. I don't remember what she said but the tone was kind. It was the last kindness I would receive for a long time.

She's staring at me with those piercing eyes. They are an intense shade of blue and seem to look right into me. I tell myself she's not a mind reader and I resist the urge to fidget. 'I'm expensive,' she says.

'I know; I called earlier for a rough idea. Money's no object. I'll pay you twice your daily rate.' At least the money is there. To be honest I'm not entirely sure Dad had a choice. I know there was inheritance due to me from my mother's death that I would have collected around the time I was arrested. It had been written into her will that we ought to be provided for in case of her death. As if she knew, which I suppose she did. I want to believe it's from him though, a sign that he cares.

'To do what? Investigate a memory that may or may not be real?' Madison asks.

'If you like.'

She shrugs. 'Why does it matter?'

'Because if I didn't kill her, it changes everything.'

'You want what? An apology? A clean record? Clearly you have money – why not just disappear, change your name, start over?'

'I don't want to. I want to find out who killed her, and why.'

'What if you're wrong?'

'Then nothing's changed. Then I'll deal with it.' I don't know if that's true but hopefully I look like I mean it.

There is another long silence. It stretches out. I hold my nerve, her gaze. She drums long, thin fingers on the table in front of her. Once, twice. I can hear the clock on the wall tick. I say, 'Please.'

She shrugs again. 'It's your money to waste.'

I resist the urge to hug her.

What I remember most about that night isn't the blood or the gore; the horror of flesh ripped open. It's not that I've forgotten it. Of course I haven't. The gruesome images still fill my head at least once a day. Sometimes when I'm awake, more often penetrating my nightmares. But they are fading now, altered by the hands of time. One thing that never changes though is the look on her face. Almost peaceful. Almost alive. Kinder somehow than she usually looked. If anyone had ever perfected resting-bitch face, it was Naomi, but that drained away with her life, or so it seemed to me. I remember holding that face, confused, not quite understanding what had happened. I kept talking to her, asking what was wrong. Even after the police officer arrived, I don't think I got it. Hours later when I was locked in the cell, in and out of an interrogation room, it sank in. She was dead. Gone, not coming back. The feel of it cut through everything else. Crystal clear.

The first thing I felt, when I realised she was dead, was relief. But then came the guilt.

I've only been out a day. Everything is odd. I waited yesterday at the prison gates for my release. My stomach was like a bile-filled washing machine. My hands were sweating. Dean Hall, my therapist, was waiting for me. He took me from the prison gates to Kingston in a sleek black car. It was overwhelming, intoxicating, and scary. I'm still heady, unsure how to pursue it. Freedom. The sharp, exquisite taste of it. I saw him stealing glances at me in the car, checking. I drank in everything, houses, shops, people, cars whizzing past the other way at what seemed to be five hundred miles an hour. I opened the window, listened to noises that seemed new and deafening. Eventually, things started to become familiar. Bus stops I had stood at, a pub that used to serve us underage – streets I had walked along, before.

I was heading to a flat owned by my dad. I'm lucky in that respect. Although he hasn't spoken to me for over five years, he seems happy to share the comfort of his finances, though not for a lawyer. I should be grateful for the money, the stability – and I am. I really am. But I want his love more. When Dean finally parked, stepped out and opened my door, I found myself frozen, stuck to the seat. He reached down, gently encircling my arm with his hand, and helped me out. Proper out. Fresh air with no walls. A woman walked by and I jumped. He kept hold of me, walking me to my door, handing me the keys, making me open it myself.

I should be relieved. To be out. And God knows I'm glad to get out of that cell. I'm glad not to have to listen to other women fighting, crying, shouting. But the thought of a new and better life still feels out of reach, like I can just about see it but I'm not allowed to touch.

I hate being here, if I'm honest. It's giving me the creeps, the whole town. Everywhere I turn feels familiar and strange. When this is over I'll leave and never come back.

3.

Madison Attallee

What a fucking weird one. I feel like I should call it in, run it past a superior, but I no longer have one. And also, fuck them, right? I'm at home. My stupid cat is trying to kill me every time I move. She's literally everywhere I'm about to put my foot. Dumb creature. She's Molly's actually. If she wasn't I'd drown her, or at least give her away. I'm going to keep her. As some kind of lure. She's what I got out of the divorce. Actually, that's a lie. I got money. Not as much as I put in. Enough for my shithole flat and my crappy office. But I didn't get any of the stuff. None of the familiar items that make a life. Rob got it all. I agreed to it when Molly said she wanted to stay with him. Not that the courts were likely to grant me custody anyway, even if she'd wanted to come with me. Either way, I didn't have the heart to have saddled her with the world's crappiest mum and then start taking away bits of the life she had left as well. Apparently the cat missed me. I reckon Rob couldn't be arsed to feed her. He never wanted the damn thing anyway.

I look in the fridge. It's pretty bare so I brew a pot of coffee and light a cigarette in place of dinner, then I switch on the computer and start googling Kate Reynolds. Nothing new. The latest article was the one I read earlier. Heavy on sensationalism, light on facts. I worked the case under DS Tom

Malone. I was impressed with him at the time. He seemed in control and unfazed. A few cases later and with a bit of experience my opinion changed. Two years ago we both went for the same promotion. I got it. He never let it go. Until now. Now he's probably gloating. He finally made DI, albeit by default. He's the kind of man who doesn't much care how he wins. Whatever. I light another cigarette. The smoke stings my eyes. I squint at the screen. So many pictures. Kate smiling at the camera. Very good-looking, on the cusp of adulthood. Everything to look forward to. Naomi, all dark curly hair and bright white teeth. Best friends. Inseparable, by all accounts.

Naomi sounded like a bitch, according to just about everyone we interviewed, though since her death she's been depicted as white as the driven snow. Often the way. Apparently she'd had a few boyfriends on the go, one of them Kate's brother. We never did find the others, though admittedly we didn't look too hard.

There's a rather vile piece in one of the nationals about genetic mental health problems. It details the history of issues in Kate's family, namely her mother who committed suicide, and her older sister Martha who has been institutionalised several times. It must have been an awful time for the Reynolds family already. Having had my own taste of tabloid fame I can imagine the damage. There's a quote from Kate's headmistress, Mrs Anselm, stating she felt the family were 'never quite right'. I remember sitting in on her interview. A chilly, formidable woman. Mostly concerned about the reflection Naomi's death would have on her school. An exclusive fee-paying establishment, Warrene Academy is set in beautiful grounds and steeped in privilege. A far cry from the grey breeze-blocked comprehensive I attended. I didn't like the feel of it though. The place had the same coldness as its headmistress.

I remember Naomi's family. She had been a doted-on only

child. Her mother Anthea was one of those child-centric yummy mummies. She must have had Naomi in her early forties and from what I gathered later on, Naomi was an IVF baby and the Andrews had been trying for a long time. She broke when we turned up at the door. That extra sense that mums have just knew why we were there before we even said a word. Naomi's father left the room. I pause for a moment letting the horror of that day sink in. I work for the victim, after all, no matter who's paying.

I think about Naomi. Forcing an image of her messy body at the scene into my mind. Later, clean and sterile, lying on a mortuary slab. Her mother losing it during the ID, a wailing sound escaping from her, more animal than human. Her little girl. Her baby. Half-child, half-woman – lifeless. Everyone deserves justice. I see Kate with her hands curled like claws; I remember prising those fingers open, the half-moon crescent cuts post-mortem from where her nails dug in as she had held her friend. Kate had been confused, dissociated. She didn't seem to recognise Naomi.

Later she sat in the interrogation room, no time for a shower, she was bloody and raw. Red soaked through a cream-coloured party dress. Laddered tights fed into sparkly high heels. The remnants of a night of fun gone horribly wrong. She looked tiny, sad, bewildered and said she couldn't remember what happened. We hadn't spent long looking into it. Why would we? A confession, then Kate's journal. Awful handwritten descriptions of a death that later came to fruition. Everything so neat, handed to us with all the loose ends neatly tied. Well, mostly.

I felt at the time we'd let her down. I couldn't have articulated it though. It wasn't that I thought she hadn't done it, though we never looked at any other possibilities, I just wasn't sure she was culpable. Ultimately, it's always the facts that decide where the guilt lies. My job is to unearth all the facts. To dig through the lives of the players, brush away the soil and see what's left. I'm not convinced we did enough digging.

Despite myself, I feel a thrill; my head is whirring. Ideas are flitting, just out of reach for now but there nonetheless. I switch off the computer, smoke another couple of cigarettes and for the first time in a long time my eyes close shortly after my head hits the pillow.

4.

Kate Reynolds

Oliver was my obsession. I thought about him every waking moment. When it first started, I was barely sixteen. Everything at home was falling apart. Marcus stropped around. Martha was almost catatonic half the time and my dad was an empty vessel. Weighted down by grief and inadequacy. I'd spend hours lying there just thinking about Oli. When would I next see him? When would he call? Should I call him? Dean said he had been a distraction from the bigger problems, the ones at home.

Then there was Naomi. One night in the pub I got there late and she was at the bar, a hand on his arm, a smile on her face. He was smiling back, leaning in close. I sidled over, slid myself between them, my back pressed against his body. She'd laughed and I'd wanted to hit her, hard in the face. I didn't though, it wasn't my style. It still isn't. I've thought more than once over the past six years that it would have been better if I'd been dead and Naomi had been in prison. She would have dealt with it, fought back. Not crumbled under the taunts of 'posh bitch'. She would have stood up for herself. Like I should have stood up to her. But I hadn't, even when she was all over my boyfriend. I'd smiled and danced and pretended everything was okay, because she was my other obsession. At the time it felt like they were the only people I had.

The night of the party Naomi had been on particularly fine form. She'd been cheating on my brother, Marcus, who thought he was head-over-heels in love with her. She wouldn't say who with but he'd found evidence. When he confronted her earlier that evening, red-faced with his anger, she'd just laughed. We'd argued. I'd backed down but it had ruined my mood, made me reckless and cross. I'd drunk more quickly than I usually would, taken more drugs. Trying to keep up with her, impress her, match her drink for drink, line for line, whereas usually I was cautious.

At some point she'd disappeared. I went looking for her, high as a kite. Everything was blurred around the edges. I was shouting her name, opening doors, giggling, unsteady and obnoxious. I passed Marcus on the stairs. He was topless, looking worse for wear, ready to hurl. And then I found her. I was almost triumphant when I swung open the door and saw her sitting there. And then everything stopped, it seemed to take me ages to notice. Or maybe it didn't, maybe it was just a second or two. Drug-time, drunk-time, unreal-time. I closed the door behind me. I don't know why. I pressed my back to it and sank down. I recall wooden floorboards on my shins, snagging my tights, then crawling to her slowly, slowly and then I was holding her head in my arms, fascinated with her face which was not right, wet blood soaking into me. I remember thinking she'd finally got what she deserved and yet I couldn't think how I'd done it.

Now I've taken a step towards proving what I know to be true, that no matter how much I might have wished her dead, wishing hadn't killed her.

My body clock is well programmed to wake up at six a.m. I doubt I'll ever sleep any later, but I am not getting up this morning. No one is rattling at my door. It's completely silent and everything around me is fresh. I breathe in and out. When

I was first locked up I'd had a cellmate. She quickly worked out that I was 'prison rich'. This isn't exactly the same as being actually rich. There's only so much you have access to, but my family had money. My dad cut all contact, but still sent in the maximum amount every week, fifteen pounds. Doesn't sound like much but you can buy a lot of drugs and booze for that inside and my cellmate wanted both. I wasn't the same as the other women. Women who shouted and swore. I was a jumpy, nervous wreck. I find my hand running along various scars on my body, ones I didn't have six years ago.

I am interrupted from these thoughts by a ringing sound; it makes me jump and I can't think what it is. I'm up and looking for its source. It goes again, shrill and obtrusive. I see something that looks like a phone by the door lighting up red. I pick it up.

'Hello?'

'Kate, it's me, I've been ringing for bloody ages. Buzz me in.'

'How?'

'What?'

'How do I buzz you in?'

A pause. 'Hold down the button.' I look and do as he says. I hear a click, and then soon enough a knock at my front door.

My hand leaves a wet imprint on the handle as I turn it. I'm wiping the sweat off my palm and onto my leg as he appears. My big brother. He has written me a letter every month for the past six years but he hasn't visited. None of them have. The one time I called him, he refused to take the call. The only visitor I got was Dean. The letters from Marcus were mundane mostly, relaying details of his own progress, my father's company, my sister's ongoing mental health issues. Often he would repeat himself. He has sent me pictures. Photos of the wedding I missed, his wife, the spitting image of our mother, his daughter who's now nearly three. My niece.

I wondered why he bothered but I treasured every word, every photo, hungrily devouring all the news and was too scared to ask in case he removed me entirely. Like my dad. I responded, of course. At first I bombarded him, with emotion, with crap, pouring my heart out. Asking a million questions, telling him I was scared. Trying to add a depth to our relationship that had never been there.

And now here he is, at the door.

'Hello, Kate.' He was nearly twenty-three when I last saw him. Into adulthood but still gangly. The years have been good to him. He is well dressed. Polished. He's lost the unsure hunch he used to have. I stand for a moment, not certain what to do next, and he reaches down and holds me, just for a second. I'm sure it feels as awkward for him as it is for me. But I squeeze back as hard as I can.

He has a bag and heads to my kitchen. He starts unpacking things I hadn't thought of – bread, milk, tea bags. 'Claudia suggested I bring a few essentials for you. We didn't know if it would occur to you. I don't suppose you did your own shopping in there.' He says 'in there' with distaste.

The last items are two mugs. He fills the kettle and makes us tea, waving sugar and milk at me in question. I stand watching him, drinking him in. Bombarded by memories. He places the two cups on the table and gestures for me to sit.

I say, 'You look well.'

He smiles. 'You look bloody thin – just like Martha. Your hair's dark.'

'I dyed it. How is she? Martha?'

He holds my gaze. 'As well as she ever is.'

The last time I saw her was the day of the party. She had been on a stay away on the actual night. Stay away was family code for the nuthouse. Dad was tying up a deal in Bristol. I guess he knew Marcus and I wouldn't manage her.

'Is she in the same place?

He sighs. 'Sometimes she's at home.'

'With Dad?'

He nods. 'We can't have her, we have Bethany.' His voice is defensive though I've made no accusation. 'She's in Sandcross at the moment.' A psychiatric ward dressed as a spa.

'I'd like to see her.'

He avoids my gaze but nods. 'You should call ahead when she's there and let her know you're coming. I've printed her details, and mine . . . addresses, numbers.' He hands me a sheet with typed information on it. Not Dad's though.

He clears his throat. 'You'll need to get a mobile phone. I trust the bank card and what-have-you arrived?'

'Yes. Thank Dad, will you?'

'Sure.'

'How are you, Marcus?'

He gives me a million-dollar grin, baring perfectly straight, suspiciously bright, white teeth. 'Life's good.'

'What's Bethany like?'

He shrugs. 'I think she's great but I'm biased.' He sips at his tea, the grin dissolving to be replaced by discomfort, and suddenly he says, 'Why are you here, Kate?'

And it's like being sucker-punched in the gut. 'Are you not pleased to see me?'

'It's not that.'

'But you were hoping never to see me again?'

'Not here, Kate. I wasn't expecting to see you here.'

I sigh. 'I know.'

'Do you? It was pretty awful after you were locked up. Fucking press hounding us endlessly. Bringing up all kinds of shit. Dad went all silent, stopped working and I had to take over. I mean, clients were leaving us left, right and centre.'

'How inconvenient.'

'Right, it was.' He misses my sarcasm. 'Now it's okay. Business has improved, we've bounced back. I married Claudia – I have her and Bethany to think about.'

'And now I'm back stirring stuff up?'

He sighs. 'Have you thought about us at all?'

'Of course I have. I've thought about all of you every day for six years. I've missed you.'

He seems intent on studying the contents of his cup.

'None of you came.'

He stands up, walks to my sink, empties out and rinses his mug. Ignoring the accusation in my voice. He says, 'I'm worried about Bethany being affected, so is Dad.' He looks again at the now clean mug, avoiding my eyes.

I wonder if my father is the same way with her that he was with us. I wonder if he gathers her up in his arms and swings her round and round until she's so dizzy she can't walk. I hope so. I sip at my own tea; it's starting to get cold.

'I'd like to meet her.'

'Bethany?'

'Yes, and Claudia.'

'Claudia obviously has some reservations.'

'The killer in the family, worse than your average black sheep, I guess.'

He flinches.

'What's she like?'

He smiles then. 'Claudia?'

'Yes.'

'She looks like Mum.'

'I thought that when I saw your wedding pictures.'

He sort of chuckles. 'I'm sure Freud would have a field day with me.'

'Is she . . .?'

He shakes his head. 'God no, she's a great mother. Dotes on Bethany.'

'Will you have any more?'

He nods. 'Probably. We don't want her being an only child.'

'Must be fun being a daddy?'

He stands, wandering around the small galley kitchen. When he stretches upwards he almost fills the whole space. 'I'll arrange dinner.'

'What?'

'For you to come around . . . for dinner.'

I feel my pulse pick up. 'I'd love that. Do you think Dad will come?'

'No,' he answers quickly. I feel a familiar stab, the pain that I can't indulge or it takes over. I think of climbing my dad like a frame, of hugging him and thinking he must be a giant. I think of his face at the police station while they questioned me. How wretched he looked in court, pale and baffled. The last time I saw him.

'I've got to get to work.' He points at the printed sheet of paper. 'Text me from your mobile when you have it, to that number.'

'Okay.'

He pauses at the door as if there's something else but nothing comes. Just a nod and then he's gone. I've missed him. I always loved Marcus more than he loved me. He could be cruel, my brother. I suppose all children can, but he was angry with it. At Mum, I think, but he'd turn it on me. I used to trail around after him anyway, looking to play, to hold on. I've missed his wedding, his child. The letters he sent weren't warm, he might have been relaying information to a stranger. Worse than that though was my dad's silence. So absolute and unbreakable. I'd left messages on his answering machine. Begging for forgiveness. Telling him I was frightened. Asking him to come.

My mother, Ruth, killed herself when I was thirteen. It's not an excuse for anything. I tried to use it one of the first times I met my therapist Dean, a get-out clause for my messed up head.

Dean laughed when I told him the dead mum story, actually laughed. I was used to people's sympathy. When he'd stopped cackling he pointed out that shit happens. I spent the rest of the session sitting in miserable, fuming silence. I had no intention of seeing him again but it was court ordered and the boredom of long days got me talking in the end. Despite hating him to begin with, he has become my only friend.

I take off my pyjamas and dressing gown and put on the greying, awful, prison-issued underwear from my backpack and my second tracksuit. This is pretty much the sum of my wardrobe.

I head into town. Walking slowly, the noise builds up the closer I get to the centre and I tread carefully, trying not to let the sounds bombard me. People whizz past and I jump each time.

I recognise Topshop and head in. In prison, I quickly realised it didn't matter what I wore. I stopped looking in the mirror the day Naomi died anyway. I found it hard to meet my own eyes in the early days of being locked up; I never knew if it was a killer looking back. Then it became habit. Now in the noisy communal changing rooms I'm looking hard. New start, new behaviour. Plus, no one's going to steal my clothes out here. I sneak glances at some of the other girls and women. Lots my age. I look like them. Normal. I look normal in jeans and a T-shirt. I pay and ask if I can change there. The girl at the till looks at me like I'm a bit odd but nods. I ball up the tracksuit, the trainers, the shabby underwear and chuck it all in the nearest bin outside.

I buy a phone next. They do a million different things now

and I am overwhelmed by the salesman's talk of apps and camera settings. I opt for the simplest one available. He sets it up for me in the shop, grudgingly, I guess disappointed by my choice and its accompanying low price. I also buy a laptop and when I get home I google Oliver. He's on something called LinkedIn. There is a photo of him. Too small for detail but I feel my heart race nonetheless. I sign up and send him a message.

5.

Madison Attallee

I wake up short of breath. My hand fires out of my bed, reaching for the bedside table, ferreting, searching. Where is it? And then I realise for the umpteenth time – it's not real. The vodka isn't there. It was a dream. I've been having them since I sobered up. They're an absolute fucker. They even have a term in the stupid rehab community: 'drinking dreams'. My shithead counsellor told me 'normal people' didn't dream they were paralytic and then wake up looking for a drink. She said it smugly as though proof of your own flawed soul was something to be bloody celebrated. I have them fairly regularly. The worse bit for me is that they combine a sort of glorified falsehood with shitty real events. And they always end the same way, with me waking up thirsty as hell, reaching for the bottle and the background thought that maybe this time it will be different. For fuck's sake. I smoke two fags then I get out of bed, put System of a Down on the stereo and sing badly while I shower. It takes me nearly a full half-hour to blow dry the mess that is my hair into something reasonable. I cut it once, thinking it might be more manageable short, and certainly more professional, but it was even more of a bastard and I sported a bell shaped almost-bob until it grew back. Far from looking sleek and sharp I'd looked even more unkempt than normal. Now I pretty much let it do its own thing. Resigned to the fact that it will always look wild. The rest of me is carefully put together; I think about my clothes and I spend time and effort on my face. It's like a disguise and I feel naked without the slap and the heels. As though if I look all right on the outside, everyone will think my insides match.

When I get in I call a meeting with Emma – that's fancy speak for 'I perch on the edge of her desk and talk at her'. Whenever I get a new client we go over the particulars. I give her a general gist of what I'm going to need administration-wise, and then she adds to it, usually with far more useful suggestions than mine. Generally this is a horribly brief process. This case is different and she is sitting ready to take notes. Her eyes widen as I outline a bit of background.

'I remember reading about it at the time.'

'It was my first murder.'

'And do you think she might be innocent?'

I shrug. 'It's unlikely, I guess, but I don't think we investigated it thoroughly enough.'

'Ah, a chance to make up for it now then.' She smiles.

'I suppose it is, yes.'

'And what's she like, Ms Reynolds?'

I like that she uses the formal address. Killer or not she's still a client and a well-paying one at that. 'She's . . . nice enough.'

'Is she different from how you remember her?'

'I only met her briefly, probably not at her finest hour either. She was pretty disturbed. And she was like that for the whole trial; the press described her as dead inside. I suspect she was in shock.'

Emma tuts. 'And yet she was sentenced for voluntary man-slaughter, wasn't she?'

'She was.'

'Dear me.'

I hide a smile behind my hand.

'She's due any minute. I'll need you to take a retainer from her today then we'll bill her weekly.' I think about how wonderful that money will be. I'm currently paying Emma's wages out of my personal account.

'Righty-ho, I'll start a file.'

'Yes, thanks. I've gathered up some old press coverage, if you could date it and see what else you can find . . .'

'Consider it done. I'll pop some coffee on.' She gets up and starts bustling about.

'You read my mind.' She doesn't drink it herself – in fact I've never seen her with anything other than water, but she seems to intuitively know when I'm running low on caffeine.

I have a good memory and I spend the next two hours writing up everything I can remember about the Andrews murder. It doesn't add up to a great deal. I wasn't the lead on the case, I wasn't even one of the major players. I had no real understanding of the nuances of a murder investigation or I'd have known that the one we conducted was pretty flimsy. It stuck with me, nonetheless, my first murder. It gave me a feel for how it would be, a thirst for solving the puzzle. This one is tricky; to all intents and purposes the puzzle was solved long ago. But I'd say there are still a few pieces missing.

Kate is better dressed than she was yesterday. Emma smiles, asks what she'd like to drink, settles her into my office and takes her coat.

'How are you?' I ask her.

She shrugs, thin shoulders rising and falling. 'I don't know really . . . It's all odd . . . like switching from black and white to colour, does that makes sense?'

'Yes, it will take some adjustment. I believe it's quite normal to be institutionalised at first.'

She laughs. 'I suppose I am, aren't I? I hadn't really thought about it.'

'Plenty of people get released and commit another crime within days so they can go back.'

'There's a certain safety in it I guess.' She doesn't sound convinced.

'You're not missing it too much?'

'No, I went to Topshop this morning and ate food with flavour in a coffee shop that looked like a restaurant.'

She smiles, though it's faltering. Prison must have been an absolute bitch for someone like Kate. She'd have stuck out like a sore thumb. I smile back at her.

Emma comes in with a tray of drinks, a jug of milk and some spoons. I watch Kate pour three spoons of sugar into her tea. She catches me looking and says, 'It's the not being rationed. I'm sure I'll be as big as a house before the month is out.'

'You should join a gym.'

'Do you go?'

I scowl at her and quickly try to rearrange my face into a less disagreeable pattern. 'I'm going to record all of our conversations. I hope that's all right with you?'

'Okay.'

'It covers you as well as me. Nothing goes further than myself or Emma. Unless I thought you were in danger yourself, or may prove a danger to others.' I give this spiel to everyone and then make them sign loads of things as well. Gotta keep your own back covered out here in lone-ranger land.

She nods. 'Understood.'

'It's going to be a lot of rehashing the past, obviously, and it's not just going to be that day. I'll need a full picture. Who was where and when. Who your friends were, boyfriends. I'll want to speak to them and your family.'

She nods but looks less certain.

'Have you seen your family yet?' I ask.

'My brother turned up this morning.'

'Did he visit you often in prison?'

'No, no visits at all.' Her eyes flutter nervously.

I tilt my head. 'None of your family?'

'No.'

It's unusual. I dealt with a particularly vile case where a juvenile sexually assaulted his own mother. When his sentence was finished his registered address was the family home. Blood is usually a strong enough tie to overcome all kinds of things.

I ask, 'Why?'

'Excuse me?'

I speak more slowly. 'Do you know why they didn't visit?'

'Because they think I'm a killer. Would you turn up?'

I think of my own mother and all the disappointing things she's done. Not murder but things that hurt, from which I'm still scarred. I think of Molly. I think of the ache I get from not seeing her. So harsh it's physical.

'Yes, I would.'

She is silent for a moment. 'I expected them.'

'So your brother turned up out of the blue after six years?'

'Not exactly out of the blue – he'd written.'

I wonder why he'd bothered to write but not shown up. Less effort perhaps. 'How often?'

'Once a month.'

'That's very precise.'

She shrugs.

I ask, 'Saying what?'

'Oh, nothing much. Updates on himself, the family.' She pauses and I think how young she looks, how frightened she must have been at eighteen. Locked up, isolated from her family. She must have felt utterly abandoned.

'Did you write back?'

'Yes, every time. I wrote letters in between to start with but he didn't respond so I stuck to once a month. We spoke on the phone a few times recently. He called when I wrote and told him I wanted to come back here.' She pauses, taking a deep breath. 'They sorted the flat out for me when I said I was coming home to Kingston.'

'So your dad is helping financially?'

She takes a sip of her sugary tea. 'Yes. I was very surprised.'

'Were you close growing up?'

She frowns. 'Not to Marcus really. If you'd asked me then, I'd have said me and Dad were close.' She blinks away tears.

'Your sister?'

'No one was close to Martha. She spent a lot of our teenage years in and out of hospital.'

'You haven't heard from her either?'

'No.'

I ask where Martha is now. Kate says she's in a psychiatric hospital called Sandcross. I make a note to call them.

I say, 'There's a history of mental illness in your family?'

'Yes, none of us Reynolds women come off well, eh?' It's a half-hearted joke.

'Marcus didn't experience the same kind of problems?'

'As Martha or Mum?'

'Either of them.'

'We were all . . . messed up . . . Especially after Mum died. Just in different ways. I got in with Naomi, then Oliver, looking for love, according to my therapist.' She laughs, it's a bitter sound. 'Marcus also got obsessed with Naomi, in a different way of course. Then he got angry. Martha cracked up.'

'Marcus was angry at Naomi?'

'Yes. She could be infuriating. They had a thing, she was cheating.' Kate flushes as though the embarrassment of the cheating was somehow her fault.

'How did Marcus find out?'

'She didn't really hide it, didn't see it as a problem.'

I frown at that. 'She knew he was upset?'

'Yes, not that it did him any good. She found other people's pain amusing.' She puts her empty tea cup on the edge of the desk. Her hand shakes slightly. I remember the days when mine used to do that. For different reasons. I pick up my coffee, enjoying its steady journey to my mouth. Sometimes it's the little things. 'Naomi sounds like a treat.'

Kate says, 'When she was nice she was really nice.'

'And when she was nasty . . .'

'Yes.'

I put down the cup and make a quick note linking Marcus and Naomi's names. 'Was Marcus violent?' I ask.

'Towards Naomi?'

'Towards anyone.'

She shrugs, little thin shoulders like spikes under cotton. 'No, not really. I mean sibling stuff, with me more than Martha. We fought but probably that's usual. He punched a lot of walls when he was frustrated.'

'You said he was angry with your mum?'

'I think so. He was quite protective over her though, even after she died. Wouldn't hear a word said against her.' She's tugging at the bottom of her sleeves and rolling her hands up into them. Lots of her mannerisms seem younger than her.

'How did your father react?'

'To Mum?'

I nod.

'He was devastated. He was really the only one of us who had a proper relationship with her.' I can see her fingers wriggling under the fabric. Worrying at a thread or button.

'The only one who was close to your mother?'

She nods. 'I realise that sounds odd, but she was never well.

She was like Martha, I suppose. Scared of her own shadow. We were always too much for her.'

I ask, 'But you loved her?'

'She was my mother.'

'So you loved her, what, out of duty?'

Kate blushes and runs a hand over her face.

'Yes, and hated her, I suppose. In equal measures if that makes sense. I don't know about the others.' She pushes the hand back into her sleeve.

'What was wrong with your mum?'

'Oh, well . . .' The hand darts out again, rubbing across her face and away. 'She was . . . morose. I don't know exactly. Something . . . happened when she was growing up. I never met her family. That's unusual isn't it?'

'Yes, I think so. Do you know why?'

She shakes her head. 'I heard whispers over the years. Dad said they weren't good people but I know she was living with them when they met. I guess he must have known them.' The whispers of the past have a habit of steering through the generations no matter how much we try to bury them. I never met my mother's parents. They never forgave her for having me. I've still managed to resent them even in their absence.

I ask Kate, 'Did Martha's . . . problems start after your mother's death?'

She shakes her head. 'Oh, no, not exactly. She was always sensitive, but things got worse after Mum died.' She's picking at her cuffs again. I don't think she realises that her hands never stay still. I bet she twitches when she's sleeping. She says, 'According to Marcus, she hasn't improved much.'

'And there was no specific incident that you know of that led to your mother committing suicide?'

'No. I've thought about it a lot, obviously. I've never really found a satisfactory answer.' The hand flicks out again.

'Tell me more about Ruth,' I say.

'She was soft, and sad. Very beautiful. My father doted on her, I remember that. Always with the extravagant gifts, nothing was too much trouble. We had a series of au pairs. A team of cleaners. He'd rush in at night and go looking for her.'

'Did she love him?'

She pauses, weighing it up. 'I don't think so. I'm not sure she had it in her.'

What must have occurred to make Ruth Reynolds unable to love her own husband? Her own children? I think of my daughter's young life. I wanted so badly to go back to work and get away from her incessant needs. And yet I loved her. It must be awful not to feel even that connection.

'Martha had long absences from school after Ruth's death. Can you tell me about those?'

Kate nods. 'Yes. She was too ill to learn.'

'Mentally?'

'Yes.'

'Must have been rough on you and Marcus, all the attention going on Martha?'

She frowns, a small line dances in between her eyebrows. 'I suppose it was. Marcus chased Dad's approval, always looking for attention. I partied with Naomi and Oliver. I'm sure you've read my journal.' She's blushing.

I say, 'It was a long time ago and we only focused on relevant passages.'

'I've regretted writing any of it since, though I'm ashamed to say I very much meant it at the time.' She tugs at the end of her sleeves, raises a hand to her hair, pushing her fringe, slightly too long, out of her eyes.

'You wanted her dead?'

'I think I did, yes.' Her voice is small, her eyes downcast.

Shoulders curled in. I wonder if it's guilt collapsing her in on herself and if so what exactly the guilt is for. Hating her bitchy frenemy or murder?

I ask again, 'But you don't think you killed her?'

She's shaking her head, wipes a hand under both eyes. Her movements are small and quick – birdlike, nervous. Hands darting in and out of her sleeves. Eyes wandering, unable to meet mine for too long. She does, though, just for a minute, and she is clear when she says, 'She was dead when I came into the room,' and sits up straighter, turning her shoulders back toward me.

'Stabbed repeatedly, just like you fantasised about in writing?'

She holds my gaze. 'I realise I don't come across well.'

'Hey, the papers don't love me either.'

She giggles at that and I can see that if she loosened up she'd be almost pretty. 'What did Marcus want this morning?' I ask her.

Her eyes stray away from my face back down to her hands. 'To avoid further embarrassment.'

Ah. 'He wants you to leave?'

'In the nicest way possible, yes.' I can't think of a nice way for your family to ask you to fuck off.

'You're not going to?'

She looks at me again, pausing. I can almost see her mustering resolve. 'Not yet. I have a purpose here.'

'To clear your name?'

'I hope so.' She quickly adds, 'With your help.'

No pressure then. I don't bother telling her how hard it's going to be to reopen a case that is six years old. Instead I say, 'Whose idea was the party?'

'Probably Naomi's.'

'You were taking drugs?' I know they had been. I saw the toxicology reports but I want to know if it was problematic or

40

recreational. Despite my own issues, I don't believe drugs are all bad.

'Yes, sometimes. Not usually like that.'

I scrawl a note. 'Naomi?'

'Oh yes, she was more . . .' Kate half smiles, 'greedy than me maybe, she couldn't get enough.'

I relate to that but I don't tell Kate. I just nod and put a question mark next to Naomi's name.

'Who did you buy them from?'

She shakes her head. 'I don't know. Naomi just showed up with various things. Usually pills.'

They had found traces of pharmaceutical speed and Valium in the girls' systems. An odd combination. I'd wondered at the time if Naomi had been buying from a doctor, chemist or nurse. I wouldn't have thought your average dealer would sell such things.

'You had a boyfriend . . .?'

She smiles at that, nodding, blushing. 'Oliver.'

'How did you meet him?'

'Naomi introduced us.'

'Where did she meet him?'

Kate laughs. 'HMV I think.'

'The record shop?'

'Yes. We hung out there loads.' She pauses, seeming to weigh something up.

I prompt her, 'Go on.'

'We used to . . . steal things.'

'From HMV?'

She blushes again, nodding.

'Why?' Both girls came from wealthy families and money never seemed to be an issue.

Kate is getting redder. 'I know it was stupid. I hated doing it; I was always terrified of getting caught and getting into trouble.' She pauses as the irony of that comment hits home.

I say, 'Right.' Little rich kids looking for a thrill. I used to shoplift food and tampons. I'd have to if I didn't manage to get the dole cheque off Mum before she hit the offie.

'Oliver was a few years older than you?'

'Yes, twenty-three.'

'And you were just sixteen at the time?'

'Yes.' She nods.

I make a note of this. I had thought this was a bit off in the original investigation. Not to mention that we had spoken to him once, briefly, and sent him on his way. I remember Malone waggling his eyebrows at him in a lascivious way as Oliver outlined a sexual relationship with Kate. When I'd asked what he thought, he'd said boys would be boys and who could blame him.

'Oliver was local?' I ask. I can't remember exactly where he lived.

'I don't know. I never went to his house. He used to come to mine a lot.' I wonder if he had been hiding his relationship with such a young woman from whoever he lived with. I can't recall us delving into who that might have been, or even where his house was. I put a large red line underneath his name.

'You thought he was cheating on you with Naomi?' She'd written as much in her journal.

'Yes.'

'Do you think they already had a thing going on when she introduced him to you?'

'I don't know.' Her eyes widen. 'I hope not, but looking back . . . maybe.' I can see her mind whirring through the past. She smiles but it doesn't reach her eyes. 'Nothing I could prove.'

'Maybe you were paranoid?'

'Maybe,' she replies.

'But you don't think so?'

'No.' Her eyes meet mine.

I hold her gaze and ask, 'Have you heard from him?'

There is a pause. 'No.' I wonder if it's the truth but I don't push it.

'He was questioned,' I tell her.

'Really?' She looks surprised enough to make me think maybe she's not lying.

'Of course – he was at the party. He said you and Naomi had been fighting, he wasn't sure what about.'

She blinks and I see something wash over her face. She frowns.

'Were there any good things about Naomi?'

She laughs at that. 'God, thinking back, I've wondered that myself. It's hard to explain . . . I suppose she was . . . fun, really fun, and she let me tag along. Before we were friends I was pretty unpopular, to be honest.' She shrugs. 'I felt like maybe I was more fun when I was with her. She was wild and exciting. We were set on different paths when we met, I think hers looked better than mine.'

'What do you mean?'

'She was charismatic, very clever. I was pretty mediocre. I had one friend, Annie Jakes. We'd known each other since we were babies. Our friendship was based on having no one else to play with. Naomi was constantly surrounded by people who wanted to hang out with her. She chose me. I was flattered.'

I scribble down the name Annie Jakes, checking the spelling with Kate, and I ask, 'Did you remain friends?'

'I tried to drop her. Probably not in a nice way. Naomi thought she was a total loser.' Kate sighs. 'Looking back I was a royal bitch to Annie. I felt she was an embarrassment.' She blushes again. 'I just wanted her to stay away. Naomi would pick on her when she tried to hang out with us, but she'd come back for more.'

'Did you love Naomi?'

'I don't know. I was very jealous of her.'

'Why?'

'She was just . . . better than me. She had parents who loved her, confidence, friends, boys liked her and she didn't seem scared of anything.'

Having met Naomi's mother, even briefly, I can imagine that her parents' world revolved around her. In some ways it can be worse than neglect. Spoiling your kids seems a sure-fire way to breed little monsters.

'What were you scared of?'

She laughs that quiet laugh again. Her busy hand covering her mouth. 'I was scared of everything.' She still looks scared now.

'Talk me through what you remember from that night.'

She does. I make notes. Then I tell her, 'I want to speak to Dean Hall about his professional work with you, with your permission, of course.'

She frowns. 'He was my therapist.'

I put down my pen. 'Look, police work, investigative work, whatever you want to call it, is an invasion of privacy. When we're looking into a crime, we invade everything and every-one involved. The criminals, the victim, their families. I'm planning on doing this with you and your life. You need to be prepared for it.'

She's biting her lower lip now, face pinched in a frown.

I tell her, 'You can walk away, you don't have to do this. Now is the time if that's what you want to do.'

She shakes her head. 'No, no it's okay. I have to. It's not like you're going to be splashing my diary on the front pages again, right?'

'No, though as we proceed the press may get wind of it . . .'
She pauses and I find I'm holding my breath.

'It can't be any worse than not knowing, right?'

I feel something close to relief, and it's not just about the finances. The dark part of me is glad to be back in the game.

6.

Claudia Reynolds

When he phones, he is fuming. I can hear it in his voice before he details the problem. He says his sister is planning on hanging around. He spits the words out and I flinch even though he isn't here. I imagine him walking around his office as he tells me of her cheek. He will be irate, red-faced. He says he will be home early today. I mutter through gritted teeth that that will be wonderful.

He isn't though, in the end. He's in a good hour after Bethany has gone to bed. He heads to the kitchen, banging about as he goes. I want him to shut up. Our daughter is asleep and I don't want her woken. I won't tell him though, no point risking it.

I wait, on hand, in the shadows, trying to keep her safe. I wait to see what he needs or wants, trying to pre-empt it. I'm doing it now. Following him around the kitchen. Closing cupboard doors behind him, getting ice out of the freezer as soon as he picks up a glass. Filling his glass, refilling. He is in a rage now. Drink clenched in one hand, the other balled into a tight fist. I murmur and nod. One ear listening out for Bethany. I had known this morning's visit wouldn't go well. Marcus has been fuming since she wrote with her release date and of her plans to head back to Kingston. He'd even phoned her to try and talk her out of it.

The big family shame. Even worse than poor Martha, or Ruth. I used to think it was dreadful what Marcus's mother had done, leaving behind three children and a husband to fend for themselves. Back in the glory days when things were black and white. When I was someone else and Marcus pretended to be too. Now I think I get it. I love Bethany, but still . . . Escape. I fantasise about it. Not suicide. I'm too gutless for that. I'm scared that I would spend eternity tossing and turning, worrying about my daughter. I imagine an accidental death. I step off the pavement and a bus comes hurtling towards me, the driver fast and not paying attention. I am smashed to pieces. I no longer exist, and I luck out twice because the afterlife is nothing. Nothing at all, just peace and silence. No gnawing in my gut, no nagging headache. It doesn't happen though. I live and breathe. I don't even get proper illnesses. No fevers to take me out. Just each day, much like the last.

'She's being fucking ridiculous; I mean she has no idea what she's done to us. What we went through. She tore this family apart.'

I nod, not bothering to point out they were already in pieces; her crime was just the icing on an already rotten cake. I wipe the side, picking up the condensation where his glass stood just a second ago. He puts it down a few inches along. He likes things tidy. Tidiness is my job. He will drop crumbs. Put drinks down coaster-less and trample mud through the house, but it had better be gone before he notices. And it is, most of the time. Bethany and I are both masters of the small space. We occupy less and less of it as time goes by. Not Marcus though. If he's in the building, you'll know about it. I used to love that about him. His physical presence. His bigness, his ability to overshadow everyone else. Funny how the things you once loved can become the things you most despise. He's sighing now. Winding down. I can drown him out to background noise. I can usually tell when I'm required, and how, by the tone of his voice. A 'yes I see' here, and an 'oh no' there. He is looking, as ever, for agreement, because underneath it all my husband is actually very needy. It's something I give willingly without thought. I learned long ago that anything else isn't worth it.

'I'm sorry, boo.' A pet name that came about years ago. Something once cute, now ugly. He's wheedling and I brace myself, still wiping the side. I feel him sidle up behind me, his hands on my hips reaching up under my shirt, warm, like liquid poison washing over my skin. I don't shudder, I carry on wiping and he grabs my breasts.

'It's not your fault, boo.' His lips, rubbery, damp, slightly cold from the drink, pressed against my neck, a thin line of saliva. And then his whole body pressing me into the counter, moving. I fight the urge to throw up. To smack his hands away, to scream. Instead I turn and smile, my arms wrapping around his neck.

He smiles back and asks, 'Shall we go upstairs?'

It's not really a question but I nod, the smile firmly glued in place, and abandon the cloth to the side. I'll come down again afterwards. Once he's spent and snoring. I'll empty the dishwasher and prepare what's needed for the morning. It's all on autopilot, an automatic reaction to my life. I know what needs to be done and I'll carry that out. Right now I am smiling as he pushes me back onto the bed. I am compliant, soft. Holding in a scream that never comes.

7.

Madison Attallee

Kate's family aren't exactly the Waltons. Dead mum, crazy sister, murderer. I'm not convinced the dad and brother are much better. It's a lot of misfortune to hit one unit. Unlucky is usually an isolated incident. I wonder if that's why the shrink ended up keeping hold of Kate's case. Maybe the material was just too rich to walk away from.

Emma's done her research on Dean, so I have a good idea who he is before I go to meet him. He's renowned in his field as one of the best criminal psychologists currently working in the UK. I'm quite sure I've read a few of his papers over the years. He must spend the majority of his time in courtrooms these days. He gets called in to give evidence fairly frequently. I was surprised when Emma told me his office is in Kingston. I'd expected a Harley Street address. Actually, it's not that far from my own but certainly a better end of town, heading out towards Ham with views of the Thames.

I am a few minutes early and stand next to my car smoking. I'm working under the admittedly stupid assumption that smoking outside means the smell won't stick to me. I know it doesn't work but I put the fag out, chew a mint and spray YSL everywhere anyway. Live in fucking hope right?

A bland blonde receptionist greets me with a half-smile and

rings through to let Hall know I've arrived. I wait, watching a screen with no sound showing twenty-four-hour news. I watch the scroll along the bottom and feel suitably depressed by it. Bland blonde's fingers run chaotically over the keyboard. Clackety-clack, clackety-clack. I glance at the clock. Hall is ten minutes late. The clackety-clack is rubbing my last fucking nerve. I'm about to make a complaint about his lateness to her when the door opens. The best-looking man I've ever seen in real life comes out from an adjoining door. He's smiling apologetically.

'I'm so sorry. A patient called and I didn't feel I could just let him . . . Anyway, sorry I'm late.' His suit is structured like a second skin and I watch him appreciatively from behind as I follow him into his office.

He sits at his desk and waves me into a chair opposite. I slump and my oversized shoulder bag slides loudly to the floor. He raises an eyebrow. I grin, aware my lion's mane hair is likely all over the place. I wonder if I have mascara goop too. I wish I'd checked now. Fuck it. He asks if I want anything to drink. I say no. He brandishes a bottle of water at me. 'I'm on the good stuff.'

'Health kick?'

He sighs. 'I do try.' Judging by his pristine condition, I reckon he more than tries. I'm pretty sure his shoulders are a result of some serious gym hours.

I smile. 'Me too.' He doesn't know my only liquid intake is coffee.

'So you're here to talk about Kate?' He smiles.

'I am, yes.'

His smile widens. 'I was so glad when I found out she was being released. Now she can start living her life.'

'How did you find out?'

He takes a sip of his water. 'She told me. I assume you know we've maintained a friendship of sorts?'

'She said you've been very supportive.'

He sighs. 'I have tried.'

'You picked her up from prison this week?'

He nods and looks embarrassed. Beautiful and kind – well, well, well. I say, 'Her family have all but disappeared.'

He nods, his pretty features setting into concern now. 'Yes, very sad, isn't it? It often happens when tragedy hits though. People assume these things band you together, but trauma can often push even the closest people apart. They were fractured before Kate's problems became so apparent. Way before Kate's arrest.'

'Her mother's death?' My phone kicks in and starts playing Guns and Roses' 'Paradise City'. Shit. I cringe inwardly and try to look cool as I ferret it out of my bag and silence it just as it hits peak volume.

He hides a smile behind his hand. 'Kate's mother, Ruth . . .' I prompt.

'Yes. I'm sure it was the catalyst for a lot of their subsequent issues, though it sounds as though she'd been unwell for an awfully long time before her suicide. Poor woman must have been desperate.'

'Do you stay in contact with all your clients?'

He laughs. 'Patients, Ms Attallee, not clients.'

'Do you?'

He pauses for a moment, hands resting under his chin. He looks like he should be on a magazine cover.

'No, I don't. My job requires a certain level of detachment, as I'm sure yours does?'

I nod agreement.

'I usually maintain it. I deal with the human mind in all its ugly, imperfect beauty. It can be harrowing . . . well, I don't need to tell you,' he muses. I shrug. This isn't a sharing session.

He says, 'To be honest, I felt sorry for Kate to begin with.'

'Did you think she was innocent?'

He shakes his head. 'No, well not exactly – I didn't think she was culpable. I'm sure you've read my initial report?'

'I have, yes.' He had stated that she was in no fit state to face a court trial. He had recommended that she continue to be cared for in a secure psychiatric unit under his supervision. That request had been denied. I guess by staying in contact he had overridden that decision to some degree.

'She was barely lucid. Didn't seem to have any idea what was happening to her in terms of legal proceedings. Her father didn't advise her. Her lawyer was certain of her guilt and so were you guys.'

'You said in your report that you felt a psychiatric facility would have been a better place for her.'

'I thought it was bloody obvious, to be honest.' I am surprised to hear him swear and it makes me warm to him. 'At the time I was working in such a facility. It would have been much more helpful to her, in my opinion.'

'She confessed.'

He's frowning at me and his voice becomes raised, ever so slightly. 'But she had no recollection of killing Naomi. She didn't give any detail.'

I ask again, 'But you didn't think she was innocent?' His report had stated that she had an unsound mind.

'Whether she stabbed her or not was irrelevant to me as a psychologist. The point was she couldn't remember it. I assumed she'd dissociated.' He sighs. 'I never meet people in their finest hour, I suppose. It's the downside to my work.'

'What's the upside?'

'Seeing improvement.'

I chuckle at that. 'I thought therapy was a lifelong process.'

He smiles widely. 'Ah, a non-believer I see.'

I shrug. 'Sometimes I wonder if we all talk about our feelings a bit too much.'

'Yes, I think we probably do. However, it's often those that say nothing who need to speak the most.' I resist squirming under his gaze.

I write a few notes on my pad, looking away from his dark eyes. 'Do you believe Kate's version now?'

'Do I believe her memories are real?'

'Yes.'

'Yes, I think they probably are and I think they were always there. They were just overwhelmed by her own guilt.'

'Because she hated Naomi?'

He steeples his hand under his chin again, nodding thoughtfully. 'Exactly.'

'When you met Kate, she needed to talk?' I push on.

'Very much so. She would have benefited from therapy much sooner. All of the children should have had counselling after Ruth died. Had Naomi not been killed, Kate would still have been heading down a bad road.' He sighs heavily and runs a fine, delicate hand across full pouty lips.

I frown. 'Bad how?'

'Her relationships were unhealthy. Naomi was an awful friend for her. Very domineering. Kate had little in the way of her own identity so was easily sucked into other people's.'

'Like Oliver?'

His eyes narrow. 'Exactly.'

'In what ways was Naomi domineering?' I ask.

'Without wishing to speak ill of someone who is no longer with us, I suspect she was a classic narcissist.' This has crossed my mind. Barely anyone other than her parents found good things to say about her, even in the immediate period after her death.

I ask him, 'Why?'

'She bullied Kate, used her as a playmate, ignored her – sometimes for days – and then acted as if nothing had happened. Kate thinks she was sleeping with Oliver. I wouldn't be surprised.'

'Really?' I give him a surprised look though I suspect he's right.

'Yes. Naomi introduced them, apparently. I think Kate was barely sixteen at the time, he was in his early twenties. Perfectly legal of course.'

I scowl at that, wrinkling my nose – sixteen isn't that many years older than Molly. 'But slightly questionable.'

He nods agreement.

'Did her dad know?' I ask.

He shrugs. 'From what I can tell, James had pretty much given up by then. He hoofed Martha off to various psychiatric hospitals and ignored the other children.'

'Grieving for his wife?'

'Oh, undoubtedly. Sounds like their relationship was terribly co-dependent. It's a term first defined by the dynamic you often see in the families of addicts and alcoholics.'

'Oh, I see.' I know all about co-dependence and alcoholic families.

'It's now thought that it's not exclusive to that community, although Ruth certainly drank heavily and had various prescriptions.' He takes a sip of his water.

I say, 'Go on . . .' trying to look like this is new to me, but thinking about my own 'family sessions'.

'Well the "non-damaged" member of the couple enables the damaged person. James was a fixer. Ruth's death would have been the ultimate confirmation of his failure. It must have been a terrible blow to him on all kinds of levels.' My ex-husband summed up in a nutshell. Capable, dependable, always there to make me look even more inadequate.

I turn my focus back to Dean. 'So why didn't James rush in to fix Kate's situation? He pretty much bailed on her.'

He shrugs. 'I wouldn't know without speaking to him. Maybe it was the wrong kind of need. Whatever the reasons, Kate was left to fend for herself.'

'But you thought she was guilty?'

'At the time, I thought she'd killed Naomi. She certainly had cause to be angry at her and the evidence pointed in her direction, as you know.'

'But you didn't think she was responsible?'

He's shaking his head now. 'Not in any legal sense. No. You saw her that day, didn't you?'

'I did.'

'Then I imagine you might have seen what I meant first-hand?'

I did, but I ignore the question. Bloody shrinks. 'Can you explain dissociating?'

'Well, like most things, it appears to various degrees. In its most benign manifestation you could consider daydreaming to be dissociating. It's the mind distancing itself from stressful events.'

I look at him dubiously. 'You think Kate was daydreaming?'

He smiles and I smile back. He says, 'No, I was just putting it into context. I think Kate was very much at the other end of the spectrum.'

'Like psychosis?'

'Not exactly. It's a fugue state, a momentary amnesia if you like.'

I make a note to look this up in more detail. I tell him, 'Kate was very confused when we brought her in.'

'Well yes, she would have been. Her perception of reality was incorrect.'

'She was checked over.'

He scoffs at that. 'Yes, they only checked her for psychosis though. This is different.'

'She claimed to not recognise Naomi.'

'Yes, nor did she seem to know how she'd got there. All quite obvious signs if you know what you're looking for.' His voice is rising; he's still cross about it six years later.

'You're saying our guy didn't look hard enough?'

'I don't believe your guy even knew what to look for.'

'You might be right there.' I think of our station shrink, Monty. An older guy even then, quietly counting down the days until his retirement.

Dean shrugs. 'I do quite a bit of legal work. The lack of knowledge regarding mental health issues never fails to astound me.'

'Police have a lot to contend with.' I half agree with him but still feel my loyalty hackles rising.

'They do. I apologise, I didn't mean to offend you.' I shrug, annoyed that I reacted at all. I can see how this guy would get under your skin. I have a momentary image of what his skin might look like under the suit. I put it away. Jeez.

I say, 'Do you still think that's what happened? To Kate?'

He pauses. 'Yes, I do. Her version of reality came back to her once the trial was over and things calmed down.'

'So now you think it's not just a responsibility issue?'

'You mean do I think she's innocent?'

I nod.

'Yes, I do.'

'Which means that there is a killer on the loose.' I don't add that they probably read the papers and therefore know exactly where she is.

He sighs. 'Yes. Innocent or otherwise I don't think now is the right time for her to be pursuing answers. Nothing brings out stupidity like mob mentality and the coverage is liable to get worse.'

'You don't think she should have come back to Kingston?' Kate has already told me he thinks this.

'Not now, no. I'm very worried about her.'

'Wouldn't you want to clear your name?'

He smiles, it's lopsided and warm. The kind of smile that could reduce a grown woman to childish giggles. I remain poker faced.

'I probably would, yes.'

'Then you can understand Kate's motivation.'

He sighs. 'Yes, of course I can and I intend to offer her support whatever choices she makes. He pauses then says, 'Kate talked about you. In some of our sessions. Said you walked her out of the room.'

'I did, yes.'

'She said you were kind.'

I shrug.

His eyes study mine. I fight the urge to look away. He says, 'I hope you can be kind to her now.'

8.

Kate Reynolds

I am walking into Kingston. It's raining a little bit, but I don't care. Every step is a reminder that I'm outside. No roof overhead, no one with keys deciding my next move, no need to watch my back. I do though. Every time someone walks past me, I jump. An internal cowering at violence about to come. I wonder if I'll ever be rid of it. I push my shoulders back and hold my head high. Tricks I learned in there. It doesn't always matter how you feel as long as you can hide it. I make each step purposeful, mentally pep-talking myself as I go, heading towards a destination I have chosen, not around and around a concrete courtyard for no reason beyond killing time. I'm walking along the River Thames. The trees rustle in the breeze. The wind is high, cold and biting, making the tip of my nose turn red. Daylight sparkles on the water. My head starts to clear, emptying itself of everything but the wind, the rain, the rustling of leaves.

My phone rings. It's a withheld number. I pick it up warily; only Madison, Dean and Marcus have my number.

'Hello.'

'Kate?' And of course he has it too, because I included it in the message I sent.

'Hi.' It's almost a strain to get the word out.

He says, 'You're out.' His voice is a low rumble. Unchanged and familiar. I feel my stomach flip-flop.

'I am,' I tell him. My own voice sounds high, and is whipped away by the wind.

'You sent me a message.'

I shrug and then realise he can't see me. 'How are you?'

'Surprised to hear from you.' His voice is low, tight and . . . annoyed? I can't think of anything to say back. I've stopped walking now. Standing stock-still. My breath held in my chest.

He says, 'You don't have a picture.'

'What?'

'On LinkedIn, you don't have a picture.'

'Oh, no. I thought it probably wasn't a good idea.'

He sighs. 'Probably not. I saw the *Comet*.'

I laugh but it's tinny and out of kilter. 'Yeah, looks like I'm famous again.'

'Hang on.' His voice becomes muffled. He's talking but not to me. I can't make out what he's saying. Before I can ask, he says, 'I have to go.'

'Okay.'

And he's gone. I'm frozen to the spot, still. The phone pressed to my ear pointlessly. He phoned me. He made contact, it must mean something. I am waiting for my breathing to slow, for the assault of memories to pass. Lying pretty, listening to him read me poetry. Waiting for his call, his visit, redeemed by his attention, his touch.

I hear something behind me but when I turn there's nothing there. I walk quickly anyway.

I order a large latte, add sugar and sit down, grabbing a copy of the paper as I go. I feel myself calm as I sip my drink and read news about other people. I have discussed my ex almost weekly with Dean for the past six years. I have agreed that it was an unhealthy relationship and one I should most definitely stay out of. I resisted the often overwhelming urge to look him up in prison, though it was easier with limited internet access and the knowledge that everything I did was monitored. I even managed a few days out in the world being free without doing it as well. I can hear Dean's voice calmly warning me about the importance of surrounding yourself with people who treat you well.

That would not include Oliver. But what he did do was excite me and, more importantly, he made me feel part of something. The mere sight of him used to give me butterflies. He and Naomi had that same quality. When his attention was on you, you felt like you were the only person alive who mattered. I miss that. His absence after my arrest was a devastating blow. I think I may have taken it harder than my family's abandonment, though I haven't admitted that to anyone. Not even Dean.

I try and push this from my mind, my eyes wandering back to the paper. All of a sudden it is pulled from under my hands. My coffee slides, spilling slightly.

'Oh!' I say, sliding my chair back, standing as I do. A hand is on the paper. I follow it upwards and I am face-to-face with Anthea Andrews.

She's aged. My God how she's aged. More than six years would warrant. The death of her beloved only child is written in every line. And she is red-faced. I instinctively raise my hands.

'Mrs Andrews . . .'

'You! What the hell are you doing here?' Her voice is low and dangerous, a whisper, but it travels and the people nearest to us have started to look.

'Please, I don't want any trouble.'

She leans over and grabs me. Her body is half on the table,

knocking the coffee fully over now. Drops of it scald me as it goes down. Her hand grabs at my shoulder, fingers digging in. It hurts but I am standing, mute, unable to move.

'You shouldn't be here.' Her voice is getting louder now. 'Go away, go away, go away,' and then she's shouting. Spit is forming at the corners of her mouth, spraying towards me. I am held by her hands, transfixed by her face. Rage, pure unadulterated rage.

The waiter is coming over and he's putting a hand on her shoulder, 'Madam, please, what seems to be the problem?'

Her eyes don't move from me; her hand doesn't loosen its grip.

'She killed my daughter.' She speaks loudly, certain and unwavering.

Silence after her loudness, and a familiar voice goes through my head. It's Janine whispering, mocking. Murderer, the scarlet letter, the brand that will never leave me. I can feel tears streaming down my face but I still don't move. We stay locked in an awful embrace. Her hand pinning me physically, her eyes burning into my soul.

'Holy shit, you're Kate Reynolds,' says the waiter. Now I can't breathe and I see his stance change, the hand that was restraining her softens. His protection removed. Everything is still and the waiter's hand now rests on her arm. Supportive.

She looks from me to him and the anger is gone. Now she is just forlorn. Her arm drops and tears stream down her face. I snatch my bag from the table and walk on Bambi legs to the door. It seems to take forever and I can still hear them whispering. Muttering.

I see Mrs Andrews through the window from outside. Crying. People coming to comfort her as they glare at me. I walk away quickly. I used to stay at that woman's house all the time. She'd bring us tea in the mornings. Nothing was ever too much trouble. I used to tell Naomi how lucky she was to have a mother like Anthea. They didn't get on though. Not really. We came home late one night when Naomi was very drunk. I apologised as soon as I saw that her mother was upset but Naomi laughed in her face. Anthea backed down, patted her daughter's arm and murmured she was glad to have her home. Naomi had rolled her eyes at me over her head. I found her careless attitude obscene in light of my own mother, by now dead but absent long before.

I'm walking so fast I'm almost running. Speeding along the river now until I hit Surbiton, not taking in my surroundings, just wanting to get home, to put distance between myself and that wreck of a woman. I get in, slam the door and pick up the phone.

'Hello?' he answers.

'Dean . . .' And it all spills out. I hear him sigh into the silence as he says, 'Oh, Kate.'

'She's angry at the wrong person, Dean. I have to show her. I have to show them all.'

'Look, you've got my office address – why don't you come in and see me?'

'I will.'

'When?' he asks.

I think for a moment. 'Tomorrow.'

'Fine, call in the interim if you need me.'

I smile despite the awfulness of it all and whisper, 'Thank you.'

'You're doing okay.' His soft voice shores me up and I'm still nodding silent agreement as I hang up. This will be over soon and when it is, I can go wherever I like. But for now I'll have to take the knocks. I repeat his words to myself. I'm doing okay. I'm doing okay. I'm doing okay.

9.

Anthea Andrews

Damian is halfway through his tenth pull-up when I slam the front door. I can see his shadow through the frosted glass door leading into the kitchen. He pauses for a moment and I wonder if he's contemplating going for more. Eventually he lowers himself and walks out into the hallway. I can feel my face screw up and tears start to flow. He's immediately by my side, helping me shrug out of my coat. I'm silent until it's off, resisting the urge to slap his hands away. I turn to face him. He looks concerned, but guarded. I figure he can probably feel the rage emanating from me in hot, cross waves.

He tries, 'Are you okay?'

I shake my head. 'No.'

'What's happened?'

'I saw her.' I feel my face contort even more. He frowns before trying for concern. I nearly don't blame him. I know I must be a parody of the pretty, smiling woman I once was. I glare at him. Lips pursed, eyes narrowed. I can feel the anger tightening my face. I am all pinched by bitterness. He doesn't ask who, he knows full well. It's been the main topic of conversation between us for months and months now. We were informed of Kate's plans to return to Kingston by the powers that be. They do that as a matter of course. Damian says he wishes they hadn't told us. But we have a right to know and it's given me months to plan, and to stew. To refresh a new and more vehement rage.

He says, 'Did you speak to her?'

I spit out, 'Of course I bloody spoke to her.' My husband's stupidity in this matter never fails to amaze me. Like he expects me to just walk right on by the vile, bastard girl who took my only child.

'I'm sorry,' he mutters. I have no idea what exactly he's apologising for and suspect he probably doesn't either. I should probably feel sorry that he has to walk on eggshells and that he says sorry all the time. But I don't. I hate him for the fact that he's managed to make some kind of peace with it. That he has betrayed Naomi by allowing his grief to shrink. That he has betrayed me by leaving me in it on my own. An extra, raw slap in the face. Proof that he didn't love our daughter half as much as I did.

I push past him and bash about the kitchen, unloading the dishwasher.

He says, 'I'll do that.'

'Don't bother, I've already started now.'

He stands uselessly, watching me, waiting for the onslaught.

I try for a few seconds to keep it in, but it's no use. I tell him. 'She was sitting drinking coffee. Without a care in the fucking world.'

I search him for a reaction and he nods. I carry on. 'It's not right. I'm not going to bloody stand for it either.'

He nods again and slides away to do I don't know what. I don't care. My mind is whirring, buzzing. Hatred beats around it like a thousand tiny moth wings, begging to be sated, fed and freed. I won't stand for it, not at all. The little bitch. And things start to ping, little ideas fizzing into existence. My head starts to calm down and my breathing evens out. I don't have to put up with this. Not at all.

10.

Kate Reynolds

I walk to Marcus's but I'm still jumpy after the run-in with Anthea. I think I hear footsteps behind me, something that is becoming a regular occurrence, but when I turn, the street is empty. I head out of Surbiton into Kingston and towards Norbiton. I should have got a cab.

The house is big, exactly what I would have expected, and it's on a private road. Not unlike the road I grew up on and not far from our childhood home on Kingston Hill. I bet he gets views of Richmond Park from upstairs. You wouldn't have any reason to come down this cul-de-sac unless you lived here. The driveway is immaculate. Gravelled, with beautiful flowers on either side. Dimly lit so I can just make them out. Two cars, a big Audi and a little Audi. His and hers. Everything says my brother is doing all right. I ring the bell and it is answered almost immediately by a woman more beautiful in real life than her pictures suggest. She is spotless, smiling broadly and, yes, the absolute spitting image of my mother. So much so that for a few rude seconds I just look at her open mouthed.

'You must be Kate?' Her voice is deeper than I thought it would be, sexier. Not like my mother's at all. I'm glad.

I nod.

'I'm Claudia. Please do come in.' I follow her and she expertly relieves me of my coat. There is an enormous picture hanging in the hallway. Clearly a professional shot of Claudia and my brother beaming, their hands on the shoulder of a small girl. A girl that is creeping down the stairs in front of me.

'Bethany, darling, don't skulk. This is your Aunt Kate.'

The girl remains frozen. Crouching near the bottom steps. She is like her mother, but pretty, not beautiful. Petite like myself and my sister. All arms and legs. I head over to her and bend down.

'Hi.' I smile. I should have brought something. Not that I have much idea what a three-year-old might like. I should have brought something for Claudia. Chocolates, wine, flowers. These are the done things. Manners I have to re-learn. There is time. Hopefully, now there is plenty of time.

She says 'Hi' back. Her voice is small and high-pitched. Intense eyes study my face. I stay low, letting her look, enjoying the scrutiny.

I say to her, 'You have pretty hair.'

She smiles. 'It's like yours.'

'So it is,' I laugh. The dye is washing away as it always does.

Claudia places a hand on the child's shoulder. 'She's fair like all you Reynolds, except for the eyes.' We are fair skinned, fair haired but with dark eyes. Claudia's are a vibrant green.

I say, 'Yes, they're all yours.'

She beams and a moment of peace seems to pass between us. My brother's voice breaks it, slicing the air. I turn to say hi but realise he isn't talking to us, he's on the phone. He waves a hand at me. Claudia is smiling, watching her husband intently. He rubs a soft hand over her shoulder and she touches his fingers. He signals to his wife that he'll be five minutes and heads upstairs, passing his hand over Bethany's head on his way. The child giggles.

'Probably work. I'm sure he doesn't mean to be rude.'

'It's no problem.'

She nods. 'We're having beef. I hope that's okay? You're not a vegetarian or anything, are you?'

'Nope, beef sounds lovely.'

'Oh, good. Bethany's already eaten. She'll go up for the evening shortly.'

I steal a glance at my watch. It's barely six o'clock. I wonder if this is a normal bedtime. We never had one. She's already in her pyjamas.

'Didn't fancy beef?' I screw up my nose and she giggles. I ask her, 'Who's on your jimjams?'

'Elsa, from *Frozen*.'

'Oh, I don't know that.'

Her eyes widen. 'It's a film,' she says as though speaking to a hopelessly stupid person.

'I see. It's your favourite?'

She nods enthusiastically.

Claudia is smiling. 'She's completely obsessed. We even get to listen to the soundtrack in the car.'

'Ah, I was like that about *Annie*. I suppose that's out of date now?'

Bethany tells me, 'Mummy loves that too. Not the new one either – the really, really old one. It's not *too* bad I s'pose.'

Claudia and I laugh. The child looks from face to face, not getting the joke. My brother comes back down and scoops up Bethany.

He says, 'Aren't you in bed yet? And why are we all on the bloody stairs?'

Claudia tells him, 'She's just going up now.' She smiles fondly at Marcus.

'Well, why don't you see to that? I'll get Kate a drink, shall I?'

He gives his daughter a squeeze and passes her to Claudia. Bethany waves at me and I wave back.

I follow Marcus into the kitchen where he pours two large glasses of wine and hands me one. I take a sip. It's cool and sharp. It's been a long time since I've tasted alcohol.

'Kids.' He's grinning. 'They need routine, even when we have visitors. I hope you understand?' I nod. He goes on, 'Claudia's good at that. Not like Mum, she used to let us run wild.'

I'm taken back to dive-bombing my siblings from bunk-beds, paint on walls, chalk on floors, hair-pulling, my mother's dejected sighs, a long stream of exasperated nannies. I see my dad coming home at the end of the day doing his best to contain it, us, tidying, whispering to Mum. Trying to keep us from being feral. There must be a middle ground. I suspect there is. I don't know it though, and I guess Marcus doesn't either.

'Claudia seems to have it all sussed,' I say, a compliment to his wife and an indirect compliment to him. He beams at me.

'She does, she does, she's ever so good.' There are photos of the family everywhere, smiles from various surfaces. There's even a calendar hanging on the wall that seems to be of them. It's open to January with a picture of Bethany beaming at the camera in full snow gear. Marcus sees me looking and smiles. 'That was skiing last year.'

I tell him, 'Bethany's a lovely child.'

'Ah yes, well that's mainly Claudia's doing, to be honest. I fund it all.' He shrugs. 'Some people might think we're too traditional, but defined roles mean order.'

Claudia comes back into the room still neatly pressed, smiling at us both. She casually refills Marcus's glass, I put a hand over mine. I remember now that I've never really liked alcohol, the taste or the effect.

He looks at his wife. 'Did Bethany go to sleep okay?'

'Yes, we read a little bit.'

'But her light's off now?'

She nods, still smiling. 'Why don't you two go and sit down – the first course is almost ready.' I take in the smooth dance between husband and wife. Claudia is what you would call a good hostess.

I follow Marcus through, traipsing in his shadow, aware of an awkwardness between us. We sit and I can see his leg jiggling under the table. I haven't made small talk for over a decade and there's little point him asking what I've been up to of late. There are many other things, big things, we should discuss, but it feels too fragile a time for most of them.

'I called Sandcross. Martha was sleeping but they said she'll call me back.'

He nods, twisting his glass in a winding circle. 'Oh.'

'She's not doing brilliantly?'

He keeps his eyes on the glass. 'Yes. Well, I did say.'

'How long has she been in hospital?'

'Sandcross is nicer than some hotels – I'd hardly describe it as a hospital.' He rubs a hand over his eyes, then says, 'She freaked out when she heard you were coming home, actually.' It's a cruel thing to say though I'm sure he didn't mean it that way.

'Do you know why?' I meet his gaze, unflinching.

His sigh both irritates and saddens me. 'We used to get hate mail, and phone calls. Someone had her personal email address. Things went directly to her for a while. Before she told us.' He's watching me. I try to remain steady though guilt floods me. He goes on, 'She was stopped on the street, and one woman followed her for almost half a mile shouting abuse.'

'Mistaken for me?'

'Yes.'

'The papers said I had a sister, I read them; everyone knew I was locked up.'

69

He shrugs. 'Not everyone reads the detail. Look at the picture, skim the headline. Teenager murders best friend in drug-fuelled frenzy. Two and two make five, or six, or whatever. You've always looked alike.'

I close my eyes, needing a break from his gaze. 'Was she frightened?'

'Absolutely terrified. Wouldn't stop screaming. The police were called. They called Dad. She was locked up for six months that time. She's a danger to herself, isn't she? Always has been. That's the thing, it's hard to protect her; it's not like Dad and I haven't tried.'

Is there an accusation in his tone, in his words? I choose to ignore it. My heart is pounding. I keep my face neutral and watch him down a second glass of wine as Claudia comes in with a tray of food.

11.

Claudia Reynolds

When I walk into the dining room I realise I have missed something. The atmosphere is tense; Marcus's glass is empty. I put the food down in front of them and refill Marcus's drink. I have made a simple starter of avocado and prawn salad. Marcus couldn't remember what Kate liked but muttered something about avocados.

We start to eat. I force the green sludge in, follow it with a fleshy prawn; I chew and chew. I find food a chore. I spend so much of my time distracted by it. Marcus is a foodie. He likes everything fresh and well prepared. When we met I was a student and I could barely boil an egg. He used to invite me to his flat and make elaborate, delicious meals. Succulent meats and tender vegetables. Things I hadn't tried before.

He sent me on a cookery course shortly after we married and I do most of it now. I can piece together flavours and textures. I serve plates of colourful, tasty fare matched with just the right wine. He cooks on a Sunday and insists on Bethany joining us. It's the only day of the week we all eat together. I dread Sundays. Her palate is a baby's – not sophisticated enough yet to enjoy what he offers her. But like me, she makes the correct noises, she doesn't criticise. My poor daughter with her haunted eyes and bowed head. I had wanted better for her, expected better. I suppose everyone feels that way about their children. Still, she won't be here forever. She'll be able to fly the nest one day. I hope she leaves and doesn't look back.

Marcus is speaking about business now. His increasing portfolio of property. He jokes that he owns half of London. Kate's chuckle seems as half-hearted as my own. I suppose the business must be part of the fabric of her childhood. Selling houses to the rich. Her father, a self-made man from humble beginnings. A builder once. I don't think she'll be heading into the company herself, though Marcus said that at one point James was quite sure she would take the reins. Marcus is playing nice but I know her mere presence has him fuming. I wonder if she knows it. There was a time when I wouldn't have wanted to meet her. She was a scary, dangerous part of Marcus's history. My parents were horrified when they found out she was his sister, and who can blame them? They got over it. Won over by Marcus's charm and obvious affection for me, their only child. He stopped bothering a few years ago and I've stopped taking their calls. They likely think I don't want to talk to them, when actually there's nothing I'd like more. But the conversations are marred by all the things I can't say. The things I daren't mention.

She seems nice. I'm surprised to even think it, but she does. She looks a lot like Martha, but somehow she's more real. Martha gives the impression that she may shatter at any moment, as though if you touched her even lightly, she might fall to the floor in fragments. Kate is solid, substantial. Bethany liked her. She doesn't know the story yet though. We're going to have to tell her, of course we are. There is a piece in the local paper already. It will spread further, and there will be repercussions. I almost agree with Marcus on that; it probably is inconsiderate of her to have come back to Kingston. But where else was she to go?

I clear away plates, refill Marcus's glass. Bring mineral water for Kate, surprised she isn't a big drinker. The meat is ready, beef bourguignon, dripping in heavy red wine and flavour. I blanche and sauté the greens, make sure the plates are heated and then I serve.

'Good grief, Claudia, this food is incredible.'

I smile. Marcus looks pleased and pats my hand as he would a small child. 'She's quite the cook, eh?'

I beam at him. I am a good pet; easily trained, easily rewarded. I think of standing, picking up the plate, throwing it at his head. I often have these kind of thoughts. A 'what-if?' sort of a game I play in my own mind. So many what-ifs. I never carry them out though. I cook, and clean and smile.

I say, 'Is it strange being back in your hometown, Kate?'

She nods. 'Do you know, it is. It's changed but quite a few shops are the same.'

'We've got something ridiculous like twenty-two coffee shops – did you notice?'

Kate laughs. 'It's a wonder they all stay in business, isn't it?'

Marcus smiles and says, 'Coffee's terribly trendy, you know.'

'It is.' I nod.

We all giggle and I'm almost enjoying myself. Marcus signals the plates with a hand wave and I get up and start clearing. He puts a tender hand on the small of my back and I beam at him. It takes me less than ten minutes but when I come back into the room the atmosphere has changed again.

'I was just saying to Kate that you don't do much in the days.'

I continue to grin, resisting the urge to list the many mindless chores I undertake in a twenty-four-hour period.

'Perhaps you two might meet for a coffee in one of the trendy caffs?'

I nearly choke on a sip of water. I don't socialise, not ever. I haven't done so since Bethany was born. Probably even before. I see Marcus and his colleagues, occasionally his dad. I take things to Martha on request.

'Oh, I would love that. How about Monday, Claudia?'

I look at Marcus who nods.

'Monday would be fine. Perhaps after I drop Bethany at nursery?' I say tentatively, still not understanding what Marcus wants from me here.

We eat pudding, the tension between them palpable. When we part ways I hug Kate to me and re-confirm our plans to meet. Marcus drops her home and I clear everything away. When he gets back his mood has darkened.

'You did well tonight, Claudia.'

I almost relax. The anger is not at me. He nods to himself, stalking around the living room. I'm curled up on the sofa. Thinking, trying to be one step ahead. He's praising me, pleased, but I remain on guard. Things can change so quickly.

'She's cracked, finally bloody cracked.'

'Oh?'

He stops, drops down near me, taking my hands in his. 'Bloody bitch has decided she's innocent, reckons she remembers things.'

I hold my breath, squeezing his hands back, unsure how I ought to react. Unsure why that isn't a good thing.

He pulls me into his arms. His thick hand unpins my hair, I feel it curl down my back and I remain still. He lifts it gently then drops it *whoosh* in my ear. He washes it for me sometimes. I used to think it was the sexiest thing ever.

'You'll be able to keep an eye on her, find out what she's up to. She's hired a fucking private detective,' he snorts. 'We'll have them poking about. For fuck's sake.' He's pulling at my hair now. It's just a step away from hurting.

'She seemed . . . nice.'

He looks at me and I stop breathing. He manoeuvres me somehow so I'm facing him. He is staring intently. 'Don't ever forget what she did, darling. Naomi was her best friend. I wouldn't even consider sending you to coffee but I need someone to keep an eye on her. She'll make trouble for us all, mark my words.'

I nod and he reaches out to touch my face. There are tears in his eyes. 'I'm sorry I'm so hard on you sometimes. You're a wonderful wife. I know I never say it. I just so want everything to be perfect.'

He's drunk. I feel tears prick my own eyes. My arms circle his body. I feel it, coming off him in waves. Pain, all that pain. I knew he was damaged goods. Stupid, stupid little girl that I was. I thought I could fix him, take it all away. We sit like that for a long time. My arms wrapped around him. I feel his tears pool on my chest and I hold him tighter.

12.

Madison Attallee

I am at Warrene Academy, sitting in front of Hilary Anselm, the same head-teacher I met six years ago. Time has not been kind and it took me a moment to recognise her. She knew who I was instantly and ushered me into her office. Though I had explained to her secretary quite clearly that I was now a private investigator, I think the head has assumed I am still in the employ of the force. I don't correct her when she calls me Detective. My chair is slightly lower than hers, a cheap psychological trick I've used myself during interrogations. I wonder if her students are scared of her or if they can see through her bullshit.

'This is about Kate Reynolds, you say?' I had been careful not to mention she was my employer.

I nod and she peers at me over half-moon glasses. 'I see she's out of prison. Poor Anthea is beside herself. They've already had a run-in. Awful, just awful.'

I know about the run-in but I play dumb. 'You mean Anthea Andrews?'

'Yes. She's never recovered.'

'It must be awful for her.'

'I don't suppose you'll be doing anything about it?'

I am cautious but tell her, 'Kate Reynolds isn't restricted

'under the terms of her release, she can live anywhere within the UK.'

'If you say so.' Her lips are pursed.

I dislike being glared at over the half-moons but I do my best to smile sympathetically.

'I'd like to get some background information on Kate and Naomi, if I may?'

'What an earth for?'

'I'm just going over some old territory, we'd like to gather as much information as possible.'

'Are you trying to get her to move herself somewhere more appropriate?'

'I'm afraid I'm not at liberty to say.'

She smiles in a conspiratorial way. 'It's good to know that the public may have a say. Perhaps you people are taking some notice of poor Anthea's petition after all.'

I am unsettled by the fact that this daft woman is a head-mistress. Of a fee-paying school, which parents must spend a fortune for their children to attend. My own head-teacher has been a driving force in my life. This woman strikes me as stupid, prissy and unlikeable. I let her think what she wants, no longer feeling guilt for not being clearer on my status. If she listened, she'd know.

She says, 'What can I tell you?'

'I'd like to know a little bit about her and Naomi at that time. The dynamic of their friendship, any concerns you may have had. I'm sure you've been over it before.'

'Yes, I have.' She sighs as though to punctuate what an inconvenience it all is. 'She was a very difficult girl.'

'Kate?'

'Yes.'

I ask, 'And Naomi?'

'In trouble too, though obviously led astray by Kate.'

That's not the version I've got so far. 'They were both allowed back in for sixth form with conditions?'

She nods. 'They were, yes.'

'Though you felt Kate was more to blame?'

She nods. 'Oh yes. Naomi started later in year seven. The
Reynolds girl was already troublesome.'

'Troublesome how?'

'Laziness mainly. It was hard to know if she was awake half
the time. They used to play truant as well, you know.'

In light of everything Kate had going on at home, I'm
surprised she made it out of bed in the morning. I don't say
that though. I nod sympathetically and ask, 'But you caught
them?'

'Oh, yes. They were awfully brazen about the whole thing.
Didn't bother trying to hide the days off. Poor Anthea and
Damian were here endlessly.'

'What about Kate's parents?'

'No, never saw them. Her mother had passed by this time,
of course.'

'James didn't come in?'

'No, and we sent plenty of letters home. You can't do much
when the family is that way, can you?'

I imagine James torn apart by grief, Kate acting out on hers.
I wonder if the letters ever made it to him. I wonder why the
school didn't try harder. Kate had been written off. I think
of my own bumpy start, of missing lessons, looking after my
mother. Trying to hold us both together. Had it not been
for the kindness and interest of teachers, where might I have
been? I contain my anger and nod at the righteous woman
before me.

'Kate's mother died just after she started here?'

'Yes, yes, awful, terrible tragedy.' Not enough to cut Kate
some slack, mind.

'Do you think that might have contributed to her behavioural problems?'

'Maybe. Perhaps the mental health problems were genetic. We had her sister here, too, before her.'

That's not what I meant but I nod and ask, 'Martha?'

'Yes, very odd girl.'

'In what way?'

'Didn't join in, only ever spoke to Kate really. It's not what we encourage here at Warrene. We need team spirit. The whole ethos is based on it. She wasn't a joiner.'

'Martha didn't come back for sixth form?'

'No, though she was due to. Kate would have been in year eleven by then. Her father sent the required notice – I think he paid for a whole term she didn't attend. Her attendance was always awful though. She was very unwell. To the point where the other girls were laughing at her.'

So they had pushed her out; she was an embarrassment. I remember feeling sorry for her when we tried to question her. She had been like a startled deer caught in headlights.

'How did Kate do, academically?'

Mrs Anselm sniffs. 'She did okay. It saved her from expulsion, if I'm honest.'

Ah, the league tables – the school's biggest selling point.

'Naomi as well?'

'Oh yes, Naomi was incredibly bright, she ought to have been looking into Oxbridge really. Both girls truanted, as I said, but Naomi could always catch up. It was much harder for Kate. Naomi's attendance also improved drastically after we spoke to her mother and father.' Mrs Anselm takes off the awful glasses and wipes them, perching them back on her pointy nose. 'Kate was a bad apple from the start – but she was brought in to me before her mother's untimely death so we can't go around blaming that, can we? She was good at evoking pity on it though. Her old English teacher thought I was too hard on her but I told him at the time she was no good.' She tuts. 'Turns out I was spot on.'

I nod, internally rolling my eyes. 'What was the name of her teacher?'

'Martin Wilson. Left ages ago, thank goodness. I believe he's at Barnaby's.' She wrinkles her nose at the mention of my old school. I suppress the urge to smile – good for Mr Wilson!

'Thank you for your help today, Mrs Anselm.'

'Not at all.'

I am shown out by her PA who looks miserable, as do all the girls I pass in the corridors. I used to envy the children who went here. They were expected to go on and do well, by right of birth and finance. I wouldn't have done well. I would have been what Mrs Anselm would have thought of as bad stock.

I place a quick call to Barnaby's and am greeted warmly by Lizzy Munroe, the receptionist. She was pretty old-school when I started there twenty-five years ago. She must be ancient by now. She says that Jessica Mason, the head, is up to her neck in paperwork but that I ought to head over anyway. 'I'm sure she'd welcome the break, love.'

13.

Anthea Andrews

Damian is trying to manage me. I watch him from under my paper. I am torn, as I always am by my husband, between annoyance and shame. Annoyance usually wins out. He's so careful, it drives me mad. He's smiling and he leans in to kiss me on my head to say goodbye. I avoid flinching just in time. I hate to be touched now. It feels ugly and inappropriate. I remember the first time he had tried for sex after Naomi was gone. I slapped his hands away. Disgusted that he would think I'd want to. What was the point? He'd tried a few more times. Now he doesn't bother.

I hear his car start and wonder if he feels relief as he drives away. He has never been career-minded, though he's always earned well. He used to go in because it paid the bills, but he was out the door at five o'clock. Keen to get home to me, his loving wife, and then his wife and daughter. For a while things had seemed complete. Now he is the first in and often the last one out of the office. Ironically he's been promoted twice since his daughter has been killed. He is earning more money than we know what to do with. Not that he has anything to spend it on. We are on an enforced penance, as he likes to put it. No holidays. No gifts. I can't see the point in any of it. He bought me jewellery and I burst into hot, angry tears. I told him he was mad to think I'd want it. Anything that sparkled was anathema to the memory of the life we'd lost. The one that had ended mine but seemingly not his.

I push the insistent thoughts away, always tinged with guilt. He expects me to still be here, to somehow be the woman I once was. She's far away now, that woman, dying a little more each day. I shower and chuck on jeans, a hoodie and trainers. My uniform these days. I used to work in an office managing people. I used to wear suits and make-up. I find it odd now that once a chipped nail could have ruined my day. I don't even look at my hands any more.

I know where Kate lives. I followed her back home a few days ago. I'd had to tread carefully. She kept looking over her shoulder, as though my hatred had a life of its own, one that whispered in her ear, making her aware of me, my footsteps in her shadow, my eyes watching her. The thought cheers me up a little and a giggle escapes from my mouth. A little tinkly bubble. I haven't told Damian about following Kate, and I'm not going to. He doesn't care. He said as much. When we were told initially he'd shrugged and said, 'Well she has to live some-where.' In that second I hated him even more than usual and I always hate him a bit. For getting over it, for letting Naomi go.

Naomi. Just the thought of that precious name makes me ache in ways I hadn't known were possible. I can only liken it to the pain I'd experienced before Naomi was conceived, when I kept losing babies. One minute my womb would be full, ripe with promises it didn't keep. Until her. My absolute beloved. A miracle just for surviving thirty-seven weeks. Thirty-seven whole weeks in my old, drying up, uninhabitable body. Naomi. I feel a red ache now – anger. Kate, out and about, carrying on as though she hasn't a care in the world. We'll see about that! I want to know what that girl's up to and I'm going to find out, no matter what. Then I'm going to make her pay.

14.

Madison Attallee

Jessica Mason was more than just a teacher to me and Barnaby's was more than just a school. My father was a myth of whom I have no recollection. My mother is a hopeless alcoholic. When my mum told her parents she was pregnant at nineteen they told her they wanted her to 'sort it out'. To abort it. She, however, was stubborn and dead set on keeping me. There have been many times since I was sorry that she had.

She had plans, I think, my mother. My early memories are of a vibrant, determined woman, quick to smile. A woman I loved fiercely. Her descent into the bottom of a bottle was probably gradual. I don't know at exactly what age I learned to hide empties, or call her work to say she was sick until she got sacked and it stopped mattering.

By the time I was ten I still had some hope. I focused on being a good girl, at home, at school. It didn't work though, and she took to going out. Something I'd once longed for quickly became my worst nightmare. She didn't go to the places I had fantasised that she would – to work, to pick me up from school, to chat with other mums. In fact, she rarely went out in the day. She headed to the pub, taking whatever there was of our dole cheque with her.

Then she started bringing people back. Men mainly. Ones who scared me. They were like her: wobbly, loud. She'd often promise to sort it out, sober up.

By the time I started at Barnaby's I'd stopped believing it and so had she. We accepted our often terrifying lives as being the norm. Horror stories were every day. My mother screaming and hitting me, trips to the hospital for cuts and falls, the odd broken bone. Endless outings to the off-licence.

I was tested at the start of my secondary education and streamed into the top groups, but by then I'd stopped trying to be good, and the rage seeped out of me, escaping from every pore and landing me in all kinds of trouble. Ms Mason took over as head at the start of my second year there. The first time I was sent to her office was for fighting with another girl. I didn't have friends but I was feared. This meant that largely I was left alone, and I left other people alone, too. This particular day was a mufti day. I had forgotten and turned up in uniform, akin to social death at that age. I overheard Marianne Branning laughing about it. On another day I would have ignored her but I'd been up most of the previous night because Mum had had a house full of people. I don't remember the whole thing but rage overtook me and by the time I was dragged off her she was a bloody mess on the floor.

That day, I was quite certain of my expulsion. I hadn't met Jessica Mason yet and she wasn't what I had expected at all. She was the most elegant-looking woman I had ever seen, one I've tried to emulate since. I flinched when I sat down opposite her, eyes carefully not meeting hers.

Jessica said, 'I've been looking at some of your work. Some of it is exceptional, though sadly inconsistent.'

I had remained silent.

'You miss homework assignments frequently, though judging by what you can achieve in class in a short space of time,

84

I'm surprised. I would have thought it would have been quite easy for you.'

I shrugged.

'You had the highest setting scores that I've seen for years.' She stared at me, narrow eyed. I didn't speak.

'You seem to have a lot of sick days. Are you unwell?'

'Sometimes.'

Her index fingers met in an arch over her lips, a pose I would later come to understand meant she was thinking.

'I don't believe you. Would you like to tell me what's actually going on?'

I had no intention of doing any such thing. I was a minor. I knew that if social services took me, Mum would have been dead, or worse, and I had come to understand by then that there were worse things than death.

'No.'

She raised her eyebrows at that but didn't push it. She told me, 'Marianne has been taken to hospital. Most of her injuries are superficial though she has a nasty cut on her eyebrow. She'll need stitches. My guess is she'll be scarred for life.'

I couldn't think of anything to say to that.

'Her parents are at the hospital. Surprisingly they have decided not to press charges.'

I hadn't even contemplated the police.

She went on, 'Her mother says she knows your mother. Apparently they used to work together many years ago. She thinks you may be having a troubling time at home, hence why they won't be involving the police. She sounds quite reasonable, luckily for you.'

I had no idea why she was telling me this.

'I'm sorry.' It was barely whispered and not really meant. I didn't have the space for remorse at that time.

Our eyes met and her gaze held mine. I felt naked in that

moment, exposed in a way I had never been before.

'Marianne won't be in until the end of the week. You will apologise to her. Here in my office, a safe environment for her. You will give her a chance to tell you how she feels about being attacked. You will also come to my office every single day for the foreseeable future until half past four. You will bring your homework with you and do it here. I will witness you doing it. I expect you to turn up to school every single day. If, for any reason, you cannot make it, you will phone me directly. You, not your mother, or you pretending to be your mother.'

I think about that meeting as I drive and it still conjures up a hundred different feelings. That day was the day I was brought back to life, and I hadn't even known I was dead. My meetings with Jessica continued throughout school life, and during my degree I emailed and called her regularly. When I got home, we had dinner once a month. She was at my wedding, standing in the photos, proudly holding my hand in exactly the spot where my mum should have been if she'd bothered to show up. She is Molly's godmother and the first person Rob rang when I was sent to rehab. She visited me once and would have come again had I not refused her. It's been nearly a year since we last spoke. Funny where life takes you, and how.

Lizzie stands and hugs me, fussing to take my coat and get me a drink. I knock on Jessica's door and get the usual 'come'. I sit and we stare at each other. Her index fingers over her lips. We'd hug if we were different kinds of people.

She says, 'You look a lot better than when we last met.'

'I think I've put on a few stone.'

'You needed to.'

I nod.

She says, 'I haven't heard from you.'

'I'm sorry.'

She smiles. 'Me too. How's Molly?'

'She seems okay. I'm only allowed to visit her under supervision.'

'For now. We email, you know.'

'I do. I'm glad, thank you.'

She smiles again. 'This too shall pass, my dear.'

I feel tears prick behind my eyes. The same words she has spoken to me so many times before. She's always been right but I'm not sure if Molly will ever forgive me, or if she should.

'You're not here to discuss Molly, are you?'

'No. I'm working on a case,' I reply.

'Oh good. You're still in private practice?'

I grin; she has a way of making everything I do sound better than the reality. 'I'm still not allowed back on the force, if that's what you mean.'

'You know full well it's not.' She sounds stern but her eyes are soft.

'I've been employed by Kate Reynolds.' I wait to see if the name registers.

'Ahhh, the angelic teen slasher, as the *Comet* dubbed her.'

'The very one.'

'I suspect you won't tell me too much, though I'd be lying if I said I wasn't curious. She was at Warrene, I believe?'

'She was, which is what led me here. Do you have a Martin Wilson working for you?'

'Ah yes, Martin is an excellent English teacher. I'm sure we pay him half what Warrene did, but he claims to be happier, so who am I to argue?'

'Having met his former boss I can see where he's coming from.'

Jessica laughs. 'Hilary Anselm. Not the most fun character.'

'You know her?'

'We mingle professionally; I don't know her well.'

'I wouldn't think you're missing much.'

She laughs again, not commenting either way, ever the diplomat. 'So you're after a chat with Martin?'

I nod as she glances at her watch.

'You're probably in luck. He should be heading out on break any minute. I'll walk you over to his class. See if we can't catch him before the bell goes.'

She points out various awards and displays as she goes. I feel at ease in her company and wonder why I have shut her out this past year. The bell blasts just as we arrive at his class and a mass of teenagers push past us.

'Slow down,' she calls out. Mutters of 'sorry, miss' respond as she rolls her eyes at me. I am greeted inside the classroom by a clean-cut, nice-looking man. He must have been newly qualified when he was at Warrene. I guess him to be at least five years younger than me.

'Ms Mason, hello.'

'Hello, Mr Wilson. Now, I'm sure you're very busy but this is Madison Attallee, an ex-pupil here and an ex-police-officer turned private eye.'

He raises an eyebrow.

'I know – terribly exciting, isn't it? Anyway, she's working on a case and would like a chat. Would you mind?'

'Of course not, as long as you don't mind talking while I photocopy?' He grins and waves a stack of papers at me.

'Fine by me.'

Jessica turns to me. 'I look forward to hearing from you, Madison. We ought to arrange our next dinner date.'

I agree and smile at Jessica. I've missed her more than I realised. I follow Martin into a small room. It's full of shelves and a large complicated-looking photocopier. If he recognises me he doesn't show it. Hopefully I'm old news these days. He gets the machine going.

'How can I help?'

'I believe you taught Kate Reynolds and Naomi Andrews?'

'The miserable Warrene years. Yes, I taught them.'

'It looks like a beautiful school . . .'

'Yes, it does, but it's pretty ugly on the inside. I nearly left teaching altogether at one point.'

'You switched to the state sector instead?'

'I did.'

'For less pay?'

He looks surprised at the question but nods. 'But more reward. Jessica reminded me why I got into the profession in the first place. Barnaby's may not be shiny, but it has substance. Although I'd be lying if I said I couldn't do with more cash.' He grins. 'Anyway, about Naomi and Kate?'

'Kate's been released.'

'Yes, I saw it in the paper.'

'I'm looking into her case again.'

'I thought it was pretty cut and dried?'

'Just tying up a few loose ends.'

His eyes narrow at that but he doesn't pry.

I say, 'I heard from Mrs Anselm that you had raised concerns about Kate?'

He sighs. 'I had, yes. Not that it did any good.'

'What concerned you?'

'Lots of things – the truanting, acting out in class. I saw her meeting a man after school, kissing him, and I say man not boy – this must have been when she was in year 11 – I'm quite sure she was just sixteen. He looked to be in his early twenties.'

Oliver.

He continues. 'I'd taught Martha before so I knew the family were troubled. Kate and Naomi's friendship was too clingy. Naomi was a very forceful girl. Kate certainly could have done with a bit of breathing space.'

'What did Mrs Anselm suggest?'

'Letting it go, as long as grades were met and fees were paid.' He shakes his head.

'What would you have done?'

'Tried to get them help. Kate had been through a lot. Naomi was a very strong personality and Kate was needy. They were suffering from opposite problems, so to speak.'

'What do you mean?'

'Kate was starved of attention, which made her meek and eager to please. Naomi was drowning in it which made her grandiose and difficult. Naomi's mother, Anthea, was absolutely convinced of her daughter's greatness, and as a result so was Naomi.' He shrugs. 'I guess the girls each fulfilled a need in the other.'

'Naomi wanted hero-worshipping and Kate was happy to provide?'

He chuckles. 'Put simply. Yes.'

I ask him, 'Were you surprised when you found out about Naomi?'

'Of course. I thought their friendship was unhealthy, but not fatal.'

'But do you think Kate was angry, under the surface?'

He grabs a pile of photocopies and loads another piece of paper, pressing various buttons. 'I can only guess, but yes, I suspect she probably was. She was bound to snap at some point.'

'You sensed something was imminent?'

He tilts his head, quiet for a moment. 'I suppose I did, though God knows I'd never have guessed what. I just knew nothing good was going to happen anytime soon unless they were helped. I think I would have dealt with them better now. Or I hope I would, with some experience under my belt.'

If only someone older and more experienced had been paying more attention to the two girls, perhaps things would have turned out differently.

15.

Kate Reynolds

I wake up with a shock to my phone ringing. I grapple with my bedside table and answer it before it rings out.

'Hello.' I know it's Oliver before he speaks, it's a withheld number again.

He sounds annoyed. 'Hi.'

'What time is it?'

'Nearly eight.'

'I overslept.'

'It happens.' Not to me. Not for six years. I don't think I've slept for longer than three hours at a time since I went in. Prisons are noisy and none of the noises meant anything good.

'How are you?' he asks.

'Okay I guess. You?'

'Yes, I'm all right. I'm on my way to work.'

'Where's work?' And then realise I know from his LinkedIn page.

'On the outskirts of town. I'm in the car.'

I wonder if he's being vague on purpose. 'Do you live in Kingston?' I ask him.

'I'm not far, where are you?'

'Surbiton.'

'Nice – one of Daddy's flats?'

'Yes.'

'All right for some.'

'What?'

'I said it's all right for some.' He's laughing. I don't join in.

'I, uh, got cut off the other day,' he says.

'Yes I know, I don't have your number or I'd have called you back . . .'

'Well, that's the thing . . .'

He's so quiet I think he's gone. I say, 'Oliver?'

'Sorry. Yes . . . Um. Thank you for looking me up. It's . . . sweet, I suppose.' And then I know what's coming. I'm so stupid.

'You're not happy to hear from me.' I say flatly.

He pauses again. I snap, 'Don't worry about it, I'll leave you alone.' I hang up before he can say anything. Then I burst into tears.

I replay the conversation in my head. I replay the conversation from the other day. I wonder how I'd invented some kind of happy reunion. I think about the dig he made about the flat and am pleased to find the tears drying up and a wave of annoyance in their place. Oliver always found it vaguely amusing that my dad had money. Amusing and useful. I remember paying for a lot of drinks and tickets. It didn't annoy me then. It's annoying me now – the implication that I somehow have a cushy deal. I've lived the past six years on a knife edge. I'm still living on a bloody knife edge. Flat or no flat, I'd rather be broke and have my family than this. And have him. Oliver. I'm irritated to find I'm crying again. I wipe away the tears. Useless. I should know that by now. Crying rarely helps.

I shower. I over-bought products but I manage to find a use for every one and I take far longer than necessary. By the time I get out I feel a little better. There's no point letting Oliver's insensitive comments and lack of interest get to me.

I'm going to meet Claudia today. My sister-in-law, being sent to connect with me in place of my siblings. My sister hasn't called me back. I try not to take Martha's silence personally – she's in a psychiatric ward, for God's sake, no matter how Marcus wants to describe it. It can't be nice. Funny that I used to envy her.

She was so absolute in her madness, so absent by it. In some ways that made her more free than I was. I was always just aware enough to look okay. I often toyed with following in my mother's footsteps. Then I met Naomi and Oliver and it was like someone had switched the lights on.

Naomi was utterly fearless. Marcus fell for her hook, line and sinker, and who could blame him? At sixteen most girls were on the verge of becoming adult, Naomi was already there. A free soul, housed in a body that made all kinds of promises. She broke his heart and laughed while she did it. It wasn't just that I envied about her, though. It was that she seemed so much more worthy than me, of love, attention. I'd look at her doting, adoring mother and compare her to Ruth. A broken and haunted woman. Naomi always seemed enough for Anthea – as though her life was utterly complete because of her child. I always thought Ruth would have been better off without us kids. Probably my dad too. I'd see her flinch when he touched her. I used to think she'd be better off dead. And then she was.

Bethany looks like Ruth, Martha and me. My mother had strong genes even if everything else about her was weak. I bet Martha dotes on Bethany when she's well enough. When we were children my sister had a host of dolls, which she was constantly caring for. I was clueless, I'd lose heads, arms, tangle hair with chewing gum. She used to hide them from me so I couldn't ruin them.

Dean had asked me if I wanted a family at some point and

I'd laughed at the idea, shaking my head. He'd asked if it was because of my mother. He'd pushed hard on Ruth and I'd struggled to answer.

I experienced her more as a background presence than an actual person. She was always there physically, but mentally she was off somewhere else. She'd be sitting on the sofa, a vague smile on her beautiful face, upstairs having a lie down, out at an appointment. Barely there, hidden behind a large glass of vodka.

She was immune to us most of the time. Whether we were hurt, fractious or ill. She'd shrug and send us on our way, to our father, the nanny, each other. Marcus took it the hardest, he devised lots of ways to get her attention. None of them worked; good behaviour, bad behaviour, everything went unnoticed. He turned his efforts to Dad instead. I thought about Mum more after she died. When I missed her, or the idea of her.

Dean was relentless with me in searching out a happy memory. For a long time I couldn't muster any at all. Eventually one came to me. Mum sitting in the garden singing. I was watching her from behind a willow tree. I'd never heard her before. Her voice was arresting. Low and rich. 'Amazing Grace' poured out of her like an instrument, sun lit her from behind and she looked like an angel. She saw me watching and stopped. I ran and threw my arms around her before I thought not to and, for the only time I can recall, hers circled me back. I remember inhaling her hair, pressing my hands against her shoulders. I don't think I had ever been that close. She softly pushed me back and stroked my face.

'Mummy, you're beautiful.'

'So are you, darling.' And then something changed. I could see it in her eyes. It was as if she came to. The wall came up again. The moment ended. She moved away, adjusting me as she went, so there was space between us. 'Run and find Anna now.'

I didn't want to, I wanted her, but when I tried again to reach her she stood, turned and went back into the house. When I told Dean about this he asked me how it made me feel. I told him it was worse than it had ever been before. Before that day I had just assumed she was incapable of affection, mothering, as though something was missing. I realised then that it was there, a maternal instinct, but just out of reach. She died two years later. I never touched her again.

I'm early to meet Claudia. Not Costa this time. It's going to be a while before I brave going back there. I don't want to bump into Mrs Andrews again. It's busy in here. Gaggles of giggly young people, students from the university, I guess. Men in suits who dip in and out with paper cups, not stopping. Women with buggies laden with colourful shapes and jingling bells. Small, bemused babies lost somewhere in the accessories, nuzzled deep in sheepskin throws, their eyes poking out. The end of rush hour. A switchover time.

I am jolted from my nosiness by Claudia. She is dressed well, less formally than before; it suits her better. I stand to greet her and take her drinks order. I watch her while I queue for coffees. She is a head-turner and plenty of men take a second glance. She either ignores it or doesn't see. Her eyes stare straight ahead at nothing. She is so still she looks like she might not be real.

I pop her coffee down and she smiles. She clicks sweeteners in and watches in horror as I pour sugar freely. I laugh. 'I know, it's dreadful. I hope it calms down, but it's so nice not to be rationed.'

She takes a sip of her coffee. 'You're enjoying freedom?'

'Oh, yes. There are so many little things you take for granted. I'm not watched or monitored – it's wonderful.'

'It must be.' There is a pause; her words seem to echo around us.

I ask her, 'You met Marcus when you were very young?'

She nods. 'Yes, twenty-one.'

'What were you doing then?'

'Studying.' She rolls her eyes as she says it as though learning is a silly pastime.

I ask her, 'What subject?'

She blushes. 'Law.'

'Wow.'

She's shaking her head, colour rises on her cheeks. 'I didn't qualify. I don't practise or anything. I got the degree, first class, would you believe.' She laughs, getting redder. 'Marcus was working for James by then and he had a sideline of student lets. A girlfriend and I rented one.'

'What happened?' I ask her. 'Did you change your mind? About law?'

She shrugs, thin shoulders rising under cream cashmere. 'I graduated, we got married. We both wanted children and Marcus was doing well financially. There didn't seem much point.'

I think about my brother. His constant need to shine. I'm not sure he would stand to be outdone by his wife. 'And then Bethany arrived.' I smile.

'Yes, she came along almost immediately. Bless her.'

'No desire for any more?'

Her eyes wander. 'Not yet.' She sips at her coffee. 'Marcus says you sat a degree?'

I shrug. 'It staved off the boredom.'

'Still, a big achievement. Especially . . . well, you know, doing it there.'

I had always assumed I'd go to university. Naomi and I had discussed where. Probably London, for the nightlife. I smile

97

at Claudia but it feels strained. 'It won't be much use with a record hanging over my head.'

'Is that why . . .? Marcus told me . . .' She's blushing furiously.

'About the private eye?'

She nods. 'Sorry, it's none of my business.'

'It's okay, it's an obvious question, isn't it?'

She waits while I try and think how to put it. 'It's partly the work thing.' I don't tell her that I don't really need to work, not financially. Dad has been awfully generous despite disowning me in every other sense.

'I assumed some provision had been made.'

I nod. 'I believe I'm innocent.'

She asks, 'Why did you confess back then?' and then apologises straight away.

'No, it's fine. I don't mind you asking. I just wish I could give you a proper answer.' I struggle, trying to find the words. I think of the things Dean has said about a fugue state. 'Everyone was saying it was me. I couldn't remember anything very clearly but I was angry at Naomi. Really angry. Well, you've read my diary along with everyone else?'

She nods.

I go on, 'My lawyer said I was definitely going down, but I'd get less time if I pleaded guilty. Dad said I should do what my lawyer said.' I sigh. 'I realise how it sounds.'

'So why didn't you tell anyone?'

'I told my dad.'

Her eyes widen. 'You're kidding?'

'No. He hasn't spoken to me since, and he refused to pay the lawyer any more money after I told him.'

She looks appalled. I feel the familiar shame broil in my stomach. Unlovable, unwanted. I hear the girls in prison laughing as another visiting day passed by and I was the only one still on the prison floor.

'Why?' Claudia says.

'He said I needed to accept my situation and get on with it.'

I take a slug of coffee. Embarrassed, though I don't know why. 'He wouldn't take my calls. Never answered my letters. Marcus wrote to me and told me to leave him alone.'

Her eyes are shiny. 'God, that's awful.' I look away, scared I might cry. She asks, 'What if you're wrong?' She blushes immediately, muttering, 'I'm sorry, it's none of my business.'

It is the million-dollar question. The one that keeps me up at night. What if I'm just mad? Like Ruth. Like Martha. But worse. Dangerous, murderous mad. I swallow and say, 'I don't think I am.'

She smiles, the first genuine one I have seen, I think. It's not like the Stepford ones I saw at the dinner table. It lights up her face. 'How exciting!'

'Oh, I suppose it is! I hadn't thought about it like that.'

'You'd have a fresh start.'

I smile back at her. 'Everyone's entitled to a few of those.'

'Do you think?'

Our eyes lock. 'I do, yes.'

We talk about Bethany for a while; she avoids talking about Marcus when I probe, aside from to reiterate what a great provider he is, and we quickly move on. When I ask after Martha she pauses.

'She's not doing well, is she?' I say.

Claudia shakes her head sadly. 'I'm afraid not. The last time I saw her she was skin and bone, to be honest.'

'Marcus says you visit her quite frequently?'

She shrugs. 'I do try. Especially when she's . . . you know.'

'Is she in Sandcross a lot?'

She nods. 'Yes, her stays seem more frequent. I'm sorry, that's probably not what you want to hear, is it?'

'But Dad looks after her?'

She shrugs. 'I think he does his best.'

'Marcus?'

'He's very busy with work, to be honest.' Claudia looks away, not quite meeting my eye. Maybe I'm not the only one they're ashamed of.

My coffee's cold. I down the last of it anyway. 'She doesn't want to see me, you know.'

Claudia gives me a sympathetic look. 'Maybe you should just show up?'

'It's up to her, isn't it? I'm not going to go inflicting myself.' I sound like a petulant child, even to my own ear. Claudia pats my hand and I blink away tears.

16.

Madison Attallee

I wake up suddenly, eyes pinging open, limbs jolting. I gasp. I feel as if I can't breathe, like I'm suffocating on nothing but air. It's a panic attack. Plain, simple, tragic and boring. I was known at the station as the Ice Maiden. The impenetrable DI. I led my team into horrific crime scenes and sat through children's autopsies. I watched other officers faint, cry and leave. I stood it all out, becoming tougher with each case. Now I am here. Lying shivering, drenched in a film of cold, sticky sweat. Unable to swing my legs out of the bed and fucking walk. Basics. Such sodding stupid basics. They are normal – the panic attacks – for someone in my 'situation'.

I've been talked through them. I know what to do. Wait. Breathe. In and out. And in and out. And in and out. I do this. Eyes glued firmly on the white ceiling, trying to rid myself of the overwhelming feeling that I'm about to die, that I'm caught up in an early death show. A warm up to the final bastardly act. Only it's not. It's all in my stupid head. I don't know how long I've been lying still, breathing, but I can feel my heart slowing down and my skin stops burning hot and cold. Finally, I can get out of bed.

I strip the sheets, pillowcases, duvet cover and shove them in the washing machine. I stand for a moment enjoying the cool feel of the kitchen floor on my feet. It's the second Saturday of the month. I get two court-designated hours with Molly this morning. I get them every fortnight and I always wake up the same way. It's ridiculous really, to be so scared of my own child. But she has the power to break me in a way nothing else does.

I was scared even when she was little, though I wouldn't have admitted it to anyone. Not in a million years. I remember the first day Rob went back to work and I was left there on maternity leave. It should have been Rob – I thought that right from the start – with his calm voice and big welcoming arms. The perfect father, and a better parent than I was ever going to be.

He left that morning and I was at the door, Molly in my arms, in my ratty old dressing gown, waving him off for the day. I put her down in her little Moses basket and then I sat and cried solidly for an hour. It was the weight of her. The responsibility. By the fourth week I had discovered that a few glasses of wine in the day passed the time, made the colicky bellows less harsh. But always when Rob got home, I was there. Dressed. Make-up on. Waiting, a smile plastered on my face. I was the one with the womb, after all.

When I finally went back to work, I knocked the glasses of wine on the head. From one extreme to another, but I was absolutely intent on proving I wasn't my mother. No way would I be Charlotte Attallee. I didn't touch a drop and I wasn't to pick up another drink until Molly was five. It was important to prove to myself that I was fine. Those dry five years said to me that I was unafflicted with alcoholism. The demon that made my mother so lacking in self-control and dignity. But I worked instead of drinking. Long hours, progressing quickly. Extra shift? My hand went up. I rose rapidly through the ranks. Leaving Molly at nursery was never a problem for me, though

I made the right noises. What I felt every morning when I walked away from my tiny baby daughter was relief.

Which isn't to say I didn't love her. God knows I loved her. I was just so scared of her. I secretly knew I wasn't up to it. As if there may be some genetic link to shit parenting. It wasn't all bad. The older she got, the easier I found it, but by that time Rob was firmly established in his role as the good one. When she cried, she wanted him and he swooped right in. I've wondered, since our divorce, about how much Rob likes to rescue. I thought he was my saviour, but sometimes I think he was a barrier to my child.

He's on time. I can see him out in reception. My caseworker is smiling at him. Giggling at something he's said. Women love my husband. They always have. Then she is there. Small, but so much bigger than she was a fortnight ago. All blonde hair and flushed cheeks. She comes in and heads straight to me, leaning in for a hug. This is a good, good day. I hold on, as if for dear life. Her skinny little shoulders are the best thing I've ever put my arms around. It's not always like this. At first she wouldn't even look at me. But she kept coming. And that has to mean something, right?

'Hello, Madison.' Her own bit of justice – I haven't been Mummy for nearly a year. The 'Mummeees' used to drive me mad. Now I would give anything to hear them. Careful what you wish for.

I ask how her week's been and she thinks seriously for a moment and tells me the ins and outs of who is friends with who and who is being left out (I'm glad it's not her). I ask what she's been doing and she says she's been very busy with Daddy and Janet. I ask who Janet is and she looks at me like I'm stupid and says, 'Daddy's girlfriend.'

I nod and manage to avoid being sick in front of her. I'm

distracted for the rest of the visit and I hate myself for it, but she chatters on and hugs me again when it's time to go. I hold on a second too long and she says, 'Ow, Mummy, you're hurting me.'

Mummy. I giggle and pretend to chase her with squeezy arms. She squeals in delight and then she's gone. I'm left sitting alone. An ache in my heart and a bittersweet feeling.

Janet. The only Janet I can think of is someone Rob works with. She's been at a few of his office events. I half remember a dark-haired woman about my age. Did she fancy my husband? Would I have even noticed? I'm not jealous. Not of Rob. That right disintegrated a long time ago. But Molly. My little Molly. I'm assaulted by images of them as a family, walking along hand in hand, some other woman doing the whole mum thing with my daughter. And doing it better, no doubt. It wouldn't be hard. Anything would be better than two measly hours every fortnight in a contact centre.

Next I get to see my shrink. He's a few doors along in this awful government building. Blood is taken, to check I'm on the straight and narrow. To check my cleanliness. Any tainted blood, which means alcohol, narcotics, prescription drugs I haven't been given legitimately, and my situation with Molly will be reassessed.

He comes in. Dr Abanol, cool, calm, collected. I immediately feel a wreck. The sweating doesn't help. But I have my 'doing just fine' shit-eating grin plastered across my face. He smiles. 'Madison, how wonderful to see you.' His eyes do their usual flick up my legs. I'm wearing trousers today. I hope it's a disappointment.

'How was Molly?'

'Fine, fine. It was lovely to see her.'

'That's good.' More smiling. Perfectly sized white teeth. A dashing contrast with his olive skin. Not a hair out of place.

My own bleached frizz is a mess. I'm quite sure I can feel it expanding with perspiration.

'And how are you?' Here comes the earnest look. Dark eyebrows knit together revealing one neat small line. His stupid, fucking head tilts to one side. The perfect picture of concern and empathy.

I mirror the look back as I always do, tilting my own head. I put on my pondering face. Intently thinking about the question in hand, as though I'm not asked it every two fucking weeks. I never tell him that I'm pissed off. Or that I fantasise about hurting Rob. That I miss the adrenalin of my job.

'I'm doing okay.' Not great, he doesn't expect great. I have supervised visits with my child, for God's sake.

'How are your meetings going?'

I haven't been to any since I last saw him. 'Oh, yes, fine. I don't even think about having a drink or anything any more.'

I do. But then I think about never seeing Molly again and it staves me. I try instead to think about everything but a drink. My favourite pastime at the moment is 'What if?' This can take many forms but is always a variation on the same theme. What if I hadn't started drinking? What if my mother wasn't an alcoholic? What if I'd never met Rob? What if I'd gone into a different career? And the biggie: what if I am my mother? But these things feel private. Not something to be shared with uber-shiny man.

'How is work?'

'Yes, going very well, actually. I have another new client.'

He beams. 'That's wonderful.'

It's a formality, a box-ticking exercise. I often think it must be as dull for him as it is for me. We while away half an hour. I leave. I assume he ticks boxes. I hope they are the right ones.

★

I get in the car and drive. I hate the place I'm headed to and yet I make a weekly pilgrimage anyway. Dutiful and sad. It's ironic after spending the morning comparing myself to her. When I get there the curtains are drawn shut. I put my key in the lock and a nauseating smell hits me as I open the door. It's human flesh, piss, shit and sweat mixed with a hundred other things. I take shallow breaths and call out, though she never answers.

She is sitting on the sofa. Smaller than ever, drowned in a huge terry-cloth robe. I bought that for her last year. It was soft and fluffy then. White like cotton wool. It's wretched now. Grey and worn. Long threads dangle from it. Her once slender, pretty legs hang out of the bottom. Paltry sticks punctuated by large postulating veins. She is a horrible colour, grey turning to yellow, and I think the same thing I always do. She doesn't have long left. And if there is a god, why doesn't he make it sooner rather than later?

The TV is on. News, turned down too low for anyone to hear. It doesn't matter. She's not watching it. There is an ashtray next to her. Butts leaning awkwardly, about to spill. Other debris is scattered around. Nothing of value or use. Packets of fast food, discarded clothing, underwear, bits of paper trampled underfoot. She shifts deep-set eyes on to me. She swigs from a bottle that rests between her legs. Cups and glasses were given up on long ago. She smiles, toothless, and pulls a cigarette out from a packet next to her. I sit down, forcing my body to ignore the filth and the dirt. I reach for my lighter, putting the flame to the end of her fag, then I reach for my own, hand shaking but feeling relief as I inhale.

'Hello, Mum.'

She nods. 'All right, Madison.' Her once beautiful, liquid, warm voice now a rasping, wheezy sneer. I can smell the booze – whisky today, strong and tangy – and I know how it would feel. I think of my body warming up and my shoulders dropping, a letting go – the envy is there. Brutal and inappropriate. Still rising even as I look at Charlotte Attallee, my ruined mother. The promises the bottle makes. The peace it can give while it steals your life.

'How are you?' I ask her, trying to keep my eyes trained on her face.

She shrugs and sucks her lips in. It gives an odd effect. Skeletal. I picture her, here, dead for days before anyone knows, the flesh leaving her, exposing the bones underneath, the ones I see now, through thin papery skin. I shut my eyes for a second. We don't say much. There's no point. But I sit and we smoke. I ask if she needs anything, knowing what the answer will be, and I give her the £50 as she requests. I'll do the same next week. Knowing the money will speed up her death. Not knowing if that's right or wrong. She doesn't ask how I am. She hasn't done for years now. I don't expect it. I used to try and clean up. Bring shopping, try and get her in the bath. I don't do that now.

I leave feeling relief, guilt and shame. I'll be back next week.

When I get home I stand in the shower for a long time thinking about Molly and my mother and myself. I try and will myself to cry but nothing comes. The hard stone in my stomach feels heavier though. It always does on these weekends. When I get out I prepare pasta which I pick at. I look at the files on my desk and open one. I have cobbled together Kate's diary entries published by the press and I open one now.

27th January 2009
I don't know what Naomi's playing at. She's supposed to be in love with Marcus. That's what he thinks anyway. She's been ignoring him for days and then I saw her talking to Oliver!! He was leaning in as well. The way he does when I tell him things.

She was all doe-eyed and serious with her stupid black frizzy hair twisting on her fingers. If I see her do it again, I'd like to snap those fingers one by one. They both jumped when I came out of school. She's such a div. I smiled and pretended I was happy to see them anyway. She was all hugs and so was he, but I bet they were talking about me.

1st Feb

Martha's ill again. I can't help. I want to shake her, make her wake up out of it but I don't. I can't. She needs to stop being such a pain but she doesn't listen now anyway. Dad is away so I put her to bed and told her not to come downstairs again until I said. She gave me the look I don't like. The one that makes me feel scared. I thought about locking her door. I have a key now, but last time she made a disgusting mess and I got into trouble! It's so unfair.

Naomi's been here for two days – her and Marcus made up. Her mum came around yesterday looking for her. Naomi used me as an excuse of course and made me lie and say my dad would be home later. She's getting on my nerves to be honest. She was laughing because Oliver hasn't phoned me and she knows I'm upset. It was all I could do not to grab my knife and put it in her. I think she's jealous of me because Oliver likes me and not her.

I watched them last night. I was walking past Marcus's room. It was pathetic. My stupid brother grinning like an idiot this morning, and Naomi grinning back. I suppose it's better than when she's ignoring him and he's all fucked up about it. Martha stayed in bed at least.

I light a cigarette and try to imagine Kate's adolescence. Not so different from mine after all. A lack of grown-ups. Something Naomi had taken full advantage of by the sounds of it. I stub out my fag, feed the cat and go back to the file.

17.

Claudia Reynolds

Marcus keeps whispering on the phone. He thinks I don't know anything's the matter but I always do. On the upside, he's being extremely nice to Bethany and me. I've got my guard up though. I've been lulled into a false sense of security before. Bethany is a lovely girl, but so quiet. And I know why. Of course I know why. It's the only thing I still feel – pain for her. I remember when I was bombarded by my own pain. Open, gashing wounds. Now I'm largely numb – which helps – but she's my weak spot. If she wasn't here I would just go. One way or another. I'm thinking about it though, in a distant way. What Kate said about prison has stayed with me. My prison may not be like hers but it's no less real.

I don't know who he's talking to and I don't care. A few years ago I would have. Once I drove myself mad wondering – trying to check his phone, read emails over his shoulder, looking for proof of what I knew to be true. Now I'm indifferent. There are other women. That takes the heat off me. I don't even have the energy left to feel sad about it. As long as Bethany doesn't find out what does it matter?

The morning passes in a blur of chores. Bethany sits at the kitchen table colouring in. She is diligent about it and I feel proud of how naturally bright she is. James is due over so I make sandwiches and snacks, which I cover and store. When he arrives I have a pot of coffee brewing. Bethany's face lights up – she loves her granddad. And who can blame her? James is a nice man. Unlike other men with extreme wealth, his own son included, he has a quiet way. I open the door and he hugs me and then bends to swing Bethany up into the air. She squeals, delighted, not even quietening down when Marcus appears. The rules change when James is here.

They head into the living room after the usual chatter. James compliments the house, how well I'm looking, how Bethany has grown. When I bring in coffee Bethany is on his lap and he's stroking her hair. Marcus is oblivious to his only child, busily discussing business. After half an hour or so Marcus says there are a few other bits he'd like to discuss, perhaps they could head to his office? I clean away cups and plates, ask if they'd like more coffee. James says yes so I put on a fresh pot. I put the TV on for Bethany.

I'm about to knock on Marcus's office door to ask if they would like cake – I made a lemon drizzle this morning – but the door is slightly ajar and I can hear them. I don't know why but I stop for a moment.

'How did she look?' James asks.

'Older.'

'Well, yes, she would I suppose. And this is definitely why she's back?'

Marcus snorts. 'We know why she's back, Dad.'

'Yes, but her mind is fuzzy, isn't it? What does it matter? It's all done and dusted.'

'What if she remembers?'

There is a silence. I'm certain they can hear my heart hammering in my chest. I start walking away to the kitchen door with soft silent feet. I cut the cake with shaking hands and put it on the tray. I walk to the office noisily this time, balancing a tray, letting the spoons jingle a bit, and I knock loudly, waiting for Marcus's response.

James grins at the cake. 'Oh, aren't you a clever thing, eh?' But the smile stops at his lips and the atmosphere feels strange.

That night I can't sleep, even though I go to bed early. Marcus doesn't follow me until much later, by which time I am feigning slumber, keeping my breathing long and even. But under it my mind is whirring. I'm thinking about how brutal my husband can be. I'm thinking about James's wife, so desperate she chose to die.

What if she remembers what?

18.

Madison Attallee

I am nervous enough this morning to want a drink. The want is bodily and all consuming. I think about the last time. Leaving Molly sitting alone at the breakfast table. Running to the nearest shop, desperate and thirsty. I think about pouring the liquid down me, unable to wait the short walk home. Of stopping just for a minute and waking up to paramedics. I think about Molly, small and scared. Not knowing what to do when I didn't come back, eventually phoning her dad. Not today. I can probably make it through today.

I dress with extra care. The years are ticking on – sped up, I'm sure, by my poor lifestyle choices, but the mirror isn't too bad, even if I'm shaking. I get in the car and I put Metallica on full blast, light a cigarette and focus only on the heavy riffs. I will see Peter. I haven't seen him for nearly eighteen months. He was a constant presence in my life. Marianne's older brother, the girl I'd beaten up at school. Marianne and I became friends after I apologised in Jessica's office for punching her. I wasn't good at it – friendship – and ours might have fizzled out sooner if I hadn't met her brother. Peter. He made me laugh when I thought I'd never find anything funny again. Soon I was going round to see him instead and we'd hang out at lunchtimes at school. He became my best friend.

My boss. And the man I cheated on my husband with.

I smoke two more cigarettes on the way with the window open for all the good it does. I spray myself with YSL and find a stick of gum. I am at the station and I feel even shakier. I sit in the car and all I can think about is him. Peter. The boy who loved me, who grew into the man who loved me. Nearly twenty years of friendship have passed and yet I could never explain to him how it was for me. He was the only person who knew about my mum, who knew what I went through. The only person I would ever let help. He was the only person I really loved.

We reached a point early on where we stopped being friends. I felt it just as much as he did, but we never became lovers. I never crossed that line. He was too precious to me to risk in that way. He was the only man I have ever been myself around. I have never wanted that from my lovers, never been able to manage it. His love was something I never felt I deserved. Surprisingly, he came to my wedding with Marianne, but to be honest I had hoped he wouldn't.

Peter sent me a text that night and told me I looked beautiful. I didn't tell Rob. I left him saying goodbye to our guests and I headed to our room. I locked myself in the bathroom at the fancy hotel that made me feel less than. I drank champagne from the bottle and I let myself feel my heart breaking just for a minute while I let it sink in that the wrong man would be waiting on the other side of the door. Then I showered, changed, made up my face and lay down next to my husband.

This is stupid. Sitting around thinking won't change anything. I swing open the door and step out; I walk towards the place that used to feel like home.

Deanie Ockham is sitting at the front desk, halfway through a call. She raises an eyebrow at me but smiles at the same time.

She waves for me to take a seat. I do. Awkwardly, unable to find where my legs should go. I cross them in the end, likely doing a good impression of a demented Bambi. She is on the phone for what feels like forever but is actually less than two minutes according to my watch.

'DI Attallee.'

I stand and almost trip my sorry arse over in the process. 'Hi, Deanie. Just Madison now, I'm afraid.'

I lean over the counter to shake her hand and I can see genuine warmth in her eyes.

She says, 'You look great. You're thin as a stick, what's your secret?'

Deanie is on a constant diet. A curvy woman always appraising everyone else's body mass as serial dieters tend to do.

I shrug. 'Stress and cigarettes.'

She laughs. 'Hey, I've got the first part down at least.'

'I don't recommend the second, they're hard to get rid of.'

She nods and sighs. 'You're probably right.'

'How're things here?'

'Oh, the usual.' She rolls her eyes. 'DI Malone's busy micromanaging us all.'

'And how's that going for you?'

Her eyes narrow. 'The same way it would have gone for you, I reckon.'

I nod, taking some satisfaction in my nemesis's obvious lack of popularity. There are some things I don't miss.

Her phone rings again, she presses a button and it stops. She says, 'I don't reckon you're here for chit-chat?'

'No. I want to see P—DCI Branning.'

She stares at me for a minute. I can hear a hundred questions churning around in her head. 'You sure about that, hon?'

'I am. It's work related.'

'Your PI business?' So everyone knows.

I try and smile. 'Good news travels fast.'

'All news travels fast. How you finding it?'

I shrug.

She says, 'Plenty of people here miss you.'

'Maybe.'

She shakes her head at that. 'Definitely.'

She looks at me intently. I stand awkwardly, suddenly aware of all my limbs again and unsure where to place them. I wonder if my face is red. I try to smile and grimace instead. Why is cheerfulness such an almighty fucking effort? I give up and let my face fall into its usual pissed off expression. Immediate comfort is my reward.

'I'll ring through for you, hon. He's in most of the day.'

I listen to her end of the call, imagining I can hear his voice. I can't, of course.

'OK, he says he'll be right down. Why don't you take a seat?'

When I see him I feel faint, actually faint. It's the effect he's had on me in recent years. The one my husband never did. But now it's something else too. Awkwardness. The sense of good stuff gone bad. Two decades of friendship ruined because I am what I am.

He smiles. I smile back and stand.

'Madison.' And I feel it again, the ache low down in my stomach.

'Hi, Peter.'

He's beaming. 'I was about to head out for lunch – care to join me?'

I nod and wave at Deanie who raises an eyebrow.

No one here knows anything for sure about Peter and me. They suspect, but the only people who really know are us. And Rob. Rob knows. We walk around the corner in silence. I light a cigarette and offer him the pack. He takes one. He is an occasional smoker. Anathema to my own thirty-a-day greed. We walk to Rosie's. A greasy spoon just far enough to avoid the rest of the team. I don't look at him but I can feel his presence. My steps two for his one.

When we get in, Marcia smiles as if I was just here yesterday. She takes our coats and leads us to 'our' table. Everything is bittersweet, tangy with my regret. She drops menus and promises to be back in a minute. Although they are never busy in here, Marcia's minutes can run into the tens. Peter looks at me. I look right back. I drink him in. He looks well, tanned. I wonder if he's been away, perhaps he was on a nice beach somewhere while I was busily writing my life story in fucking rehab. It's been over a year since I saw him, perhaps closer to fourteen. I haven't counted the days without him. I had put him somewhere else but now the pain of his absence washes over me.

'How are you?' he asks. He's looking at me, into me. The same intense eyes he had at fourteen, the same look of concern when he'd come and help me clean my mum up. When he'd come and hold me, back in the days when I still cried.

'Better,' I say too quickly. He waits. I sigh, 'I'm okay.'

'How's Molly?'

'I don't really know. I see her for two hours every fortnight. She seems okay.'

He shakes his head. 'Christ.'

Marcia appears from nowhere and asks, 'You know what yer having?'

I don't think I can stomach food and tell Marcia, 'Oh . . . Just coffee for me, thanks.'

Peter says, 'I'll have coffee too and a club sandwich.'

We don't say anything else until the coffee arrives. She has brought Peter's sandwich and a plate of biscuits which she puts pointedly in front of me. One of those people who seems to need to feed, even when it's not asked for. I realise I'm hungry and reach for one anyway.

He says, 'I've tried to call.'

He has as well. Endlessly to start with. I didn't have my phone for the first twenty-eight days while I was locked up. No outside contact is another of the stupid rules. When I came out, I had dozens of missed calls from him. Voicemails, text messages. He wrote a letter that went to my old house. Rob opened it, read it, and came around to the flat, banging at my door. It's been a year since I went into rehab. I've been out for sixteen months.

'I know,' I say.

'I found your new address, thought about coming around.'

'I'm glad you didn't.'

He sighs at that. 'Are you . . . did the . . .?'

'I'm not drinking.'

He nods. 'I'm glad.' And I know he is.

I smile in an effort not to fall apart and tell him, 'I get tested every two weeks. Court ordered.'

'That's awful.'

I fiddle with the paper napkin on the table, tearing away at the corner. 'It is as it is. I left Molly alone in the house.'

'You nipped to the shops.'

'To buy vodka, Peter. I nipped to the shops to buy vodka. At seven a.m. And I didn't make it back.'

'I know.' He looks away from me. I shouldn't snap at him. It's not his fault he always wants to see goodness in me. And it's not his fault that there isn't any there.

He pours us both a coffee, adding just the right amount of milk and sugar to mine. He slides it over to me, then he says, 'I'm very much hoping it is, but I don't think this is a social call?'

I shake my head.

'Not that it isn't nice to see me though, right?'

I find myself trying not to smile. 'Not that it isn't nice to see you.'

He smiles. 'Okay, what are you after, Attallee? If not my perfect body?'

I laugh as he spreads his hands wide to show all that I'm missing out on and my nerves evaporate. This is Peter. The boy whose bedroom window I used to climb into in the middle of the night. My first kiss. My last shag.

I sip my coffee. It's too hot. 'I'm working on a case.'

He says, 'Good, and without an awful boss to get in your way, right?'

'Right. The last one was a tyrant.'

He nods, looking deadly serious. 'So I've heard. But with a perfect body, yeah?'

I giggle. 'Peter.'

'Sorry. Your case?'

'Kate Reynolds.'

He thinks for a moment. 'God, the angelic teen killer?'

I nod.

He says, 'Malone ran it. Made his name on it, just before my time here, must be five years ago or so.'

'Six.'

'Right, we've had the mother of the victim in, I believe. Anthea Andrews. Reynolds is out, back in the area.'

I nod. 'Yep.'

'Odd choice of location, nothing we can do about it though.'

'Anthea hasn't hired me – Kate has.'

He frowns now. 'What for?'

I take another sip of my drink. 'Reckons she's innocent.'

He doesn't look convinced. 'And you?'

'I don't know. But she pays well and it's not another divorce case.' My voice sounds more defensive than I mean it to.

He still looks dubious. 'So she wants to what . . . clear her name?'

'Yes, and find out who let her take the fall.'

He leans back in his seat. A woman at a nearby table looks at him appreciatively. I glare at her, full of the same rage I used to get when Peter would half-heartedly get a girlfriend. She looks away. Peter doesn't notice, and asks, 'Does she have any evidence?'

'Not really.'

The woman is getting up and leaving. She shoots me an anxious sideways glance. I feel instantly guilty, and simultaneously annoyed.

'I wasn't involved in the case, but as I recall it was pretty open and closed.'

I nod. 'She was found clutching the body. The knife a few feet away. She'd been drinking, taking drugs. Couldn't say what had happened when we took her in.'

'She was sent down on manslaughter, right?'

'There were diary entries. They got leaked to the press, and the jury were equally unimpressed.'

'That's right. Pretty open and closed.'

I nod.

He's studying me. 'Except, you're not convinced.'

I shrug, he laughs. 'Come on, Madison . . . it's not just the money, is it?'

'I don't know. I mean it is mostly the money. I've been in business for six months and we're haemorrhaging cash.'

'Do you need some help?'

'No.' I scowl at him. Getting back on topic, I say, 'It was all just so easy.'

He raises an eyebrow at me. 'Usually the most obvious answer is the right one.'

'Usually, but you still have to dig a bit for evidence. Look,

I don't know. It was the first murder I ever worked. I was the first on the scene.'

'And what? You didn't like her for it?'

I shake my head, trying to put it into words. 'Not exactly, and . . . I just thought there had to be more. No history of violence then she just goes and kills her best friend.'

'Okay. We're not going to be reopening it with no evidence.'

I roll my eyes at him. 'No, of course not. That's why she came to rent-a-cop.'

'Hey.'

I shrug. 'It's true.'

'So what do you want from me?'

I take a deep breath and just say it. 'I want to look at the files.'

He looks like he might laugh.

I go on quickly. 'Look, I know it's not usual, but the case is old, and solved. A member of the public could request those files.'

'Then request them,' he says, frowning.

'It might take months.' I sound whiny.

'Madison,' he groans.

'How about you let me look and I put in a request?' I smile at him. 'If it comes to anything we can say I went through proper channels.'

There are some police who will never, ever bend the rules. Peter isn't one of them, but this is a big ask and I know it.

'Christ. Let me look over them first.'

I grin from ear to ear. 'Thank you.'

He says, 'Did you expect me to say no?'

I glance around, trying to avoid his eyes. 'I don't know.'

'I don't think I've ever said no to you in our whole lives.'

My face burns red as I think about the last time he didn't say no.

'Thank you, Peter.'

He sighs. 'It's okay. Can you stop ignoring my calls?'

Now I'm looking at the table, which is no use because I can still feel him staring. 'I don't have anything to give you.'

'And I don't want to take anything. I just want to have you in my life. However that works for you.'

I pour more coffee for us both and say, 'I heard Rob came . . . to the station.'

'Yup.'

'I'm sorry.'

He laughs. 'I'm more sorry for you, he must have been a prick to live with.'

I don't want his bloody pity. 'You didn't meet him at his best,' I snap.

'I've met him before.'

'Not properly.'

He scowls. 'We were never going to be friends.'

I sigh and say, 'He hates me.'

'You didn't do anything wrong.'

'I cheated on him.'

Peter says, 'You should never have been with him.' The certainty in his voice makes me wince.

I start standing, grabbing my coat. He's there moving my seat back. He pays the bill and we walk back to the station. The angry words about Rob are between us and neither of us speak. My head is racing with a hundred thoughts, things I don't usually let myself think. If Peter and I were ever to be, will he forgive me for marrying Rob? Will he love Molly? I push them aside. They're irrelevant because I'm not going there. I offer him another cigarette but he shakes his head.

'They'll kill you, you know.' I frown and he takes my hand, squeezes it, lets it drop.

We hug at my car. Longer than we need to. He says he'll be in touch about the files, then I watch him walk back into the station. He turns and waves and I get in my car.

19.

Kate Reynolds

I wake to the sound of the paper hitting the doormat. I instinctively jump up, throwing off the cover and landing on my feet next to the bed. Then I remember where I am and feel something swelling inside. Not exactly happiness but not far off. I am getting accustomed to waking up out here in the outside world more quickly than I thought I might. I get back under the covers, enjoying lying here in my own bed, wide enough to stretch out on.

I became so accustomed to being trapped and feeling claustrophobic that I didn't even notice it. Lots of people say prison is a cop-out. Not harsh enough. In some ways they seem right – I had a television with five channels, I could make phone calls. I was one of the long-termers surrounded by other long-termers, who generally want less trouble than their petty counterparts. But I had to share a cell. With Janine. Janine was big and angry and aggressive. My accent annoyed her, my hair annoyed her, the fact that I used 'fancy words' annoyed her. And she had a whole horde of other girls who liked to be 'annoyed' by whatever she was annoyed by. It was six months of sheer hell. I was already panicky and lost, missing my home and family – confused as to where they were, wondering what the hell had happened, if I had killed Naomi and somehow forgotten

– and worse still – whether I had enjoyed it. A gang of them waited for me to come back from the showers one afternoon and beat me so badly that I was on the hospital wing for two weeks. I cried solidly, whimpering for my dad. I kept asking if anyone had called him and didn't believe them when they said they had. Because he would have come. He should have come. I wouldn't tell the guards what happened – I knew better than that – but I begged and begged for a single cell and after I attempted, pathetically, to strangle myself with a bed sheet, they gave in. Despite the ineffectual choice of tool, I almost succeeded. Janine had been out on exercise so I knew I didn't have long. I wouldn't have been able to hang myself. They make sure you can't, nothing is high enough. Instead I wrapped the sheet around my neck and then around the toilet bowl and I crawled towards the door until it tightened and then I pushed myself forward a bit more. If I hadn't passed out I might have done it.

Once I was on my own, it wasn't non-stop violence at least, though the threat was always there. But I wasn't free. I didn't feel the wind in my hair or my legs taking me somewhere with purpose. I didn't lie aimlessly in bed in the morning knowing I could get up and do what I wanted. I sat on my bed, locked in for twenty-three out of every twenty-four hours. But those twenty-three were spent in dread of the one where someone might get me. Those twenty-three hours were spent alone with my own head. So I'm savouring the little things – clean bedding that smells like it has met softener, shampoo in nice bottles, scented soaps. And time. Oh my, the feeling that my time belongs to me again after so long when it didn't is amazing.

I am no longer owned, trapped by someone else's rules. In that way, I can't think of a greater punishment than prison. I ate when I was told, woke up when I was told, and went where

I was supposed to go and when. I was detained at Her Majesty's pleasure. Held firmly in a place not of my choosing for six years. All of my adult life to date. Years that I'll never get back. It doesn't end there either. I will always be a criminal, branded by the invisible scarlet letter. Murderer. My sentence will never be spent, I must always declare it. I'm rehabilitated enough to stand on the periphery of life, but not to join the party.

I get up, boil the kettle, drop water over a tea bag and grab the paper. There is a photo of me on the front page. It's the one all the papers used back in 2011 where I look like the teenage psycho from Poison Candy. Anxiety bubbles up like acid. I try to swallow it down. There is a picture of Anthea Andrews just next to it. She looks tearful and broken. *Continued on page four* . . . I read it knowing I shouldn't. I call Dean, barely able to breathe, barely able to use words. He tells me to come to his office.

When I arrive his receptionist smiles and ushers me in. His 'office' is more like a living room with a desk in the corner. The main part of the room is taken up with sofas, which he waves me onto, then he boils a kettle and makes me tea. He has his ever present bottle of water.

'How are you?' he asks.

I can still barely breathe as I say, 'Did you see it?'

'Yes, I had Linda nip out and grab a copy. I'm so sorry.'

I'm shaking my head, trying to clear away the cobwebs and the fear. 'You warned me this would happen.'

He looks soft, concerned. 'I'm not glad it is happening though.'

'I know that. Maybe you were right. I should have gone far away from here.'

He sighs. 'Maybe, but it's started now.'

'What, you mean it's too late to go back?'

He shrugs but doesn't offer an opinion either way. He's worried about me though – I can see it in his tense shoulders. He walks to his desk where there are bits of paper in various piles. I watch him from the other side of the room. He is straightening the papers and tapping the bottom of the pages on his desk, and then putting them into neat stacks alongside each other. I wonder what he's working on. I don't think he'd tell me if I asked.

I say, 'I don't think I can. Stop. I'm here now, aren't I? I've signed a contract with Madison's company.'

I watch him shuffle, tap, stack and he says, 'I'm sure you could get out of it.'

'I'd have to pay her.'

'Probably.'

'I've caused this much trouble already,' I sigh, 'I don't want it to be for nothing.'

'Then I guess you carry on.' Shuffle, tap, stack. 'How did coffee with your sister-in-law go?'

I smile and tell him. He is nodding in approval and I'm pleased to be able to have something good to say for once. I think about mentioning Oliver but I don't. Dean wouldn't approve, and I wouldn't blame him. He was always scathing of Oliver and considered him to have taken advantage of me. He'd consider it a step backwards to know that I had contacted him again.

I talk about Bethany instead and I tell him Martha doesn't want to see me and that I'm not going to push it.

He nods. 'It's just for now. Who knows what she's thinking.' He carries on with his papers. Shuffle, tap, stack.

I say, 'God, I'm sorry, I'm distracting you. I'm sure you've got better things to be doing than sorting me out.'

He laughs and comes and joins me on the sofa. 'Relax. I'm researching for a particularly dry paper. To be honest, the distraction isn't unwelcome. Besides, I've said before that I'm here for you and I mean it, okay?'

'Thanks, Dean.'

He smiles, his head tilting to one side. 'Now, absent family and bad press aside, how are you?'

'Everything feels a little bit strange,' I admit.

'It's going to.'

'I like being outside though. I like walking, and I don't have any Janines to worry about.'

He smiles. 'That's great. She can't get you here and the main thing is she didn't break you. None of it did.'

'This town's giving me the creeps,' I say. 'I can see memories everywhere, but it's like they belong to someone else. Like another girl lived that life and now I'm someone else with a new life.'

'You are a different person now.'

I nod. 'I suppose I am.'

He asks all about my family and he says it's good that Marcus is trying to include me. He was always more positive about my brother's letters than I thought he should be. I guess Dean is always trying to keep my morale up. He says, 'These are good things, Kate.' I don't tell him my own thoughts about my brother and my suspicions of the man he's become. I don't mention Claudia's Stepford-wife smile and the picture perfect home. It feels disloyal somehow and besides, maybe some people's lives are that perfect. Maybe I'm just jealous.

'I know, I know, they just don't feel like my things yet, if that makes any sense.'

'Well they are. This is your life, start getting used to it.'

I smile agreement. He's right, of course he's right. 'I'll feel better once the investigation's finished.'

He frowns at that. 'You should make a decision to feel better now. You have to be prepared for the fact that nothing may come from it. You need to live now, not wait to live. Haven't you waited long enough?'

If only I could. I ask him, 'What are you doing for the rest of the day?'

He laughs. 'Working.'

'And tonight?'

'Probably more of the same.'

'Not going to divulge any more than that?' Our friendship has always been one sided by its nature. I'd be lying if I said I wasn't curious about his life.

He laughs again. 'I should be getting on now, if you're all right?'

I'm not. But I need to go. 'I am.'

20.

Anthea Andrews

I feel even more aggravated than usual. I watch the Reynolds girl, swanning about as though she hasn't a care in the fucking world. Meeting up with a woman for coffee. Then she walks along the river. I see her stop a few times and lift her face up to the sun, look at the flowers around her – things I don't do any more, things my beloved Naomi will never do again. The bitch. The walk along the river takes Kate into a tall modern building. I wait until she goes in and then I wander by, looking at the placard on the door. Dr Dean Hall.

I recognise that name. I remember him from the trial, trying to plead in Kate's defence, saying she wasn't of sound mind and should be sent to a psychiatric unit for help rather than prison. For murder! Why would she still be seeing him? Maybe she is mad. Tortured, like her mother and sister who I had always pitied. I don't pity her now – I don't pity anyone. I hope that Kate is mad, demented, in pain, even though it can hardly be a fraction of what I go through each minute, each hour. A glance at my watch tells me I need to get a move on.

I poke my head around the door. Damian scowls at me before he can stop. 'You're late.'

'I'm sorry,' I answer, not meaning it. 'I lost track of time.'

He's about to bite back at me when Marilyn steps in smoothly. 'That's fine. Anthea, please do come in and we can get started.'

I plaster on a smile and take a seat next to him. I feel my leg brush against his and I move back, quickly rearranging myself into as small a space as possible, still smiling my fake smile. He flashes one back at me and pats my knee.

'Damian mentioned that you saw Kate this week?'

Of course he mentioned it. 'I did, yes.'

'That must have been tough for you,' says Marilyn, leaning her head to one side.

I don't say anything for a minute. Anyone watching would probably think I was taking a moment to compose myself. I feel my jaw tighten. I use the pause to steady myself. To try and push the rage in before I lay in to our stupid, ridiculous counsellor.

'Mmmm.' I manage to nod.

Marilyn asks, 'Did you speak to her?'

'I did, yes. I told her she ought to bugger off.'

That's an understatement and I know it. In reality I had totally lost my shit. I can't tell this woman that though. I only attend these ridiculous sessions because Damian insists.

Marilyn leans forward and as she does her blouse slips and the top of her bra is exposed. I catch Damian looking and watch Marilyn sit back, subtly readjusting as she goes. I am almost amused as I watch my husband look longingly at another woman's breasts. I suppose once I would have been jealous. Now I don't give a shit. I find I'm suppressing a grin.

Marilyn says, 'Did seeing her make you feel angry?'

I snort a bit, unable to hold in my contempt, and I hear my voice start into a tirade of sorts. Eventually I stop and glare at Marilyn and then Damian who is now busily looking at Marilyn's legs. For God's sake. Though in fairness I don't even shave mine any more. I'm struck again by odd amusement and

I almost giggle. I wipe a hand across my smirking mouth and then I fan my face. It feels very hot; I wonder why the others aren't looking uncomfortable.

'And you, Damian?'

'What?'

'Do you feel angry that Kate is back?'

He shrugs. 'I feel angry about a lot of things.'

Marilyn nods. 'Like what, Damian?'

He sighs and says, 'No, I don't think that's right, I'm not angry, I'm upset. Upset that I've lost my daughter and that she seems to have taken my beautiful, fun wife with her.'

I roll my eyes and say, 'He doesn't care about Naomi. I've told you this.'

He sighs and I turn to him. 'Well, you don't, do you?'

Marilyn chimes in, 'Damian, Anthea asked you a question.'

He sighs again, fidgets and shrugs. 'What's the point?'

'In what, Damian?' Her voice is low and soothing.

'Being angry. It's not going to bring her back, is it?'

I tell him, 'You never loved her as much as I did.'

He opens his mouth to say something and then closes it again. He knows I'm right.

'Do you think that's true, Damian?'

He says, 'I'm sure no one can love a child as much as their mother, but I loved her, of course.'

'You just don't miss her that much, right?' I snarl.

He goes back to staring out the window. I burst into tears before I can help it and Marilyn makes soothing noises at me, which is stupid. The tears aren't sadness, they are my anger. Leaking out. If this therapist was any good surely she'd get that?

Marilyn asks, 'Anthea, do you think Naomi would want for your life to stop just because hers has?'

Damian says, 'I'm pretty certain that that's exactly what Naomi would want.'

I turn on him then. My hand moves as if of its own will before I have a chance to stop it. It swipes out across his face, hard. Marilyn is up and out of her seat, seeing if he's all right. I watch them and suppose I ought to feel sorry for the red mark burgeoning across my husband's cheek. For the new level of badness I have levied onto our marriage. Instead I feel like laughing and as I feel the uncontrollable smile spread across my face I hurry out of the small room. Once I'm in the corridor I erupt into bubbly giggles.

We came in separate cars so I am able to speed away before he comes out. The giggling subsides and the anger re-roots itself deep in my bowels. I toy with feeling sorry for Damian, trying to weigh it up, see how it feels. But I find I don't have the capacity. I park and walk into our house. I look around, as I often do, in wonder. That once we were happy. And we really were. There's no denying that we had a good marriage. Solid. Damian never so much as glanced at another woman then, and I took his devotion for granted. I loved him. I really did. But I loved Naomi so much more. I head upstairs and get into my daughter's bed, imagining I can smell her. I slide my body under the covers and cry quietly. I must fall asleep because I am woken by the sound of Damian coming in. He pops his head around the door and I keep my breathing long and even. I hear him whisper 'I love you' before he closes the door and leaves. I almost feel sorry for him.

21.

Madison Attallee

If I'm looking at the front page of the *Comet* with dismay, I can only imagine how Kate must be feeling this morning. I light a cigarette, inhale, then I hear the office door open and Emma comes back from lunch. Crap. I throw the cigarette out the open window a second too late. She's too polite to comment. I stand and mutter that I'm going for a fag, dropping the paper on her desk as I go. It's cold but at least it's not raining. I really need to stop trying to smoke inside.

I'm certain Kate will feel like shit. I've had my fifteen minutes and they were pretty ugly. Disgraced cop, drunk on the job. People lapped it up.

There was one incident with a woman I remembered vaguely from a playgroup I'd been to with Molly. She accosted me on the street. The rage and bile were falling off her, disproportionate to her lack of involvement. I'd done nothing to her personally. I guess it was the affront to motherhood, abandoning duty. I can't forgive myself, and I'm not sure Molly ever will, but it's bizarre that strangers pick up the resentment and nurse it like their own.

Emma tuts at the paper as I get back into the office. 'Poor love.'

'She's a convicted killer, you know, Emma.'

She presses the paper back onto the desk and tuts again. 'Looked like a scared child to me.'

I hide a smile. I'm getting more used to her. She's not squeamish and she's not judgemental, both of which will stand her in good stead here.

I ask, 'How did you get on with the party list?' We've been working our way through a list of people who were at the party the night Naomi died. Most don't want to see me. I've spoken to two so far, neither of whom were particularly helpful. Both reiterated what I already knew from Kate.

'No more meetings as yet, I'm afraid. You've got Annie Jakes shortly though.' The friend that Kate had dumped for Naomi.

I get to the food court in Bentalls early and sit and wait. Annie is one of those unfortunate young women. Bad colouring, masses of pimples and she's dyed her hair an ungodly orange colour which might have looked cool on someone else, but on her it just highlights the redness of her skin. She sits heavily in front of me.

I smile. 'Hi, thanks for seeing me.'

She shrugs. 'Sure, why not. Nothing else to do at lunch.'

'Where do you work?'

'HMV,' she scowls. 'Probably not for long though.'

'Are they closing this branch as well?'

The scowl may just be her expression. It's not helping her out. 'Dunno, probably.'

'Have you had lunch?'

The scowl deepens. 'I'm on a diet.'

'Coffee?'

'Caramel latte. Please.'

I go up and order then put the drink in front of her, she adds sugar. My kind of diet.

She says, 'So why are you investigating this now?'

'Oh, just some loose ends that have come up.'

'You that pig that got sacked, right?'

'That's me.' I smile at her.

She slurps noisily at her drink. When she puts the cup down there's a faint line of foam on her upper lip. It makes a sort of head on one of her pimples.

She smiles a bit, which does little to improve her looks. 'Guess you gotta take what work you can get now, huh?'

'Yup. Mind if I take notes?'

'Nah, course not.' She sips again and licks the foam off the pimple this time.

'So you were at Kate's party?'

'Yeah.'

'You were friends with Kate?'

The frown is back, 'I was, but not so much once she met Naomi.'

'She ditched you?' I try to sound sympathetic, though I can imagine that Annie made it reasonably easy.

She snorts. 'Yeah. I don't want to sound shitty or anything but Naomi pretty much told her what to do.'

'And Kate did it?'

Annie shrugs. 'Pretty much. She used to be all right.'

'But not by then?'

Another shrug and a loud sip. 'I dunno. No, not really. Not when she was around her anyway. Naomi was pretty popular. I think the parties were kind of her idea. Kate didn't have many friends before she knew her, to like, invite, y'know?'

I nod that I do know. 'So, what do you remember?'

'Kate being wasted. She was snorting something with Naomi. Coke, I s'pose.'

'Was that new?'

Shrug, frown, slurp. 'Dunno. She didn't used to do it when we hung out, but like I said she'd pretty much ditched me.'

'Was her boyfriend there?'

'Yeah, Oliver was there. He made a joke about me being fat. I nearly left but then I got chatting to Martha outside.'

I pause at that. 'Martha? Are you sure?' Kate had been quite adamant that Martha was away that night.

Annie's looking at me like I'm thick. 'Yeah, I know who Martha is. I've known that family since, like, infant school.'

'Of course, sorry. Where was Martha?'

'Out the back. I stepped outside, after Oliver was being a shit. Like I said, I was going home. I could walk to mine through the back garden.'

'Right.' I've looked up the layout of the surrounding properties and know that she could indeed just stroll across.

'She was in the garden. She made me jump actually, cos it was pretty dark.'

'What did she say?'

'I dunno exactly. We like, said hi. I asked if it was too loud for her, she was, you know . . . kinda fragile.'

I nod. 'Yes.'

'She said it was. I told her about Oliver being mean, said I was gonna go home.'

'Did you?'

'Yeah, I left. Was gone before it all kicked off.' She sounds disappointed.

'Probably best.'

She shrugs and says, 'Look, it's not good to say but plenty of people weren't that sad.'

'About Naomi dying?'

She shrugs. 'Hey, I get it sounds harsh but she wasn't a nice person, get me?'

'I do.'

'I was surprised Kate hadn't snapped earlier, to be honest, way she spoke to her.'

I nod sympathetically.

'I should call her,' Annie says.

'Kate?'

'Yeah. See how she's doing.'

I smile. 'I'm sure she'd be happy to hear from you.'

'I'd better get back.'

I get in the car and dial Kate's number.

'Hi.'

'I just spoke to Annie Jakes.'

She pauses. 'God, how is she?'

'She said Martha was there that night. At the party. You said she was locked up.'

I hear her take a breath in. 'She was. She was always away when Dad was. Well, usually. She was there in the day. I didn't see her all evening though.'

'Annie reckons she spoke to her in the garden.'

'She can't have.'

I pause.

Kate says, 'Annie must be mistaken.'

I say perhaps she was and I hang up, not pushing it, but I'm quite certain that Annie was telling the truth.

I turn up the stereo. Richard Ashcroft is moaning that the drugs don't work. Tell me, brother. I try to check the calendar on my phone and simultaneously switch lanes. Someone beeps and I shout ineffectually. I need to speak to Martha Reynolds.

22.

Kate Reynolds

I'm back at Dean's office. It's in danger of becoming a second home.

'I remember you talking about Annie,' he says.

The guilt bites at me. 'Yes, she was probably my best friend before Naomi. When we were younger. Our back gardens were joined.'

'But you didn't really like her?'

'I don't know. She was . . . convenient, I guess. God, that makes me sound horrible, doesn't it?' I think about the bullying in prison – the beatings were bad but sometimes it was just the sniggers and the whispered comments that hurt the most. Naomi and I used to do that to Annie. It made me feel big. I guess that's how Janine and her gang felt about me.

Dean is sympathetic. 'It makes you sound honest.'

'I had sort of hoped she'd go to a different secondary school. Her parents talked about sending her out of the borough.'

'But she ended up at Warrene?'

I shudder at the memory. 'She insisted she didn't want to be away from me.'

'Ah, and then you met Naomi?'

I nod. 'And dropped Annie like a ton of hot bricks.'

'Relationships change,' he shrugs.

I smile, grateful for his support, for his faith in my inherent goodness. I say, 'I know.' But inside I'm remembering Annie's face when she tried to tag along at lunchtime. I'm remembering Naomi laughing at her and me joining in. Gaining false self-worth from someone else's misery. I remember feeling ashamed and then cross that she wouldn't just go away.

I ask Dean, 'Why would she have said Martha was there?'

'I don't know, maybe she's getting confused.' Dean is always giving everyone the benefit of the doubt.

'It's unlikely though, isn't it?'

'I don't know.'

'It doesn't matter,' I say. 'Madison's going to see Martha today anyway.'

He nods. 'I thought you said she was in hospital again?'

'Yes, she is.'

'Maybe you should see her first?' he suggests. 'Explain who Madison is?'

'She doesn't want to see me.'

'What?' His brow knits in concern. I look away.

'I called and the nurse, or whatever she is, said she wasn't ready but that she'd call me.'

His frown deepens. 'But she's agreed to see Madison?'

I grin. 'I doubt Madison's asked in advance, to be honest. She should be there by now.'

He seems not to hear me, but then he looks at me, concerned. 'Are you okay, about her not seeing you?'

I shrug. 'Maybe she's scared.' I don't add what I hope, that maybe she feels too guilty to see me after six years of silence.

I know where I'm going when I leave Dean's. I planned it last night when I found his work address. He's an IT manager. According to his school dates he's also at least four years older than he said he was. There's a coffee shop over the road. It gives me a perfect view of the front of his offices. I sit, order tea and hover behind the *Daily Mail*, the only paper they have. I wonder if this is how the rest of my life will be? A series of coffee shops. If I don't manage to prove my innocence I will be a murderer forever. Which means I'll stay unemployed. That scarlet letter will follow me.

At least Dad is willing to fund me, so far anyway. Dean says I should be grateful for it. He contrasted my freedom with that of my fellow inmates. They'd leave, get parole and spend a lifetime having to declare the sins of their past. An instant barrier to any kind of success. It's not like that for me. Dad has conveyed via Marcus that my account will remain full. Marcus even hinted the other day that if I were to consider relocating, a house would be paid for in full and put in my name. I was cross at that. They should believe me, surely? They should have my back. Every day I sat in that damn cell waiting. Expecting the key to turn, to be told it had all been a big mistake and my dad to be there having fixed it all. Every night I'd go to sleep on a pillow damp with my tears, wondering if I was so bad that he just stopped loving me.

Oh God, there he is. I glance at my watch, 12:30 p.m. I watch him walk out, glance at his own watch, cross the road. I'm sinking into my newspaper. For a moment, just a moment, I think he's seen me. I almost ready myself and am about to lower the paper when I see him wave. Then a woman appears on the other side of the glass. His side not mine, and I watch her wave back and he walks over to her. They smile, linking arms, heading off. I'm up and out before I have time to think it through.

I follow at a distance. It's busy enough for me to blend in. I hear her laugh, snippets of words, but nothing concrete. They go into the park. There are fewer people here, but I'm too absorbed to worry about it. They sit on a bench and I walk just inches behind them. Their hands are joined, resting on the back. There is a ring on his finger and a matching one on hers. I feel a sharp pain in my stomach and I must make a sound because she turns around. She looks at me, doubled over, then asks, 'Are you okay?'

And I'm frozen stupidly to the spot and he's looking at me over her shoulder and he looks as sick as I feel. Now she's standing and I see what I had missed. A bump. A baby. He's going to be a dad. They are a family. Oliver's family. I'm turning and running. I can still hear her shouting after me but I can't stop. I run so hard and so fast that my legs nearly buckle. The tears come then. I am on the side of a big field, near the Millennium Park. I remember when they planted it. I remember coming here with my dad, wandering to the playground over the field, him pushing me higher and higher on the swings, the wind in my hair. Years later Naomi and I used to come here to smoke cigarettes, weed, whatever we had. Hidden and furtive. She'd kiss boys and I'd wait, awkward. Trying to be nonchalant, until Oliver came along.

His wife. That woman is Oliver's wife. I don't know why I'm so surprised. Only my life has been on hold. For everyone else it's carried on. Well or otherwise.

The sky has turned angry and grey. The heavens are going to open. I walk slowly back to my flat and when the storm comes the rainwater mingles with my tears. The first night I slept with Oliver it was during a storm like this. We were in my room, everyone was out and it felt like it had been raining for weeks. Maybe it had. It was painful and sweet and surprising. I knew then that I loved him but I guessed he didn't feel the same. When I get out of the bath I have four missed calls. It's him. I turn my phone off and climb into bed, listening to the rain hit my window and thinking that I'm still that stupid little girl all these years later.

23.

Madison Attallee

I can't get hold of Kate. I've left a voicemail. I have found Oliver and it turns out he's married. Living over in Chessington, not far from her. I'll be going to see him, but I figure I should let her know first. I don't think I'll call him in advance. I have a bad feeling about him, the same feeling I had at the time.

I'm on my way to Sandcross. Martha refused Kate's visit, but I won't give her the same opportunity. I know she hasn't spoken to her sister yet and that she's in a bad way. Well, you don't end up in the nut-ward on a good day, I should know. I'm enjoying smoking and driving. Courtney Love is screeching about Miss World and the sun's almost out. I'm singing badly and flicking ash all over the place. Fuck it. There should be some upsides to not having to car-share with a kid any more.

I'm greeted at reception by an insanely happy Irish nurse who introduces herself as Denise. She grins at me as though we're old friends and asks how I've been. I smile and say fine. The grin widens as though in genuine delight. I wonder if she's been at the happy pills. I follow her down a long hall.

'Martha's in grand form herself today, so wouldn't you be in luck.' She continues to chatter inanely. Since she doesn't pause for breath I assume no response is required on my part. I sneak looks into various rooms and glimpse ornate ceilings and calming plush sofas. Everything is very bright white. Not sterile though. It's all warmed up by carefully hung paintings and colourful vases of flowers. I have to remind myself this is pretty much the same as the place Rob dumped me in, even if it is better dressed. A nuthouse is a nuthouse, after all.

My first thought is that Martha looks a lot like her sister, though she's much thinner. She's that kind of stick shape that lets you know she's not okay. It's a look I sported myself a few years ago. She looks up when Denise pats her hand and introduces me. I offer my own hand which she takes limply. Her whole demeanour is soft, sunken and slow. Her eyes are glassy, too shiny, from the meds. The lovely mongy meds.

'Hello, Martha.'

'Hello.' She looks at me blankly.

Denise beams at bugger all. 'Well, that's grand. I'll be off, though I'm just a beep away if you'll be needing anything.'

'I'm Madison Attallee. I'm doing some work for your sister Kate.'

'Your name is unusual.' The words come out in slow long syllables.

'I don't think I've met another Martha, to be fair.'

She smiles but it's vacant. 'It was my grandmother's name.'

'It's nice.'

She shrugs. 'Daddy's mum. I never met her, sadly.'

'My mum chose Madison after a place in America she always wanted to visit.'

'Did she?'

'Visit?'

She nods. 'Yes.'

'Nope, 'fraid not.'

'That's sad.'

I shrug, getting out my notebook and pen, resting them on my lap. 'That's life.'

She leans forward, reaching for a glass of water. I hear her sip, swallow; it all seems such an effort. She says, 'I always thought travelling might be fun.'

'Have you done much?'

'Hardly. This is as far as I ever get, I'm afraid.'

I smile. 'You've plenty of time yet.'

She doesn't smile back, but looks at me as though I'm very, very stupid. 'I'm not very well.'

'You might get better.'

She shrugs, her stick-like shoulders rising and falling under a silk dressing gown. 'Did Kate hire you?'

'Yes.'

'So she's not in prison any more?' She's been told this on a few occasions.

'No.'

She takes another slow sip of water and then rests the glass precariously on her knee. 'How is she?'

'She's okay, I guess. I'm reinvestigating her case.'

Martha leans forward and slides the glass onto a coffee table. 'Why?'

'Because she thinks she's innocent.'

'Are you the police?'

'No. I'm a private investigator.'

She blinks like one of those dolls that shuts its eyes slowly as you lean it back. The effect is unsettling. She says, 'I'm glad someone's helping her,' though she doesn't sound glad.

'Why? Do you think she's innocent?'

She shrugs. 'I don't know.'

'You were at the party that night?'

'Was I?'

'Yes.' I tell her, 'You spoke to Annie.'

'Annie Jakes?'

'Yes.'

'Did I?'

'She says you did. Don't you remember?'

She shrugs again. 'It's been a long time.'

'It's been a long time since you spoke to Kate as well.'

Her glassy eyes meet mine. 'I'm not a very good sister, am I?'

'I don't know.'

'I asked to visit her.' She turns wide eyes on me. They look damp but it could just be whatever chemical cosh they have her on. 'Daddy and Marcus thought it would be a bad idea. Now it's too late.'

'Why?'

She shakes her head. 'I'm not very well.'

Fuck. This girl hardly knows what's going on right now. 'Did Kate have a lot of parties?' I ask.

'They weren't Kate's parties, they were Naomi's. Naomi was a horrible girl.' Her small pale face screws up crossly.

'In what way?'

'She was loud and could never keep to herself. She was jealous of Kate, you know.' Her eyes narrow.

'That's not what Kate thinks.'

'Kate was utterly besotted with her.' She is studying me now, looking alert for the first time since I arrived. She says, 'You were in the paper. It said you had some kind of a breakdown?'

'I did, yes.'

'I'm sorry.' From one fucking nutter to another.

'I'm sorry you're here,' I tell her.

'You shouldn't be, here is safe.'

'Home isn't?'

She shrugs.

'Kate is keen to see you,' I say.

She sighs. 'Soon.'

'Kate thought that you were away the night of the party.'

'Yes, I was here.'

'Well, Annie seems to think you were home that night. She saw you in the garden.'

She stares at me a second too long. 'She must be mistaken.' Her voice sounds clear now, definite, and I wonder how much of the confusion is an act. It must be a pretty good get-out clause. *Nope. Too crazy. Leave me alone.* Maybe I should try it.

'She seemed pretty sure.'

Martha shrugs, looks out of the window and away from me. 'She was probably drinking.'

'Why? Were they all quite out of it?'

'I don't know. I'm sure I was here.' Her face is screwed up in concentration.

'When did you find out Kate had been arrested?'

'I can't remember – Daddy must have told me.'

'Seems like the sort of thing you'd remember.'

She wipes a frail hand over her face. I can see all the veins. It's the hand of a woman many years her senior. 'I forget things.'

'Like your sister being locked up for murder?'

She shakes her head as though trying to clear it and says, 'Lots of things. Lots of things.'

'What's wrong with you?'

'I have anorexia and depression.'

'And memory loss?'

She reaches for the water, but changes her mind. I watch her eyes dart around the room, avoiding mine. I wonder if she has that fugue state that Dean was talking about. Perhaps he should come in and assess the crazy mare.

'Was Oliver there that night?' I ask her.

Her eyes dart around the room again. Everywhere but mine. 'Probably, he was always at ours.'

'What was he like?'

146

She's busily looking out of the window again. 'I don't know. I didn't know him well.'

I prompt her, 'He was a friend of Naomi's.'

'Was he?'

'You must have known that.'

She wipes that small shaky hand across her brow. 'I feel tired.'

'Kate and Naomi argued that night, do you remember that?' I push.

She shakes her head. 'Ask him, I don't know. He'd know.'

'Ask who? Oliver?'

'No.' She's shaking her head quickly now, side to side. 'No, no, no, no.'

'Martha.'

She stops, stares at me, wide-eyed.

'Ask who?'

'Him, ask him.' Her eyes are wide. Frightened. Her voice is high and loud.

'But you were there?'

Her voice is quiet now, pleading, 'I'm tired. I think I need to rest. This wasn't a good idea. I'm not supposed to speak to anyone. You should have rung. They would have told you that.' She's pressing a call button hanging on a rope around her neck.

'Why aren't you supposed to speak to anyone?'

She shakes her head.

'Are you not allowed to speak to Kate?' I ask.

'No, I can't speak to Kate. She's causing trouble. I'll get in trouble too!' She continues pressing the call button.

I press her. 'Who, Martha? Who will be cross? Marcus? James?' I throw names, looking for a reaction.

Her eyes close and stay shut.

'Martha?'

'This isn't a good idea.' Her voice is almost a whisper. She's like a child.

Denise appears and Martha tells her, 'I'm very tired now, I think I ought to sleep.'

Denise pats her hand. 'Well, that's fine, dear, you get yourself to bed, I'll see your friend out.'

Denise eyeballs me until I stand. I put a card on Martha's bedside table. 'If you ever think of anything, Martha.'

She doesn't look up at me or move.

Denise shuts the door behind us and ushers me along.

'Is she always like that?' I ask her.

'Like what?'

'Confused. She seemed perfectly lucid one minute and freaked out the next.'

She sighs and stops walking. 'What was she confused about specifically?'

'The night of Naomi Andrew's murder, for one. She doesn't seem to know where she is or where she's been and she's convinced someone's going to be cross at her for talking to me.'

Denise says, 'You're not an old friend, are you?'

I pause and then tell her, 'I'm trying to help her sister, which might in turn help her. I'm a private investigator.'

She glances at me and seems to make a decision. She shrugs, a sad look on her face. 'She has good spells and bad spells. She's an unfortunate case though, I'm afraid. Martha's been boomeranging backwards and forwards for years. You can see for yourself she's all skin and bone.'

'Is that normal – to never get better?'

She sighs at that. 'Sometimes. More usually with the schizophrenics and psychotics.'

'Which she's not?'

'No, she has a diagnosis of anorexia.'

'You don't agree?'

Denise starts walking again; I follow. She says, 'I'm not a doctor.'

'But you don't agree with her diagnosis?'

'I think not eating is a stress thing with Martha. She's not your average weight obsessive. Not that it's really about weight, even for those girls.'

I say, 'She's been in and out of here for years – aren't the doctors concerned about her lack of progress?'

'The therapists here leave her alone, we're more like a holding pen for when she becomes a danger to herself.'

That's dreadful, I think, and ask Denise, 'Isn't it their job to make her better?'

She nods, lips pursed in a thin line. 'You would think so.'

'Look, like I said, I'm trying to help her sister. I get the impression you care about Martha, and helping one might help the other so if you've got anything to tell me that you think might help . . .'

She doesn't speak for a minute, but continues to walk. Then she sighs, stops and says, 'James stopped the treatment.'

'Her dad?'

'Yes.' She nods.

'When?'

'After Kate got arrested. They brought Martha in the day after. James said she was very upset and he didn't want her being bothered, just well fed, well looked after.'

Bloody hell. 'And nobody questioned him?'

She tuts at that. 'They did and he just paid more money, made a large donation. So we hold her.'

'Are you sure about that timeline? That she was definitely brought in after Kate's arrest?'

'Oh, yes. We'd all been talking about it. It made the paper the day she was arrested, if you recall.'

'Do you have records of when she arrived and how long she stayed?' I ask her.

'Yes, I would have thought so.'

'Can you check them for me?'

She shakes her head and I can see worry lines jumping up at the corner of her eyes. 'I don't think I should . . .'

'Please.'

An official-looking man walks up alongside us. 'Hello, Denise.'

'Dr Tibbett.'

We walk along behind him in silence until we reach reception. I pause as if to shake Denise's hand and slip her my card. I keep eye contact and say what a wonderful job she's doing with Martha.

24.

Claudia Reynolds

Everyone is out – Marcus is at work, Bethany at nursery. I rush through my chores. Blood is pounding around my body. I can feel it in my veins and my ears, making my heart race so hard I'm surprised I don't die. I have a purpose today and mixed in with the ratcheted anxiety there is also excitement. I scrub, hang washing, and hoover everything to within an inch of its life, then I marinade chicken, peel potatoes and shell peas. I am expert at these things. Perhaps one day I will have a job as a housekeeper.

Marcus keeps the key to his office in our bedroom. It's in a shoebox at the back of his wardrobe. He thinks I don't know but I watch everything. The house is my domain – I know every nook and cranny. Except the office. The office is a foreign land. His, not mine. He'd laughed when he was setting it up and I asked why. He'd said everyone needs a room of their own. So said Virginia Woolf, I responded, but he didn't get the reference and he scowled at me for being a smart ass. But we'd giggled. Those were the days when he laughed things off. I even pouted and asked where my room was. 'Darling, the whole house is your room,' he'd said, and I felt like the luckiest girl alive. The whole house. Still beautiful now. More so than it once was and yet it holds me captive, a perfectly decorated prison. My golden cage.

I have the key. It swims and wriggles in my sweaty hand and I wipe it on my skirt. By the time I am standing outside the door I am unsure. He could come home, it's happened before. Not often. He used to come back on his lunchbreak for sex. That stopped a few years ago, thank goodness. Everything is loud, my breath rasping in and out, and the pale blue door looks too bright. I have to do this. I force my hand to reach out and it slips before I can get a proper grip. I hear the handle click as it turns and feel like my lungs might explode, but once I am in my breathing evens. I feel better . . . victorious. Oh, I know I haven't achieved anything. Not really, but I'm so used to being the perfectly trained obedient wife. I'm tempted to trash the place – to just go through smashing things up. The pictures of him on the walls, smug-faced at various events with clients. I want to rip his degree off the wall. Stamp on it, mourn for the loss of my own education. The things I might have been. But not now, now I need to look.

It's a long process. Each thing I touch has to go back exactly how it was. I go through every drawer. There are receipts in one of them for lingerie and dinners. All in the same pile, paper-clipped together. A mistress. Not the first, and certainly not the last. I pretend not to know, but I always do because his insatiable demands lessen for a time. I am grateful to these women for a moment's peace. There's nothing much else here, it's all business-related – things I don't know about, large sums of cash. I have no idea how much we are worth. I find a book of accounts and flick through it. Profit is dipping. It's still good, but nothing like it used to be in its heyday. He signs off a lot of lunches, some hotel stays. I put the book back, hit by how pathetic it is that I don't know my own financial situation, and the complete trust I put into someone who hates me.

I open cupboards, the filing cabinet. Nothing. I'm left staring at the safe. I try Bethany's birthday, no. Mine, no, and it says three tries and I'm locked out. That means I have one left. It will be her, Ruth. But will it be her birthday or the day she died? I go for the latter – always the darker option with my husband – and it clicks open. The blood starts rushing again. My hand reaches out to see what's there and almost, almost freezes. A photo album. Lots of pictures of Ruth, the family, the siblings. My heart aches just a little bit, for the frightened-looking little boy in these photos, gripping hard to his mother's hand.

She was beautiful, Ruth Reynolds. Truly a work of art – high cheekbones, wide-set eyes and full lips, though they never seem to smile. They were younger even than us when they married, Ruth and James. Seemingly he rescued her from some unpleasantness at home, though it's never discussed further than that. Marcus always said they were happy, but I doubt it. She has the same bird-like quality as her daughters. They would be her miniatures, but their colouring is different, less striking. I look like her, I know that. I'm not being big-headed. Beauty certainly hasn't brought me a better life as I had assumed it would, but it's there nonetheless. I know what Marcus liked in me. A fixable version of her, and I've played the part beautifully, moulded into what he wanted. Still, it seems not to be enough.

I put the album back and reach underneath. I pull out a scrapbook, filled with all of the articles relating to Kate's arrest and subsequent trial, mingled in with legal documents, which I skim. God. Papers relating to Martha and her many sections. Bills from the asylum they call her spa. Careful, careful, a quick look and put them back. I've been in here for half an hour, my hands are starting to dampen again and I want out. Something else, right at the back – a notebook, no, but something. Bound in canvas, covered in butterflies, worn over time. I pull it out, careful, heart racing. I open up the first page and my blood turns to ice.

DIARY OF NAOMI ANDREWS
KEEP THE FUCK OUT!!

25.

Kate Reynolds

I dream that I am in prison and Naomi is chasing me, trying to tell me something, but she has no mouth and all I can hear are her muffled screams. I wake drenched in sweat, convinced I heard my door close. I am holding my breath. Everything is dark but I see my clock glowing: 3.30 a.m. I get out of bed as quietly as I can and head for the front door. It's shut, but when I turn the handle it's unlocked. Perhaps Oliver crept in. Maybe he's cross that I found him. His wife. I know he can get around locks. He used to show up in my dad's house all the time. Appearing from nowhere.

Did I forget to lock up when I came in? Maybe. I lock it now and turn on all the lights. I drag the duvet off my bed and into the living room. I turn on the TV and watch the light drift in. As the sun comes up I finally fall asleep. When I wake up it's eight and I feel calmer. I probably left the door unlocked, maybe even open. Thinking it was Oliver is me being para-noid. Though I wouldn't have put it past him to do something like this six years ago, he's a grown man now. With a wife and a child on the way. I shudder now at what used to excite me.

I get to Madison's office. Emma takes my coat. Madison is on the phone but waves at me to take a seat as she stands to head outside. Emma perches on the edge of Madison's desk and asks how I am.

'I don't really know,' I say.

Her face is kind, open. 'I would think that's to be expected, isn't it? Plenty of adjusting to be done, eh? And all this to be sorted before you can really relax.'

I half whisper, 'I'm worried I might be wasting your time.'

'Well, now, I wouldn't say righting wrongs is a waste of time.'

Emma's nice. If she was your mum I reckon you'd end up with a much better life than the one that I have. Madison comes in exhaling a puff of smoke. She sits down heavily, dropping her phone on the desk with a clatter.

'Your sister's pretty out there,' she says.

I smile at her bluntness. 'She always was.'

'The hospital confirmed that she was brought in the day after the party.'

'No, she was there already. I'm sure of it.' I can't even bring myself to dwell on what that means.

'How do you know?'

I try to think back. 'Marcus told me, I think.'

'When? Before or after your arrest?'

I feel sick now. 'After.'

'Right.' A pause. 'She wasn't a fan of Naomi's and didn't like Oliver much either.'

'Martha?'

'Yes.'

My heart starts beating a guilty tattoo. 'They weren't very nice to her.'

'How?'

'They made fun of her.' I blush, not adding that I joined in. I don't suppose I have to, Madison's not stupid.

She says, 'Sounds like Naomi wasn't nice to anyone. Martha must have been an easy target.'

I sigh. 'Yes, I suppose she was. Do you think Martha was there that night?'

'Why would Annie lie?'

'I don't know, to stir?'

She narrows her eyes. 'Really? All these years later?'

'You said yourself she's still mad at me.' It sounds pathetic even to me.

'Yeah, at you, not Martha, which is who she's implicating.'

I can't even take that on board at the moment. Implicating.

'I sent Oliver a message on LinkedIn,' I say, changing the subject.

'Great.'

She's being sarcastic and I don't blame her, but it's better out than in I think, so I keep going. 'Then I waited for him outside his work.'

'Even better.'

'I saw him meet his wife.'

Her eyes narrow. I feel embarrassed saying this stuff aloud, but I force myself to go on. 'He saw me, and he's been calling a lot since then.'

'Saying?'

'I don't know; I haven't spoken to him properly. He didn't want to speak to me before.'

'Now he does?'

'He probably wants to tell me to stop stalking him.'

She looks cross, but her voice is even when she speaks. 'Good, don't stalk him and don't take his calls. I'm fucking serious when I say that.'

'I think someone came into my flat last night.'

'Why?'

Tears prick the back of my eyes. 'The door was unlocked. I thought I heard it shut.'

'Might you have just forgotten to lock it?'

I nod. 'I might have.' But I don't sound convincing.

'Jeez,' sighs Madison.

I go on, 'Oliver used to turn up at my dad's – he'd always find a way to let himself in.'

'Brilliant.'

'He's four years older than he said he was.'

Her voice is cross now. 'Stop stalking him. I'm going to visit him today.'

My phone beeps before I can respond to that and I check it.

'Oliver?' Madison asks.

'No, my sister-in-law – she wants me to meet her today.'

'Well, go do that – meet in a public place and stay out of trouble.'

I ask softly, 'That bad?'

'That fucking bad. Keep your phone on and pick up if I call.'

'Okay,' I reply, numbly.

I get to the park at almost exactly the same time as Claudia. She has a worried look on her face, but she still looks amazing.

'Hi.' I wave.

She physically jumps and immediately says, 'Sorry.'

I recognise that jump. It's the inbuilt warning system of the hunted. It's how I reacted to every movement in prison, every time Janine brushed past me. When she whispered 'boo' I'd break down.

'Hey, no problem, I shouldn't sneak up on people. No Bethany?' I ask.

'She's at nursery on the other side of the park. I probably have about an hour.' She glances at an expensive-looking watch. 'Let me buy you a coffee?'

'Thanks,' I say brightly.

'I would have invited you to the house but it says in the

calendar that Marcus is working from home today, though no sign of him yet.'

'Okay.'

We walk through the park and into the café in companionable silence. She orders coffees. The boy who takes the order is all fingers and thumbs. He sneaks furtive glances at her as he steams the milk. She smiles at him when he brings them over and he turns the colour of beetroot.

'Shall we walk?' she suggests.

'Can do.' I smile.

'I know it's a bit chilly, but I spend so much time cooped up inside.'

'I know what you mean.'

'God, of course you do, sorry, I didn't mean . . .' She stops, flustered and looks at me apologetically.

I laugh, 'Claudia, it's fine.'

She nods and we start to walk.

'Are you okay?' I ask her.

'No, not really.' She glances at me and I give her what I hope is an encouraging look. 'Tell me about Marcus and Naomi,' she says.

'You don't know?'

'I didn't, I might now. I think they were involved?'

I shrug. 'Yes, they were sleeping together.'

'Did Marcus . . . did he love her, do you think?'

I try and think about that for moment. 'He probably thought he did. They were kids really.'

She nods. 'What was she like?'

'Generally, or to him?'

'To him, I suppose.' She shrugs. 'No, generally.'

'Not so good. She found other people's feelings amusing.'

'God.' Neither of us speak for a while. We walk, drink coffee, and then she says, 'Our life is a lie, you know.'

I don't know what to say to that, so I keep quiet and she goes on, 'I suspect you might have guessed how.'

I don't even want to say the words, the ones that had been nagging. It's all too perfect, too contained and I know enough about my brother to know that he's a mess. That it has to come out somewhere. I ask her, 'Does he hit you?'

Her beautiful big eyes shine with tears. She nods. 'I was young and naïve when I met him, not that it's any kind of excuse. I never for one second thought I'd grow up to be the kind of woman who stayed. I've had plenty of opportunities to go.' She sighs. 'I thought it was best not to.'

'For Bethany's sake?'

'Yes, although staying hasn't really done her any favours. Financial security is cheap when your safety isn't certain. I've never told anyone.'

'So, what's changed?'

She tells me about a conversation she heard between my dad and my brother, Marcus asking 'What if she remembers?' I feel tears prick my own eyes. When she tells me what she found in his safe I feel them escape and drip down my cheeks.

'I need you to bring me the diary,' I tell her.

'I know.'

'Will you?'

She nods. 'Yes, but I have to make it safe for Bethany. He'll know.'

I take her hand and give it a squeeze. 'You'll come to me. We'll talk to Madison and she'll know what to do after that.'

'I was right to tell you, wasn't I?'

I nod. 'I'm glad you did.'

She presses her hand deeper into mine and squeezes back. I look down and see finger-sized faded brown bruises round her wrist, like a hateful mockery of a beaded bracelet.

'I'll call when I can,' she says, before leaving to go and pick up Bethany.

I ring Madison and tell her shakily what Claudia has told me, what she has found.

She says gently, 'It might mean nothing.' But I don't see how that can be. I walk slowly around the park, trying to clear my head, but my heart is too heavy for silence. I feel the awful fear creeping in. Like I'm about to be suffocated by it. My knees start to turn into jelly and I manage to make it to a bench. I slide down, pulling my phone from my bag. My hands are sweating so much it slides away, onto the floor. I wipe my hands and pick it up and then I ring Dean.

'Kate, I was just thinking about you.'

I smile and feel my pulse slow, already feeling better for hearing his voice. 'All good things, I hope?'

'Of course. How are you?'

I sigh and tell him about the diary. When I'm done, there is a long silence and I say, 'Dean . . .?' wondering if we've been cut off.

He says, 'Sorry. I was just mulling it over. Marcus certainly is a mystery, isn't he?'

I laugh. 'That's one way of putting it. Dean, I feel so let down.'

'They've been letting you down for a while now, Kate.' He says it gently, but the words still hurt.

'I know.'

He says, 'Look. You're doing well, far better than I thought you would. Don't go getting depressed now, okay?'

'Okay.'

He says, 'Everything will be fine.'

I feel better by the time I hang up. But it takes me a few minutes before I stand and walk home. Looking over my shoulder as I go.

26.

Anthea Andrews

I know that I have crossed some sort of line. I couldn't stop myself and I didn't really want to. I'd known I was going to do it. I've been researching how to pick locks for over a week and found it surprisingly easy to get information once I found the right forums to ask. So I went with it, knowing it would keep playing out in my head if I didn't. I left while Damian was asleep. I purposefully parked a few doors down so he wouldn't hear the car start, not that he'd have woken up. He never does, and I'd 'slept' in Naomi's room. He leaves me when I'm there now. At first he used to come in and lie behind me, sharing the pain. Now he finds it maudlin. The time limit on his grief has expired, apparently.

I spend a lot of time in that room, absolutely determined to remember everything about my daughter. To always keep her firmly in the forefront of my mind. Naomi was a wonderful girl. Even as a toddler she had been miles ahead of the other kids – she had been early to walk, to talk. Once she could communicate she'd bark out orders to me and Damian and we would smile at each other over her head, amused by her bossiness. Clever little thing. As she grew she mastered things quickly but then tired of them. Swimming, then gymnastics, a phase of ballet. She'd tire of friends as well, when she outgrew them, as I always saw it. Other mums complained occasionally and I told them what for; they were just jealous that their daughters weren't Queen Bee.

Damian had warned me that I was spoiling Naomi. That she was a girl who needed limits. But children need love. Especially children like Naomi. Special ones who weren't even supposed to be born. It was the only thing we'd ever argued about. When Naomi became a teenager it had got worse and I had found myself keeping things from him. Naomi's 'high jinks', as I tried to think of them, became more and more outrageous. I told myself she was just a teenager. They're notoriously difficult. I have no doubt it was a phase she'd have grown out of.

I had been so intent on getting into Kate's flat last night that once I was inside I hadn't known what to do. I left the door ajar and crept into the bedroom and watched her sleep, this stupid girl who had almost lived in our house at one point. I'd thought seriously about killing her, then and there. That's probably what I'd been thinking all along really. I'd looked at the pillow next to her and almost felt my hands grabbing it, lifting it up, pressing down on her face. But something held me back and I looked for just a minute, no more. Then I left, shutting the door harder than I'd meant to on the way out. I'd hurried down the stairs, out onto the street and to my car. By the time I got back home it was four a.m. and I knew I wasn't going to get any sleep, so I watched the sun come up, pleased that I had the option. I'll wait and see what the little bitch is up to and then I'll kill her. I'm half smiling by the time Damian comes down and he smiles back as he makes us both coffee.

27.

Madison Attallee

Peter brings the files. He catches me unaware at home and before I can think straight I've agreed to him coming in. I make coffee, my hands shaking. It feels strange having him here in my flat. We chat about nothing. When he says he probably ought to go I agree, but neither of us move. For a second I think he's going to lean in to kiss me and I'm ready to push him gently back. He doesn't though; he takes my hand instead and says, 'I know now isn't the time.'

After he's gone I sit for a while in silence, smoking, thinking. I think about us, him, Peter. I think about him on his bike, driving his first car. I think about phoning to tell him I was getting married. The awful silence and my pissed off voice saying 'Aren't you going to congratulate me', knowing how I'd have felt if it had been the other way around. Unable to be any kinder. He'd hung up.

Peter joined the police force shortly after he left university. He suggested I join and I'd gone along to an open day to keep him happy. Much to my surprise it had sounded varied and interesting, and I was temping and directionless at the time. Sure I wouldn't last in an office but determined to do something. I loved it. From the day I started. The busyness. The messiness. Dealing with criminals and victims. I seemed to have an affinity for both. Peter was posted in the city but I stayed in Kingston, never wanting to be far from Mum. I met Rob, we had Molly, and then Peter ended up back here. As my boss. Just after my drinking had reached a new level and my marriage was on the rocks.

I have a box of photos. Of him. Us. Being kids, turning into adults. I haven't let myself look at them for over a year and I don't let myself now, though the longing is strong. Almost as strong as the desire to open my flat door, run down the street after him and throw myself into his arms. Fuck this shit. I put on Led Zeppelin and I turn it up loud. I light another cigarette, drink Appletiser wishing it was wine, and think to myself that I'd probably cry if I was capable.

Early the following morning my phone beeps, waking me up. It's Peter, asking how I am. I text back that I'm fine. He asks me how long I'm planning on punishing myself. I'm not going to respond to that. My phone beeps again.

'Not letting yourself be happy isn't going to make Molly love you any more.'

If he was here I'd punch him in the face. I learned enough in the nuthouse to know that my behaviours are pretty predictable. Even my mental health issues lack originality. I smoke and stew and ignore Peter's messages, hoping it will hurt his feelings. Because I'm an immature prick.

It's nearly seven thirty a.m., but it's still pretty dark. Soon the moody sun will shine through my flimsy curtains and then I'll have to get going. I drain another cup of coffee, smoke another fag and step into the shower. I let the scalding water wash over me, hoping it will take last night's regret with it. I struggle getting the box of files down the stairs and into my car. By the time I'm done, I'm sweating and my blow-dried hair is fucking frizz again. I wonder why I bothered showering.

I drive to my office with Garbage blasting 'Stupid Girl' out of the stereo. Thanks a million, Shirley. It's only eight o'clock. Emma won't be here for another hour or so. I half-drag, half-carry the box in, trailing mud from outside along with me. Shit. I ineffectively wipe at it with some kitchen roll, could be worse.

I feel a little charge go through my body when I take the lid off. How fucked up is that? It's not a bloodthirsty thing though, not exactly. I used to have a hard time explaining it to Rob, but what gets me hooked is the puzzle. The things that lead people to do the awful crimes that used to land on my desk. The choices people make, or don't know they're having made for them. What it is that makes us tick, so to speak. Nine times out of ten the perpetrators are normal, born just like the rest of us. Along the way something gets lost, broken, their actions veer from the right track. They become unhealthy. Damaged, and dangerous.

I start with the pictures. Normally I'd walk a crime scene first, get a feel for it. This one's long gone but I work to pull the images back as I remember them. Naomi leaning against a wall, eyes glazed and looking straight ahead. That thing that made her who she was now gone. If you looked quickly and ignored the blood she could have been a sulky teenager – she could have been bored, or pissed off. She could have been alive – if you didn't look too closely, and if it wasn't for the blood. It was everywhere. I remember that, stepping into the room and the sticky feel of it under my feet. I wasn't wearing shoe protectors, it messed with the scene-of-crime officer's job later.

I look at the photo of Naomi, no Kate by this point. I'd led her off. But she had been there initially, holding her limp friend in her arms. Both girls red and slippery like a bad Hallowe'en costume. Kate had smiled at me as I opened the door. Another kid had already found them, the one who phoned us. He had left a pile of vomit outside the door, followed later by my colleague's own contribution. Malone questioned him. The poor kid hadn't known when he rang whether the girls were alive or dead, maybe someone had just been hurt? I knew as soon as I stepped in. You can smell it, death. I bent down and said 'hi' to the smiling girl. She had carried on smiling and asked if I might shut Naomi's eyes. I said I couldn't. The other officer had given up at the door. Evacuated his stomach and stood shaking. I knew I had to get Kate out, this smiling gruesome child. I knew she was about to be arrested. The knife was inches from her knee.

When DI Malone arrived he found me outside the front of the house half holding Kate up. He would congratulate me later for my smarts. He walked in with a team, then came back out seconds later and arrested her. She didn't look all that surprised. Then she smiled at the other officers and half waved at the crowd of teenagers and gathering parents who were watching. Someone managed to get a picture. It made front pages everywhere. I was sent home to shower and change and get some rest. I didn't, though, get rest. I was back, scrubbed and fresh, adrenalin pumping, waiting to see what happened next.

Next in the box are Kate's mugshots. Some of the blood had been wiped away, but not all of it, and she's still smiling. Back to Naomi – washed and on the autopsy table, looking young and womanly at the same time. I sat in on that autopsy. It was brutal. I was there when her parents came in first to identify her, even worse. The report is here. I flick through it. Death was caused by one fatal stab wound to the neck, although many other injuries were present. More stab wounds. The person who killed her had been pretty mad, pretty determined. It's no easy thing to stab another person. It goes against instincts that are ingrained.

Kate's father took two hours to get to the police station. We were unable to question her until he arrived. I didn't sit in on the interviews, so when I open the transcripts they are new to me. There is a recording. I put it into my own Dictaphone and hit play. Malone went at her hard. Her father barely stepped in. He urges her to answer a few times when she pauses, but other than that James stays out of it. What kind of parent doesn't move heaven and Earth to save their child from a horror like that? She giggles at one point. He hisses her name and she stops. I don't think I would have handled it the way Malone did; I like to think I might have been kinder. She was checked by Monty, a shrink we use at the station. He's pretty vacant, always stressed and seems to think badly of everyone. He said she was fine. I think his exact words were something like, 'Perfectly fine, little cow even laughed.'

I'm amazed at how little was collected. By my estimation the whole investigation was flimsy. Naomi's parents were handled with kid gloves. Marcus was only spoken to once, despite Kate telling us he had been in a sexual relationship with Naomi and was prone to jealousy. Oliver was questioned for all of fifteen minutes. There was one visit made to Kate's school, which I had been present at. Mr Wilson wasn't spoken to. As I recall, we apologised to Mrs Anselm and promised not to take up too much of her time. I've had to work with Malone many times over the years. What I initially mistook for confidence on his part is actually just bravado. A front to hide the truth that he is sloppy and lazy in his work. Work that matters, damn it. He'd always been ambitious though, wanting the accolade that promotions bring. I was doing most of his legwork for years before it occurred to me that I could probably do his job. He's never forgiven me for taking what he saw as his promotion.

The office door opens and Emma comes in, bringing a blast of cold with her. She quickly surveys the muddy floor and the leaning stacks of paper. I try to look nonchalant. She smiles, hangs her coat, pops on coffee and appears as if from nowhere with a mop I didn't know we had. The floor is sparkling in no time and she offers to help with the documents.

'Sure. I'm gonna have a fag.'

'Righty-ho.'

I'm only outside for five minutes. I smoke two cigarettes, thinking it will save time later. When I get back in the stacks are already somewhat neater and there is space on the big round table I'd plonked it all on.

She carries on stacking while I keep sieving. She has started piles based on type of document. She inhales sharply as I pass her the pictures. Half an hour in she says my name.

'Yes?'

'Marcus and Naomi's relationship is mentioned by several people, yet it doesn't seem to have been followed up much. Would that be normal practice?'

'No.'

She tuts. 'According to your diary you're seeing Marcus this afternoon?'

I nod.

'At his office?'

'I am.'

She hesitates before saying, 'I wonder if it's worth calling the wife first, in light of what Kate's told us.' Naomi's diary.

I grin at her. 'You know, that might not be a bad idea.' Emma may prove to be more useful than I give her credit for. Even if she does speak like a Victorian spinster.

28.

Claudia Reynolds

The phone rings and I almost drop to the floor. Idiot.

'Hello?'

'Is that Claudia Reynolds?'

My stupid hand is shaking. 'It is.'

'Madison Attallee. I believe your sister-in-law said I'd be in touch.'

I can barely breathe but I manage to say, 'Yes.'

'Are you all right?'

'What do you mean?'

She pauses then says, 'You sound ... I don't know, breathless.'

'I'm fine.' I can't begin to explain all the ways that statement isn't true.

'Kate told me what you found.'

'Yes.' My voice is barely a whisper.

'Do you have it in your possession?'

'Well, not exactly. It's here. In the safe. If I take it . . .'

'Kate said you're planning on going to stay with her for a while.'

'Yes.'

Her voice sounds softer now. 'That seems like a good idea. Why don't you get your things together, for you and

Bethany, get the diary and we'll all meet at Kate's later?'

'Okay.' I'm nodding as though to convince myself as much as her.

We say goodbye and I need to sit down for a minute. Bethany is napping. I switch on the baby-monitor to make sure she's okay and then I head into the office. There's a Post-it note on his desk with a telephone number on it and a kiss. This is how brazen he is now, how little my feelings matter. Or perhaps he figures I'm so well trained I wouldn't dare to come in here.

I remember the first time it happened. It was one of the admin girls at work – not quite his secretary but close enough to be a cliché. Bethany was only a few months old. I almost didn't blame him. I was milky, frumpy, in that state that new mothers find themselves in, being boring and preoccupied. The violence hadn't really begun by then. Somewhere in my mind I had reasoned it was the stress of becoming a parent. We hadn't discussed it since. I had stopped being wary.

I called my mother and sobbed down the phone. She was without judgement and asked if I wanted to stay in the marriage or not. I said yes. The thought of it being just Bethany and me seemed untenable. She was at the house an hour later and I left Marcus a note. On the same kind of pink Post-it as the one I had found. Tacky and pathetic. Very like the one I'm looking at now.

The stupid girl had signed it, the one I found years ago. I knew her name because she often rang Marcus with schedules and appointments. I'd picked up the phone a few times. I left the disgusting, explicit words on the kitchen table along with my own saying we would be at my parents. The insult was made worse by the tone. It was dirty. Something Marcus hated from me in the bedroom. A side of my own nature I had given up, now providing only the chaste wife.

He called that evening, devastated, and asked me to come

home so we could work it out. Mum was pleased, she said marriage was all about hard work and that in the end it would make us stronger. I headed back home, full to bursting with hope and forgiveness. I walked in with Bethany sleeping in my arms. He took her upstairs and laid her down in her cot while I sat expectantly, preparing myself for the apologies and preparing to be an understanding wife. What he had done was unforgiveable, but I was so madly in love with our daughter I could see how he felt pushed out.

When he came back down the stairs he didn't look sorry. He looked cross. I opened my mouth to speak but he was on me before I had the chance. Still to this day it remains one of the most brutal beatings of our marriage, and there has been much brutality. When he was finished he spat at me. Somehow it hurt just as much as his fists and feet.

'You will never, ever leave me again. How dare you?'

I couldn't move for the rest of the evening. I lay prone on the floor, battered and bloody. He went to bed and I stayed where I was. At one point I wet myself. Hot acrid urine soaked through my clothes, warm at first, but icy cold by the morning. He woke early, put me in a bath and washed me with such tenderness it nearly broke my heart.

Bethany cried when she saw me. I had only glanced briefly in the mirror but I knew my face was raw with one large black eye. The rest of the bruises were on my body, harder to spot. I couldn't go out for nearly a week and even then I sported large Jackie O shades. He never marked my face again.

I should have left that morning. I think maybe even Marcus thought I might. When Mum called that afternoon I assured her things were okay, that we were going to work through it all, just as she'd suggested. She sounded so relieved and I desperately wanted it to be true. I had Bethany now. I had vowed the day I discovered she was growing inside me that she would come from a happy home, like mine. Two parents had to be better than one. I would make this marriage work. I'm saddened now, by that decision made all those years ago. The things stolen from my daughter have been far greater than I could have imagined. It's nearly time, I know now that I have to get away. Even if it is nearly four years too late.

29.

Madison Attallee

Marcus is the managing director of Reynolds Estates, a property investment company started by his father back in the days when you could make a fortune from very little. James has stayed on in his role as CEO, though from what I can gather the day-to-day running of things comes down to Marcus. James is rarely in the offices. When I arrive I'm met by a large glass building – new premises the company had taken over five years ago. The reception is a wide, airy, open space with not one, but three efficient and neat-looking receptionists. I walk up and am greeted with a row of smiles. I smile back, telling them Marcus Reynolds is expecting me. They call for his PA and lead me to the 'waiting area', letting me know she'll be with me shortly.

She takes a few minutes to arrive and is beaming when she does. She gives me an unasked-for commentary of who does what on each floor as we go. I nod politely and then I end up in another bloody waiting area. Ashley, apparently, asks if she can fetch me a 'refreshment'. I say I'm fine. I am kept waiting for another five minutes, then her desk phone rings and I'm sent through.

The office is impressive. Beautiful views, more glass, lots of pictures – Marcus and James, Marcus, Claudia and Bethany.

Claudia looks a lot like Ashley, the PA. They look like a perfect catalogue family in the pictures, but then Rob, Molly and I might have looked like that to outsiders. He walks around the desk and takes my hand warmly in both of his. He is very good-looking. Chiselled, dark, tall, well dressed. Too shiny for my tastes.

'Please sit. Did Ashley offer you a drink?'

I smile. 'Yes, I'm fine, thank you.'

He smiles back with even perfect teeth that must have cost a fortune. 'Good, good.'

'Thank you for seeing me, Mr Reynolds.'

'Marcus, please. Mr Reynolds is very much my father.'

'Of course. I understand he's in the process of retiring?'

He shrugs. 'I think he'll go for what you might describe as semi-retired. I can't ever see Dad letting go completely, to be honest. I suspect he'd get bored.'

'And you'll take over as CEO?'

The grin is on again. 'That's the plan.'

'I guess you're already pretty much in charge?'

He laughs. 'I suppose I am.'

'Your other siblings weren't interested in joining the family business?'

'Martha's done bits and bobs over the years. She's not cut out for work. I understand you've visited her yourself so you can probably see why.'

'Yes, I visited her. I also heard they'd ceased her treatment a few years ago?'

His face sets in harder lines. 'I think you must have heard wrong. Sandcross offers fantastic ongoing treatment, though we have come to accept that Martha will never fully recover.'

'From what?'

'I beg your pardon?'

'Never fully recover from what?'

He shrugs. 'Whatever it is that ails her. Anorexia is most likely, in itself, life threatening, and probably depression as well.'

'And your father doesn't think psychiatric treatment will help her any more?'

His eyes narrow. 'I'm sure my father and the staff at Sand-cross have come up with the best care plan for my sister. We pay them enough.'

I smile from ear to ear, almost enjoying myself. 'I'm sure you do, it's a beautiful place.'

'Yes, it is.'

'So Kate won't be coming into the fold either?'

He kind of snorts. 'If you mean "Will she be working here?" I'd say it's unlikely.'

'She's quite well educated now, as I understand.'

'I think you probably know that she and my father no longer speak.'

'No happy family reunions since her release then?' I ask.

He is silent for a moment, no longer smiling. He holds my gaze. I stare back and smile. He asks, 'Did you work on the original case?'

'I did.'

'But you're no longer on the force?'

'Nope.'

He is starting to smile again, a bitchy little twitch at the corner of his mouth. 'Were you sacked?'

I smile wider and tell him, 'I left.'

'Before you were sacked?'

I shrug. 'Maybe, guess we'll never know.'

His voice is lower, quieter. 'I get that you probably need all the work you can get, and I get that Kate is probably paying you a load of money, but even you must see this is a pointless endeavour?'

I don't say anything.

He carries on, 'I have no idea why Kate feels the need to dredge up the past, as if she hasn't caused us all enough pain.'

'Were you close?'

'Sorry?'

'Were you and Kate close?'

He sighs. 'I don't know, we were siblings, we shared a childhood, our time together was inflicted on us.'

I say, 'She's not someone you would have chosen to hang out with?'

'Probably not, no.'

'You liked Naomi though.' It's not a question.

He regards me with open contempt. 'I did, yes. It's not a secret that we dated for a while.'

'Kate seems to think you were madly in love with her.'

He laughs. 'I was very young. I didn't know what love was.'

'You were the same age your wife was when she met you, weren't you?' I smile. He doesn't say anything. I ask, 'What was she like?'

'Naomi?'

'Yes.'

Something on his jaw slackens just a little. 'She was very outgoing, very attractive.'

'Sexy?'

He laughs, trying for affable again. 'Yes, I guess she was.'

'And Kate was quite a quiet girl before they met?'

'I suppose so. Hardly an angel though – she and Naomi certainly liked to party. She had a much older boyfriend, probably not the only one.'

'You mean Oliver?'

He nods. 'Yes.'

'What was he like?'

'He was arrogant.' I nearly laugh out loud at the irony of this man calling someone else arrogant.

'Kate thought Naomi was sleeping with him.'

I see colour rise on his cheeks and I go on. 'Why did you break up?'

'We didn't.'

'So Naomi was still your girlfriend at the time of her death?' For fuck's sake, Malone.

He wipes a hand over his face, visibly paler than when I first came in. 'I'd hardly say girlfriend, like I said, we were kids.'

'But emotions can run high in younger years.'

'If you say so.' He glances at a large, ugly watch, probably a few grand's worth. 'Is this going anywhere?'

'You told the police that you and Naomi were no longer an item.'

'Did I?'

I nod, not taking my eyes off him. 'Yes.'

His eyes dart around the room. 'Well, like I said, it had fizzled out.'

'Kate thinks you had an argument with Naomi that evening.'

'Kate thinks lots of things, doesn't she?' he snaps, and not waiting for an answer goes on, 'Silly bitch can't remember the night in question though, can she?'

I don't say anything.

He continues, 'She was knocking back the drinks like a lunatic. It never surprised me that she lost time.'

'Yet she says she was normally quite sensible. She said she'd been telling Naomi off, about Oliver. And you.'

He waves a hand as though to dismiss my words but says, 'Maybe.'

'Kate says she thinks she might have been depressed, looking back.'

He makes that snort again. 'Mental health issues seem

178

abundant in Reynolds women.' A cruel statement about his own family, along with 'silly bitch', and he doesn't even seem to have noticed.

I say, 'But not the boys, eh?'

'Excuse me?'

'No mental health problems on your part?'

'Of course not.' He pulls himself up in his chair, hand waving at his ostentatious surroundings. 'Look around you!'

I ignore that. 'Kate says your wife is nice.'

'She is, yes.'

'Has a lot of accidents.'

The air in the room seems to change.

'I don't care for your tone, Ms Attallee.'

'What do you mean?' I make my eyes wide and innocent.

'Our time is up.' He buzzes and Ashley appears, ready to see me out.

As I am being ushered through the door I turn to face him. 'The past has a way of catching up with us, Mr Reynolds, no matter how far away we think we are.' I hold out a card. He ignores it, and me. I leave it on a shelf by the door.

I follow Ashley to the elevator and she follows me in. 'How is he to work for?' I ask her.

'Oh, great, really great.'

'You look like his wife.'

Her smile wobbles enough for me to suspect more than a working relationship. She doesn't say anything else until we're at the front doors where she waves me off with an overly bright smile.

30.

Claudia Reynolds

I take the diary. It has a pretty, cotton cover with embroidered butterflies on the front. Seeing it again, I realise it is the same as the one Kate wrote in, its picture splashed all over the papers. They must have bought them together, or for each other. I put it under my jumper in the waistband of my trousers and carefully lock the safe behind me. I leave the office and close the door. Bethany is engrossed in *Little Princess*. I watch her for a moment and feel that familiar swell of love.

I ask her, 'Are you okay?'

She nods, not looking up.

'We're going to go over to your aunt's shortly.'

'Oh, good.'

'We're going to have a sleepover.'

'Yay!'

'It might be for more than one night.'

She nods, still facing the TV, 'Okay, Mummy.'

'I've packed some of your things – we mustn't forget Matilda.' Her rabbit, she's clutching her now, engrossed in her programme. I tell her, 'I'm just nipping upstairs.'

In my own bedroom I empty my sports bag and throw in a few bits. I take the diary out of my waistband and add it. My phone ring. It's Marcus.

'Claudia?'

'Hello, Marcus.'

'That PI was here.'

'Yes, you said she would be coming.'

There is a silence. The diary is poking out the side of my bag. I push it in and zip the bag shut. I feel tears wetting my cheeks. There are so many things to say and yet no point in saying them. I think about our wedding day. I was full of hope, and so very desperately in love with the man on the end of the phone.

'I'm so sorry, Claudia.'

I can barely breathe. 'Why are you sorry, Marcus?'

He laughs, it's a bitter sound. 'Where do I start?'

'I don't know.' I can see his face smiling eagerly at me, full of hope and excitement, saying 'I do'. I picture him with Bethany, not knowing how to hold her when she was born, standing prone and unsteady, her gurgling in his arms. My heart feeling light, full and happy. I imagine him with Naomi, gawky and young, not grown into himself. Oh God. Why are we this? When did we become this? What could we have done differently?

'I owe you so many apologies, Claudia.' He sounds hoarse. I wonder if he is crying. I need to get going. I need to get Bethany and our bags and go. But the phone is glued to my ear. My breath is held. I'm waiting, though I don't know what for.

'I love you, Claudia.'

I had no idea that he still had the power to break my heart, to untie me, but I am undone.

'I love you too, Marcus.' And in that second I know it's true, just as much as I know it's the last time I will ever tell him.

When I hang up the phone I feel something new, I feel free. I text Kate to tell her we will be there in half an hour. I load and turn on the dishwasher, my head buzzing, alive, frightened, hopeful, full of love and hate for Marcus. Sadness for the boy he was and who he is now. I am about to call Bethany when I hear the front door click. Oh no, Marcus must have come back. I go out to the hall, but there's no one there and the door is closed.

I call to Bethany. She doesn't answer so I start towards the living room where the *Little Princess* song is playing. Her episode must be up. Then pain shatters inside my head. I am blinded by it, stung. I drop forwards, balancing on my knees. I can't work out what's happening. I open my mouth to call my daughter's name again and it's suddenly full of foul-smelling material, dry and scratchy on my tongue. I inhale because I have to, breathing in something pungent and disgusting, then I feel a hand grip the back of my head and a knee in my back. Oh God. I try to say Bethany's name again but there's nothing and then everything fades to black.

31.

Madison Attallee

I get off the phone to Kate. She sounded steady. She's been shopping for Claudia and Bethany's visit. She says she's looking forward to it. I'll meet them at Kate's later and we'll try and figure out if there's anything useful in the pages of Naomi's journal.

I get in the car and my phone rings almost immediately. I'm about to ignore it, but it's Rob. I put him on speaker, start driving and turn down Skid Row.

'Hello, Rob.'

'Madison, how are you?'

'Fine, thank you. Yourself?'

'Yes, good thanks.' He clears his throat and I can hear phlegm rattle up and down. It's an annoying habit.

'Is that all, Rob?'

'Well, no.'

It's like pulling fucking teeth. I balance the phone on my knees and light a cigarette. Immediate calm.

'Are you smoking?'

'Yep.'

He sighs. I inhale and exhale loudly, taking a petty pleasure in it.

He says, 'Molly and I are planning a holiday.'

'Nice, anywhere good?'

'Just Spain. A friend of mine has a place there.'

I wonder if the 'friend' is the wicked stepmother. She's probably not wicked, she's probably really nice. My stomach lurches. I have an itchy feeling behind my eyes.

'Okay, well, thanks for telling me.'

He quickly adds, 'We want to go for fourteen days in the summer.'

'Ah, so I'd miss my Saturday?'

'Well, I can't be scheduling our lives around a few hours with you.'

'Those hours are important to me, Rob. Hopefully for Molly too. It's all we get.'

He sighs. 'Well, right, and we . . . I . . . was thinking, after speaking to Molly, of course, that perhaps she could come to you the Saturday before we leave. She indicated she might like to stay.'

I nearly lose my grip on the wheel. 'Rob, are you toying with me?'

'Look, we'd see how it goes, of course, but if all goes well perhaps it would make sense. The reports say you're sober?'

'As a judge.'

The thought of waking up with Molly is almost too much to bear. She would be there at the start of the day. It would be how it is for normal mums and daughters one morning every fortnight. A chance to try to be a mum. I make all kinds of deals with a God I don't believe in in my head. I'll stay sober, I'll even go to those fucking meetings if I can just have this . . .

'Fine,' says Rob. 'I'll get the details passed to my lawyer.' Everything via the law these days.

'Who is she?' Oh shit, it's out before I can stop it.

I can imagine his face, a frown, narrowed eyes but secretly

pleased. Oh shit, I've given him the satisfaction. I can never keep it in.

'Janet, from the office,' he says. 'You've met her a few times. She's nice. Easy going.' The implication being that I'm not.

So she had been biding her time. I feel a stab of jealousy, sharp and awkward. I picture her in the park with Molly, tangled in the sheets on my fucking bed. Everywhere I was, everywhere I left an imprint, she'll be slotting herself in, changing the shape. She gets to spend fourteen days with my fucking daughter and I get to be grateful for the odd night. I manage, 'I'm pleased for you.'

'Thanks.'

There's nothing left to say after that on either side. I'm not pleased for him. I'm sad for me. Cross that some other chick gets my life, even if I did make a royal mess of it. I know it's my own fault, the whole thing. If I'd have done things properly, walked away of my own accord, without a bottle in my hand. If only, if only . . . We wouldn't be together, Rob and I, but I would have been with Molly. No court gives dads custody unless the circumstances are extenuating. Like mine. I try to focus on the good news. I get an overnight. Molly has a father who loves her, and he's a good dad even if he is a prick generally. She won't be consigned to a shitty incapable alcoholic mother. Her childhood won't be the long, lonely stretch that mine was. She even gets a new fucking mum. I feel it deep down in my gut. The kind of raw gnawing rage that nothing other than vodka can relieve. I light another cigarette and drive too fast; I turn up Skid Row loud enough that the windows rattle.

Turns out our man, Oliver, had a few run-ins with the law as a minor. Emma's made fast friends with Deanie who deals with a lot of the research at the station and happened to have a little bit of time on her hands yesterday afternoon. The files are sealed so I don't yet know what the run-ins were for. But I know someone who might.

I pull in to the Guildhall, which houses the too few social workers who service the borough. Liz Martin comes out when I text, a file under one arm and a packet of Marlboro Gold in her other hand. She waves them at me. 'Tell me you haven't given up?'

I shake my head. 'Not even considered it.'

'Good, we're a dying breed.' She laughs at her bad taste joke and lights up before she's fully out the door. 'God that's good. I keep having these insane days where I start worrying about my health, throw a pack out and "give up". All it means is a crap morning for everyone in the office and I'm running to a newsagent by lunchtime!'

'Yeah, they're a difficult one to kick.'

She laughs. 'The stress from this place'll kill me quicker than a bit of nicotine.'

'How is it?'

'Same as ever – too many people needing help, not enough of us to do it properly. They've axed half the team, given us a load of new people to look after. Bloody cuts. It's a living nightmare! How are you now?'

She hasn't seen me since I left the force. I shrug. 'Okay. It's odd working alone.'

'Yeah, well, at least you don't have to deal with that prick Malone any more.'

I laugh. 'True enough.'

'And you're not on the piss either so win-win.' She's not one to mince words but the bluntness still makes me flinch. She adds, 'I got the notes on Molly, sorry, love. It's a small town, isn't it?'

'Guess so.'

'I've made you a copy of the file you wanted so you can

keep it, unofficially mind, so don't be taking it public.'

'Okay.'

We head to a stand in the middle of the market place. She queues for coffee and brings two steaming cups to the table, sloshing scalding liquid as she goes. 'You were in luck, a good pal of mine dealt with the lad back in the late eighties now. The whole family are on file as there was an adoption involved.'

'Oliver was adopted?'

'Looks like it. I haven't read it in detail.' She opens it up. 'Right, so, Amelia Horfield specialised in counselling incest victims.'

'Jesus.'

'Yeah, crappy work, but someone's got to do it. Better than working with the offenders, and she was pretty good by all accounts.' She coughs. 'Well, the Horfields had been foster- ing the boy they adopted for years. They already had a son of their own who was pretty much the same age as the boy they fostered.' She pauses and blows her nose. 'In fact it looks like both boys must have still been under one when they initially took him in. No other children. Obviously no problem them getting a child – a therapist and a banker, of all things, married, already parents. Like a dream for us, I would have thought. However, the paperwork suggests it's a bit more interesting than your average adoption.'

I take a sip of coffee – Americano, which means too many shots of espresso. Why can't anywhere just sell filter coffee? I drink it anyway and say to Liz, 'Go on.'

She pauses to sip at hot foam. She makes loud slurping noises and coughs again. A rattling smoker's phlegm-fest. I hear my future.

I say, 'You could try injecting, Liz.'

'Ha ha, look, I don't have time to wait for it to cool – you want the information or not?'

I laugh. 'Sorry, go on.'

'Right, so it was a bit of a complicated case.'

'Complicated how?'

'The boy was the son of one of her patients.'

My head joins the dots. 'So a produce of incest?'

Liz nods. 'It's a safe assumption, right?'

'God.'

'The boy's mum was a Ruth Hanover, later married and became Ruth Reynolds.'

'Shit!'

'Name mean something to you?'

'It does. Jesus.' I try and take it in. Ruth Reynolds. Kate's mother. Ruth was a victim of a male relative. And Oliver. Oh Jesus. Oliver would be Kate's half-brother. I don't divulge this to Liz, instead I ask, 'Okay, so what was he done for?'

'Breaking into the Reynolds' house, sometime around 1999.'

'Fuck,' I mutter, then ask, 'So they knew who it was?'

'Well, no, actually. It was the husband who pressed charges.'

'James?'

'Yes. Claimed not to know him at all.'

'So what? Ruth hadn't told him about her having Oliver?'

Liz shrugs and lights a cigarette, coughing seconds later. It puts me off lighting my own. 'Doesn't look like it.'

Liz's phone rings and she's instantly into an intense conversation. She hands me a printout of some of the paperwork. Oliver's name has been carefully blacked out, he was a minor. Liz mouths that she needs to go. I nod, sitting. I do light up in the end and I drink the shitty too-strong coffee. I take the cup back to the stand and suggest haughtily that they ought to do filter. The girl smiles and says they do Americanos. I scowl at her. There's no fucking hope.

How the hell am I going to break the news to Kate that Oliver's her big brother?

32.

Kate Reynolds

Claudia should have been here hours ago. I've called and sent messages. I wonder if Marcus has got to her first. I'm tempted to head down to his office. They've relocated, apparently. I remember the old offices – dusty, dark-wooded. My dad, busy. 'One day you'll be here, Kate, you all will, sitting where I am.' I think of Marcus now, the only one who made it.

Oliver keeps ringing. He left a voicemail saying, 'I need to speak to you, it's really important, Kate . . . there are things you don't know . . . things I have to say. Call me. Please call me.' I have no intention of calling him. When I sent that message on LinkedIn I had had some stupid idea in my head that we might pick up where we'd left off. But I'm not a child any more. I'm old enough to realise that a man who is married with a child on the way probably isn't going to enhance my life, and he didn't seem interested anyway. Looking back, I don't think he ever did. He rings again. I pick up and then hang up so he can't leave a voicemail. If he comes around I won't let him in. I think about the sense I had that someone was here and I put the chain across my front door. A few seconds after I do so the doorbell rings. I am frozen until I hear Madison's voice.

'I can see the shadow of your feet under the door,' she calls.

I open it, ready to laugh at myself but the smile stops when I see the look on her face.

I am reeling as she tells me about Oliver. Little things begin to sink into my mind: I remember laughing when he'd 'guessed' where my bedroom was the first time he'd visited; finding him in my father's study looking in a drawer; distracting me when I asked him why; asking about my mum. I thought he'd cared. About me. It's too much and the thinking builds to an unbearable point. I feel the contents of my stomach rising up and I run to the bathroom. When I come out Madison is still sitting awkwardly on the arm of my sofa, studiously avoiding eye contact. I suppose there's no easy way to tell someone they've committed incest.

'He's been ringing,' I tell her, and laugh. It sounds far away. 'He said he needed to tell me something.' I laugh again, wishing that a wife and a child were the biggest problem with Oliver and me. My disappointment over my first and only love. Oh, the halcyon times of moments ago.

'You didn't know,' she says lamely. I'm about to respond when my phone rings: Marcus's landline, thank goodness.

'Claudia?'

There's no answer but I can hear breathing, another voice mutters something cross in the background and all of a sudden the breathing stops and my father is in my ear. 'Kate?'

I had no idea until this precise second just how much I've missed him.

For a moment I can't speak. I am three years old with a bloody knee, his big hands picking me up and kissing it better. Hiding behind a door, watching him work at his desk. Larger than life. Inhaling the scent of his aftershave. My small arms curling around his neck. I am all of these things and then I am eighteen. Sitting in a police cell watching anger and shame in his eyes. Waiting for a rescue that never comes.

'Daddy.'

There is a pause, then he clears his throat. 'I hate to call with bad news, under difficult circumstances . . .'

'What's happened?' I can hear Marcus saying things in the background.

'Calm down, for heaven's sake!' To Marcus not me. I think I hear a sob. I'm sickened when I realise it's my brother. I don't think I've ever heard him cry.

'Claudia and Bethany are missing . . .'

My head tries to make sense of this. 'Maybe she's gone out?'

He sighs. I can still hear Marcus gibbering. 'It doesn't look that way. There seems to have been a struggle of some sort. I'm putting your brother on.'

I feel panicky. I don't want him to go. 'Dad—'

'We'll speak later.' His voice is soft and I believe him.

'Kate?' my brother says, sounding frantic.

'Marcus, what's happening?'

'I got home and the front door was wide open, but her car's here and bags. I . . . I think she might have been planning to go somewhere. With Bethany.'

Here, she was coming here, I think. 'Maybe she got distracted and had to nip out?' I say instead.

'She hasn't fucking nipped out, and everything's a mess. She wouldn't leave it like that, or the door open.'

I shut my eyes. 'What do you want me to do?'

'The police won't help until someone's been gone for twenty-four hours, for God's sake. Said what you did. But the fucking door's open, the lamp's been knocked over . . .' He's near hysteria.

'Marcus,' I say sharply.

'Your PI . . . can your PI help?'

'She's right here,' I say without thinking.

'Well, fucking well put her on the phone!'

I flinch as I hand the phone to Madison. I'm always on the receiving end of someone else's rage. Naomi, if I didn't do what she wanted; Janine, just for having the cheek to be alive; now my brother, who left me well alone when I needed him and my dad. I feel my own anger swelling. Dean used to joke that one day it would just explode out of me and be apoplectic. But it never has. I've always kept my cool, or remained a fucking doormat. In the end Janine left me alone because I faded into nothingness. Naomi kept me in favour as I was agreeable. Marcus kept writing his cold letters once a month and I didn't stir things up. I wonder if this is who I'll always be.

I hear Madison say she'll go to Marcus's house. As she leaves, with a sympathetic hand on my shoulder, I feel useless. I dial Dean and then I change my mind. No. I can't tell him this. I'm too ashamed. I sit and cry. Awash with disgust about Oliver, the only boy I'd ever been with and how tainted it all is now. He must have targeted me specifically. How sick is that? And how easy I was to get to. How in need of affection that I took it up on the first offer. I feel it again, the swell of it. Anger. I find I'm not crying any more and I feel fuller somehow, bigger. I start cleaning my flat – every nook and cranny, until everything is sparkling and then I pray quietly to whatever there might be that Claudia and Bethany are okay.

33.

Anthea Andrews

I'm waiting outside Kate's flat. I'm drinking coffee from a flask, eyes narrowed, hands clenched. I've been here for a couple of hours with the car radio on, not really thinking much, when that blonde woman turns up. The investigator. She'd be gorgeous if she frowned less, not that I can talk. I giggle and the sound startles me. The woman runs a company called MA Investigations. I think it's laughable that she'd take on a convicted criminal. She must be desperate. I watch her sit on the bonnet of her car and chain smoke about three cigarettes, then she opens the door and leans in. She comes out spraying herself and sliding gum into her mouth. I have always thought smoking to be a stupid habit and this sort of nonsense confirms it.

When the investigator leaves, Kate doesn't come out for ages. I am on the verge of giving up, but there she is. I follow her to the shrink's office, and then I follow her home. Twice Kate turns as though she can feel my eyes boring into the back of her head. I'm careful not to stop and run, continuing on instead with casual, slow steps, looking the other way. I am masked in baggy clothes, my face shielded by a baseball cap. Soon. It will be time soon. The thought buoys me and I feel not exactly cheerful, but certainly less sad.

34.

Claudia Reynolds

I open my eyes and pain shoots through my head. It's over-whelming and for a few seconds I think I'm going to vomit. I don't. I shut my eyes tightly, willing everything to stop spin-ning. When I open them again I let my focus come together slowly. Light seeps in, unfamiliar blue walls greet me. I don't know where I am or how I got here. I remember being at home, packing . . . then . . . Oh God! Bethany! I'm scrambling now with an urgency my limbs aren't responding to. My head is saying *move* but it's slow progress. I'm on a bed. It's not mine. It's making moving even harder. I half-slide, half-fall off it and then I'm on wooden floorboards on all fours. The room is small and sparse. The bed is a single. There is another one next to it. On top of it is my daughter. Oh, thank God. I try to push myself up sideways and fall with a bang, but I don't feel the repercussions anywhere on my body. My limbs feel odd, fizzy and wobbly. As if they were made from cotton wool, not flesh and bone. I can't seem to control them properly but I have to.

I am on my back now, stranded and stupid like an upturned ladybird, ridiculously trying to right myself. This is no good. I force myself to breathe in and out. The same way I do after Marcus beats me. When I'm in my own home, scared and wounded, needing to fight through the pain. Mind over matter.

My hands become ready and I grip the edge of Bethany's bed. I pull myself up and there she is. Relief floods me when I see her chest rise and fall. I drag myself upright, onto the bed. All my muscles shake in protest and then I flop down, close behind my daughter. I manage to wrap an arm around her before it all goes black again.

35.

Madison Attallee

The house is exactly what I was expecting. Very much like mine and Rob's, classic Surrey. A beautiful exterior but, as I well know, appearances can be deceptive. It's not like the tower block I was raised in, on the other side of town. That looked exactly like what it was. Matchboxes piled, one on top of the other, full of poor people. Poor of pocket, poor of soul. It's what happens when you make ghettos. When the battered and bruised only have each other to look at. No. This is a different world. One I was a part of briefly. When I was a little girl I used to lie in bed and wish to be transported out of my life into one like this and for a while I made it. I don't think it suited me though. Now I'm nowhere, in some sort of limbo between the two. At least I'm not back where I started, I guess, and at least that second bedroom will be getting some use soon.

I ring the bell and Marcus answers. He is far removed from the calm, cool, collected man I met at his office earlier. He is dishevelled. A worry line cuts down his face.

'Hello,' he says.

'Hi,' I reply sombrely.

I follow him into the living room, where another man stands as soon as I enter. He looks similar to Marcus but smaller, older, less polished. He takes both of my hands in his as his son did earlier today. The gesture from him feels more genuine.

He says, 'Thank you for coming.'

'No problem.'

Before James can say anything else Marcus blurts out, 'She was going to leave me.'

I take out a pen and paper and sit. 'What makes you say that?'

Marcus stands and leaves the room, then comes back in with two bags which he places at my feet, pointing at each in turn: 'Claudia's; Bethany's.'

I start to go through them. A few essentials for a few days away. My heart sinks when I see a teddy bear and the books the little girl probably chose for herself. Something's gone very wrong, but despite Marcus's poor husband act he's still pretty high on the suspect list. I repack the bags. James runs a hand over his face.

I ask, 'Do you know why she was planning to leave you?'

He holds my gaze. I wait.

'I might have been neglectful of her.'

'No other reasons you can think of?'

'It's reason enough, isn't it? Look – can you bloody find them or not?' He stands, pulls himself upwards and uses his height to look down at me.

I stay sitting, looking up at him and resist the urge to wink. 'I can try,' I say.

'Well, surely you should be out looking then, eh?'

'Marcus!' James says, putting a hand on his son's shoulder, almost physically pushing him down. He turns to me saying, 'We're very grateful for your help. I realise it goes beyond what, er . . . the things Kate has employed you for.'

Marcus starts to speak again and James silences him with a look.

'Ms Attallee, we will of course pay you for doing this for us, on top of whatever you've already agreed with Kate.'

I shrug. 'I can't make any promises. There isn't much to go on.'

'We realise that. What do you need?'

'Honesty.'

There is a long pause. Marcus's huffing breaks the silence.

'We've told you everything we know,' James says.

I don't believe that for a second but I smile anyway. 'Can I look around?'

Marcus frowns and looks like he might speak. James nods. When Marcus gets up to follow me I smile again. 'I'm okay, thanks.'

He doesn't sit. I guess he's weighing up what is more important right now. I'm surprised when he slumps down again, shrugging. 'Don't mess up my office.'

'I won't touch anything.'

The house is big and beautifully decorated but it's not warm. You'd have a hard time believing a three-year-old lived here. There are no toys downstairs. The office is the only room where there is any mess and most of that is on the desk. A pink Post-it note with a phone number and a kiss. Claudia must have seen it when she came in for the diary. I pick it up and slip it into my pocket. You never know. Women can get awful crazy when a man's involved. Marcus will probably realise I've nabbed it despite my promise not to touch. If he wants to ask me about it though, he'll have to have a conversation about whose number it is. The thought makes me smile.

Most of the downstairs is open plan – one large space that combines a beautiful country style kitchen, a large living area and a huge table and chairs. The office, a more formal dining room, and a small bathroom and a conservatory are the only separated rooms. None of them look used except the open-plan part, but there is no dust, nothing out of place. Imagine cleaning rooms you don't even use.

Upstairs there are two spare bedrooms, also clean, with fresh bedding in each. Bethany's room is lovely and full of toys and books. There are drawings on her desk of three people, two small ones with long hair and a giant with short hair. There are letters on a page next to it. A A A A A, B B B B B, C C C C C. They should have been at Kate's now, safe. I quell my anger. It won't help right now. Her chest-of-drawers is filled with little girl clothes. I get a thump in my chest remembering Molly at this age. All arms, legs and defiance. I have to find this kid.

The master bedroom is huge. I open a walk-in closet filled with stunning clothes. I browse a few labels – they're all designer. I open a few drawers, frilly, lacy, impractical knickers. High-heeled shoes line the bottom of the cupboard. Jimmy Choo, Westwood. Another walk-in is filled with suits.

As I'm walking down the stairs I notice a plant pot at the bottom on the window ledge on its side. A small line of soil spilling along the white sill. I take a picture on my phone and check the area around it. Nothing else seems amiss, but I don't think the plant would have remained askew on Claudia's watch. I get back downstairs, aware of two sets of eyes following me.

'Well?' from Marcus.

'Nothing to suggest where they might be, I'm afraid.'

He sighs.

I say, 'I'll take the bags with me, if you don't mind?'

Marcus looks as though he might speak when James steps in. 'Very well.' He picks them up. 'I'll walk you to your car, Ms Attallee.'

Once we are outside he says, 'You mustn't mind him.'

'He has a short fuse.'

James turns to face me. 'Do you have children, Ms Attallee?'

'I do, yes.'

'They break your heart, don't they?'

I don't reply.

He heaves the bags into the boot of my small, impractical car. They barely fit.

'Marcus has always had a foul temper. When he was a little boy he used to get into rages he couldn't control. He'd get so worked up I thought he would explode. Nothing like the girls. I had hoped he'd grow out of it. He seemed to, when he met Claudia. He settled down, was happy even.'

'But it didn't last?' I think of Naomi's bloody body, stabbed to tatters and the anger it would take. I think about Claudia and what she's told Kate. I'm still unsure what James's role in this is but I know this man is lying about something, and yet I don't dislike him.

He shakes his head sadly. 'I don't think so. I try to stay out of their marriage.'

'Like you've stayed out of Kate's life?'

His eyes avoid mine. 'We don't always get parenting right.'

'I guess we don't.'

I leave with the feeling of having found out nothing and been tasked with the impossible. I was due to see my mother this afternoon but I'm not going to make it. She's probably forgotten anyway. I start to drive, light up a cigarette, inhale deeply, dial my mother and put the phone on speaker. She picks up but doesn't say anything. For fuck's sake.

'Mum?'

'Yes?' Crackly, dry.

'It's Madison.'

'Oh.' Not 'hi'. Not 'how are you?'

'I was supposed to come and visit you today.'

'Fine, I'll see you later.'

She's about to hang up. 'No, Mum, wait a minute.'

'What?'

'That's why I'm ringing. I can't make it – some work stuff has come up, but I'll be there at the weekend.'

'Okay.' And she's gone, no feeling on it either way. I know better than to take it personally and yet I still feel it, a little sting somewhere. Her indifference isn't personal, it's not about me. Shit, I, of all people, know that. I have to forgive her. Somehow I have to. If I can forgive her, maybe Molly can forgive me.

When I get back to the office, I ring Peter. He confirms that Marcus Reynolds called to report his wife missing. 'Went totally ape when we said we couldn't help.'

I laugh at that. 'I'll bet.'

'I'd assume they've just left, wouldn't you?'

I fill him in. Telling him of their escape plan, the diary, the packed bags left, the upturned plant, and the open door. I tell him about Marcus and Naomi. He sighs when I say Malone didn't really delve.

Eventually he lets out a low whistle.

I say, 'I'll be investigating it, obviously we wouldn't bother at this stage.'

'We, the police?'

'Okay, you.'

He pauses. 'Sorry I didn't mean it to sound that way.'

'I know.'

'How can I help?'

'You can't. You guys will have to look into it when it hits forty-eight hours, I suppose.'

'A lot can happen in that time.' I can hear the concern in his voice.

'Yes, I think it's already started,' I reply.

'Do you figure the husband for it?'

'Well, I would say he's certainly high up on the list but there's this ex of Kate's who seems to show up in everything.'

'Your spidey sense doesn't like Reynolds?'

I laugh. 'No, it's not that I don't think Marcus is a total shit. But I'm more interested in Oliver Horfield.'

'Kate's boyfriend?'

'Yes, he's shown up recently. Harassing Kate now.'

'Wanting to rekindle a beautiful thing?'

'Not exactly, and he has a wife,' I say, and then fill Peter in on the incest aspect.

He appropriately mutters, 'Fucking hell.'

'Right. I've been trying to contact him at his work, been on holiday apparently. No answer on his mobile and I'll be driving to his house shortly.'

'Is there a history of abuse with the husband though – Marcus?'

'Yes, not documented, but Claudia's pretty much confirmed it to Kate, not to mention the affairs.'

He lets out another low whistle. 'Oliver seems a good place to start, especially since it looks like he was stalking the whole family. I'd do the same.'

'Ha, you won't ever find yourself out here in lone-ranger land.'

'In some ways you have more freedom.'

I laugh. 'I guess it has its upsides.'

There is a pause that's too long, then he says, 'Are you free later for dinner?'

I want to say yes. I so want to say yes. I think about Janet and Molly and Rob. I sigh. 'I'm going to be up to my neck in it, sorry. The priority is finding Claudia and Bethany – you know as well as I do that this time is going to be crucial.'

'Another time?' he tries.

'Sure.'

I don't mean 'sure' though. I mean 'leave me alone'. Peter is more than I can bear right now. The thought of him fills me with love and fear in equal measure, and I do love him. I always have. I think about how shit I feel every time I speak to my mum, or drop Molly home. The burden of the people I care about is already too much. I can't manage him as well because the chances are it won't work out. Oh, it'd be fun for a few months; exciting and new. I'm always good for a few months. Then I'd turn on him, like I turn on everyone. And he'd disappoint me as much as I would him. It's what people do to each other and I can't take the upset. When I get upset, I drink, and when I drink, I lose control and Molly needs me to be in control. Or at least be able to look like I am.

I force away the other thought that whispers in my stupid mind. The one that says maybe this time it will be different.

I can't take the risk.

36.

Claudia Reynolds

'Bethany.' My voice is scratchy, dry, barely a whisper; my throat feels as though I've swallowed razor blades. I try again. Nothing. I move my arm, so heavy it hurts, and I shake her as hard as I can, which turns out to be pretty softly. I'm rewarded though. She rolls over slightly, her eyes flutter and open and she looks right at me, glassy but okay.

'I'm very sleepy, Mummy,' she mumbles, and she's gone again.

I must drift off because the next thing I know Bethany is saying, 'Mummy . . . Mummy.'

I force my eyes open and look at her.

'Where are we?' she asks.

'Shhhh, baby, everything's okay,' I say, but my blood feels icy. I remember a firm hand pressing something to my face. We were at home. I was going to leave. Finally, I was going to leave. I was taking the diary to Kate. I'd spoken to Marcus. He must have found out; he has done this to us. His own family.

'Mummy, my throat hurts.'

The door opens and I instinctively try to close my arms around my daughter but they are too slow.

'Hello, Claudia.'

For a second I'm confused. Not Marcus. Not a man at all. I find myself looking directly into familiar eyes.

I say, 'You!'

'Hello, Claudia,' she repeats with a smile.

'Martha, what are we doing here?'

She ignores me. 'You have to stay here for now.'

My head is fuzzy and I can't think of the right things to ask, though there are many, many questions quivering just outside the fuzz. She sits on the bed opposite us, still smiling as though we were all having a friendly visit.

'Do you both feel okay?'

'No, I feel funny, and Bethany won't wake up properly. You drugged us.'

'Oh, no.' She shakes her head like a petulant child. If I had the strength, I'd hit her.

'I wouldn't do that to you.' There are tears in her eyes. 'I wish he hadn't had to, but you wouldn't have come, would you? If we'd just asked?'

Marcus. No matter how far he goes, I think he can't go any further. But there's always another level.

I glare at her; she says, 'I know it doesn't feel nice, but of all the things he might give to you it's not the worst, oh no.' She shudders at something in her own head.

'Martha, what's happening? Why did you want us to come here?'

She looks at me and seems almost surprised by my presence. 'The diary. We had to take the diary.' I almost laugh. At my own stupidity. At the thought that I might have managed to do something that my husband didn't know about. Of course he knew I'd been in there.

I can feel my daughter heavy in my arms, she's gone back to sleep. 'Martha,' I say.

'Yes, Claudia.' She's smiling, an insane, unreasonable smile.

'How did you know I had the diary?'

'Oh, *I* didn't know! He told me.'

'How did he know?'

She laughs, a mad, high-pitched sound. 'He knows everything, he's always watching.' Oh God. Her life isn't so different from mine.

'Is he watching us now?'

She nods. 'Of course.' Her hand waves to the top corner of the room, there's a camera there. She giggles, that awful sound again. There must be a camera somewhere in the office.

'I think I've been too long; I'm supposed to be quick. I brought you food. It's on the table. You'll start to feel better soon, I promise. It wears off. I should know. There's a bathroom at the back of the room. And there's a telly.' She hands me a remote and stands to go.

'Martha . . . wait—'

'Claudia, I have to go, I told you,' she frowns.

'You have to help us . . . please!'

Her frown fades and she kneels by the side of the bed, turning her head at an angle so we are eye to eye. 'I am helping you. Just do what I say and you'll be fine. Don't do anything to make him angry.'

'How would we make him angry?'

She shrugs.

She stands again and goes out of the room. I keep calling her name even after the door closes and I hear a lock turn. I keep calling in my croaky voice, until Bethany wakes up and asks why I'm shouting and then I smile and stroke her hair and tell her not to worry, that everything will be fine. But my heart is racing.

37.

Kate Reynolds

I feel a familiar pressure build on my chest. Fear: cold, uncut, clean and fresh. It's non-specific, it's about nothing and everything all at once. I remember the same feeling when I realised my new home would be prison, that Naomi was dead, that it was my fault. It didn't happen during the trial or while I was on remand, it all seemed dream-like then. Dean says I dissociated, a coping mechanism. Then the wonderful numb detachment left, the first night Janine climbed down onto my bunk and held a pillow over my face, just long enough that I thought I was going to die. So that defence is long gone. Everything is horribly real. That night has come back to me with startling clarity. The first time I remembered it was during a particularly sleepless night, only a month after I had been sentenced. I thought it must have been a dream and Dean had agreed that that was likely. But it had happened again, and then it came to me in the daytime and I knew it wasn't a dream. It coincided with the numbness wearing off. Dean suggested later that I had been in shock. That's when I'd called my dad. The last time he spoke to me until now. The day he shut me out. The details became clearer, but I took a risk when I went to Madison. My memories might have been false after all. But look where they've led. The more I think about it, the more I understand that the knowledge was always there. Buried in my subconscious.

I call Dean; he's the only one who will make me feel better. I tell him about Claudia and Bethany. He asks if I'm okay and I say I am. But I'm not. Not really, though I feel better for talking to him. The more Madison has uncovered the clearer it is that many things have been covered up. Oliver is Ruth's son. He is my brother. Martha was at the party that night. Marcus and my dad are involved. The worse thing about it all is that I still love them, especially my father. These awful undeserving people, who not only left me in my hour of need, but may have had something to do with putting me there. In prison even Janine's messed-up relatives turned up every two weeks. She delighted in the fact no one came for me. Except Dean, and they all knew he was my therapist. The sting of abandonment is no less now. It still hurts just the same six years on. It's not normal, is it, to treat your child that way? No matter what. Betrayal.

Then there's Oliver. The other person I loved. My brother. He is my bloody brother and he knew that all along. I loved him. I trusted him like I trusted them all. I think Dad and Marcus must have known. I can only think that even though she's dead, James was looking out for his precious Ruth. Her reputation even in death was to be upheld even as mine was shattered. It must be that. I can't go so far as to think they knew I'd go into the room, but they didn't come rushing to save me either. Naomi must have known something. It wouldn't surprise me. Her favourite currency was information. If she held your secrets she could use them against you. My guess is she tried to do this with Oliver.

Madison has asked me to wait an hour to come into the office but I am restless and the walls of my flat are closing in. I grab my coat and bag and head out. It's cold but sunny and I walk. I walk aimlessly out of town, to green trees and the river, trying to untangle the mess in my head.

My phone keeps beeping, it's been doing it since yesterday. I try and scroll through, there's a text message and a voicemail. Oliver. Sounding desperate, panicked. 'Kate. Please, we need to talk. We really need to talk.' Silence. A sound like a sob. I stop walking. 'Please, Kate, phone me back.' He leaves his number. The message ends and the time it gives is just before Claudia and Bethany disappeared. Oh my God. I dial the number. It rings and rings. I dial it again. No answer. He's got them. It's not Marcus. I call Madison in a panic, barely able to breathe, barely able to speak. She tells me to stay put and in twenty minutes her black sports car screeches to a halt and she gets out.

I'm sitting on the floor. Sweating, panting. Madison takes one look at me and sits down next to me. I'm surprised when she takes my hand, locks her eyes with mine, and says: 'You are okay. You are not dying. It's a panic attack. You just need to breathe in and out, and in and out.' I stay focused on her eyes and I can feel my heart slow down and my breathing return to normal. I whisper, 'Oliver. Voicemail.' And I hand her my phone.

She listens, hands me back my phone and helps me into her car. When she starts the engine, rock music blasts out of the speakers. I nearly jump out of my skin. She turns it off quickly and apologises, mumbling that it helps her think.

'Mind if I smoke?' she asks. She still hasn't said anything. About him. About what we are going to do.

I do mind, the smoking, but I nod that I don't and she winds down the window and lets in cold winter air as we drive along. The cigarette smells disgusting, but I can see her loosen with every puff. Maybe I should try it.

'Start at the beginning,' she orders.

I do, adding again the feeling I had had that someone was

in my flat earlier in the week. The other feeling of being followed, being watched.

'You should have told me.'

'What, that I had a feeling?'

She laughs. 'Look, this whole investigation has been based
on you having a "kind of" memory that may or may not be
real, so any other feelings you might have I want to know
about, okay?'

'Okay.' I wind down my own window, trying to get air but
breathing in nicotine instead. I smile and say to her, 'Looks like
I might be onto something though, doesn't it? Bet you're glad
I'm innocent?'

'I figured you might be.'

I'm surprised at that. 'Really?'

She shrugs, inhales, exhales, flicks the fag butt out of the
window. 'Yup. Doesn't mean we don't need proof though,
does it?'

'The police wouldn't have touched this case again.'

She sighs. 'Lucky for you I'm not the police then.'

'Did my dad and Marcus know anything about Claudia and
Bethany, do you think?'

'I don't know. But they're definitely hiding something,
protecting someone.' It's what I've been thinking but I still
feel like I've been punched in the stomach. Like the world is
caving in around me. Oliver. My brother. Did my dad know?
Did he know when Oliver was coming to the house? Surely
not. Naomi. She's the key, I suppose. Naomi, who Marcus was
in love with. Marcus, who is lying. My dad, who is lying. My
head is spinning.

'Ruth,' I say suddenly.

'What?'

'The only explanation can be that Dad is looking after Ruth's
reputation.'

'Ruth's dead,' Madison says.

'Can you think of another reason?'

'Not yet. Maybe he had something on them.'

I frown at her. 'What do you mean?'

She shrugs. 'Look, we're not done. But there's something there. I get your theory about Ruth but I'm not into it.' She must see my disappointed face because she adds, 'I'm sorry, this must all be very tough for you.'

Tough is an understatement, but I say, 'It's better to know, isn't it.' Although I still can't quite work out if I agree with that idea.

Madison calls the police. I'm alarmed to see her balancing the phone precariously between ear and shoulder while driving way too fast. She tells them that Oliver Horfield has taken Claudia and Bethany and that she believes they are in immediate danger. My stomach starts doing a nauseous dance.

Madison is still talking to them as we park and I follow her into the office, thinking a lift with her is like a near-death experience in itself. She leaves me with Emma who clucks around. She feels motherly, though I realise when I look at her face that she's probably not that much older than me. She makes me tea and adds sugar without being asked. She takes my coat and gently squeezes my shoulder.

Madison's office door slams and Emma flinches slightly. She busies herself tidying around me and then stops, sniffing the air above her. She tuts. 'Smoking out the window again. I daresay it'll be the air freshener next.'

As if on cue we hear the spray. We're both giggling, despite the situation, when Madison comes out. She frowns but ignores it.

'According to Oliver's company he's on annual leave,' she says. 'Took it at the last minute – apparently got a good deal on a late booking.'

'But his phone was ringing.'

She looks at me as though I'm stupid. I fall in a second too late. 'Have you tried calling his house?'

'Of course.' She scowls at us both. 'No answer. I'm going around there now.'

My heart is racing. Oliver sounded crazed and hysterical, a man on the edge, and who knows what he'll do next. We have to find Claudia and Bethany. We're running out of time.

38.

Madison Attallee

The house is modest. At the end of a quiet cul-de-sac. Pretty, bland new-builds, nothing special. But they must be expensive, everything here is expensive. I knock on the door of Number 48 and a woman answers. On first sight she's quite plain but then she smiles and it's as though the whole area around her lights up.

'Are you Louisa Horfield?'

'I am.' Still smiling.

'My name's Madison Attallee, I'm a private investigator. I wonder if I might have a quick word with your husband?'

The 100-watt smile falters. 'He's not here.'

'Do you know where he is?'

'At work.'

And this is where I have to be a shithead. 'I'm afraid he's not, I've already checked. They said he's on annual leave.'

Her hand darts quickly to her belly, cupping the underneath. I realise she is really, really pregnant. Great.

'How far along are you?' I ask her.

She looks down. I know that feeling. You hold that child and don't even know you're doing it.

'Eight months.' We both look at her bump.

'I suppose you'd better come in,' she says.

I pass photos in the hallway. Her; a man I assume is Oliver – tall, very blonde. Unlike Kate, though their colouring is similar. A photo of their wedding day.

I follow her into a large open-plan kitchen. Another big family living area, not quite as grand as Marcus and Claudia's, but still all the rage. I remember ours being built. Rob's excitement as the bricks went up. Him trying to enthuse me with magazines and textile plans. I barely noticed when it was done. I wasn't there enough to enjoy the space. She puts a kettle on and waves a mug at me in question.

'Coffee, please.'

She gets out a cafetiere and fusses with water and milk, bringing it to the table. Instant would have done. She pours us both a cup.

'I'm only on one a day. I know I ought to be off the caffeine, but I can't pack it in entirely. I'll be sorry if this one's hyper, eh?' She smiles but it's strained now.

'Is it your first?' I ask her.

She nods. 'Yes. Well, I've lost three.'

'I'm sorry.'

'Why are you here?' she asks, quickly changing the subject.

I weigh up what to tell her. 'Do you know the name Kate Reynolds?'

She screws up her face. 'I recognise it but I can't think why.'

'She was in all of the papers a few years ago, six, to be exact. She was charged with the manslaughter of her best friend, Naomi Andrews.'

'God, yes. I remember. I didn't live here then.' She sips at her coffee, cupping her hands around the mug.

'So you didn't know Oliver then?'

'No. We met . . . I suppose it must be four and a half years ago now.'

'Where?'

'Online. Look, I don't mean to be rude . . .'

'Oliver was involved with Kate,' I tell her.

She stares at me blankly. 'The murderer?'

'I think she's innocent.'

She blinks, coffee held an inch away from her mouth.

'He never mentioned it?' I ask.

She puts the cup down. 'No. Was it serious?'

'It was to Kate.'

'God. Wasn't she just out of school?'

'Eighteen at the time of her arrest.'

'So, he must have been . . . a fair bit older than her.' It's not a question.

I give her a moment while she does the maths figuring out there are twelve years between them, then I say, 'They'd been seeing each other for a couple of years by then.' And watch while the bomb hits. Sixteen is different to eighteen, especially when you're dealing with a man pushing thirty.

I see her shudder at the implication, glad I don't need to mention at this stage that Kate is his sister as well and that I think he's probably a murdering kidnapper.

'Why are you telling me this?' she asks.

'Why do you think he didn't mention it?'

'I don't know, maybe he was embarrassed. I didn't expect full disclosure – I certainly didn't give him a blow-by-blow account of all my exes.'

'Were any of them convicted of manslaughter?'

She frowns. 'Look, Oliver's not . . . he doesn't talk too much about his feelings.'

'Has he always been that way?'

'Aren't most men?'

I don't answer.

'I didn't meet him at the best time – for him, I mean,' Louisa says.

'Why?'

'His mum had been in an accident. She's never recovered.'

'What happened?'

'A car accident, she was brain damaged. Lives in a home now.'

'His dad?'

'David's a nice man, very quiet. Had a big job in the city but he had a breakdown after Oli's mum was hurt. He pulls shifts in Sainsbury's to cover the cost of her home.' She quickly adds, 'We have offered him money.'

'He won't take it?'

'No.'

'Where does he live?'

'David?'

I nod. 'Yes.'

'Around the corner. In fact, that's probably where Oliver is right now. I'll call him.'

She's up and grabbing for the phone before I can stop her. I hear her leave a message, adopting an enforced cheery tone.

'Maybe they've gone to see Amelia – sorry, his mum,' she says, sitting back down.

I repeat, 'Kate says she's innocent.'

Louisa stares at me. Her coffee sits untouched and her hands are resting on her bump. 'I'm sure Oliver would be happy to help with any enquiries you have,' she says.

'Kate's sister-in-law is missing. Claudia Reynolds.'

Something flickers on her face and her mouth drops open. She closes it quickly.

'So is her three-year-old,' I add.

'God.'

'If there's anything you can think of that might help?'

'What – do you think Oliver took them?' She laughs. 'He's the nicest man I know.'

'But he doesn't talk to you about his feelings – maybe he's bottling things up. He didn't tell you about Kate.'

'That's neither here nor there. I trust him completely. I'm having his child, for Christ's sake,' she says, her voice rising.

'But you have no idea where he is?'

'I don't like what you're implying and I think you need to leave.' She's out of her seat and getting to her feet. 'If you leave a number I'll make sure Oliver calls you when he gets home.'

She hurries me to the door. I hand her a card and take her hand before she can stop me.

'Do you have any friends nearby?' I ask.

'Why?'

'Humour me.'

'I have an aunt a few roads over.'

'Think about staying there, just until this blows over.'

'Get out.' She snatches her hand away. I'm pushed over the threshold and the door slams.

My phone rings just as I pull up at the office. It's a number I don't recognise.

'Hello?'

'Is that Madison Attallee?' Soft Irish tones.

'Yes. Is that Denise?' The nurse from Martha's hospital, Sandcross.

'Sure, how could you tell?'

'Your accent,' I tell her.

'Ah.'

'Are you okay, Denise?'

She pauses, then says, 'I am. I can't be long – I've just nipped out.'

'Okay.'

'I'm not sure if I'm out of turn to call you or not.'

'I'll keep it between us if I can.'

'Martha discharged herself, yesterday.'

'Okay.'

She hurries on, 'Normally her dad would be here to get her, but she just went on her own, like.'

'Is that unusual?'

'It is.'

'But she's allowed to? I mean she's not on a section or anything?'

'Well, that's right, I just . . . it didn't seem right, and I tried to ask her . . . if she was okay, what was happening, you know?'

'What did she say?'

'She said she was fine and there was no need to call her dad, she'd make her own way.'

'Okay, I'll be discreet, but I'll try to find out if she's shown up.'

She asks, 'Would you let me know?'

'Of course.'

I don't call Marcus or James to check. I'm quite certain that even if they knew where Martha was neither one would tell me. I get in the car because it's too cold to stand outside and light a cigarette. I sit for a few moments in silence, trying to assimilate a thought that's forming, but just out of reach. I'm on my second fag by the time it hits me. Martha. James and Marcus would have no real reason to protect Oliver, but what if Oliver had been using not just Kate, but his other sister as well? I think about James paying the staff at Sandcross, asking them to leave her be and I wonder if maybe there's a good reason. I hit dial on the last number on my phone.

She picks up on the second ring.

'Hello?'

I balance the phone dangerously between shoulder and ear and say, 'Denise. I'd appreciate you not mentioning this to James or Marcus right now.'

'Right, okay.' I'm relieved when she doesn't ask why.

39.

Kate Reynolds

Dean is waiting in the reception at his office. I promptly burst into tears when I see him. I've been holding everything in and now it empties out of me. He sighs, puts a gentle arm around my shoulders, walks me into his office and settles me down. He makes me tea, sipping from a water bottle and taking a chair opposite.

When Dean called I'd told him everything about Oliver and how I'd contacted him on LinkedIn.

'Why did you message him?' he asks.

'I don't know.'

He sighs. 'I wish you'd spoken to me.'

'I knew what you would say.'

He sighs again. I feel shame wash over me, that I've managed to make a bad situation even worse and that I may have caused Claudia and Bethany's disappearance. I gave Oliver a way in all those years ago and by reigniting his attention I've let him back in again. I think it must have been him following me, so he'd have figured out that Madison was investigating it all again. If he's broken into my flat who knows what he's found, and I'm pretty certain I led him to my sister-in-law. My niece. God.

I say, 'Oh, Dean, what have I done?'

He pats my hand but doesn't say anything to alleviate the guilt.

Which makes me want to say more – to explain. I tell Dean in detail who Oliver is, that Madison has discovered he's Ruth's son and who that means he must be to me. He watches. His face betrays nothing and I find even saying the words makes me feel rotten all over again.

When I am spent he says, 'I'm so sorry.'

I say, 'I'm an idiot.'

'You're not an idiot. Your mother caused all of this long before you were even born.' His voice is sharp.

'Do you think my dad knows? Maybe that's what he's been hiding.'

'It's hard to know; they definitely seem to be hiding something. From what you've told me James was always out to protect Ruth.' Dean shrugs. 'Maybe he's still doing that now.'

I think about that and I agree. Ruth's still stabbing my heart and she's been dead for a decade, for God's sake. Oliver must have been obsessed with her. And us. I shudder when I think just how mad he must have been, or desperate for that love. I wonder if he thinks we got what he didn't. He'd be wrong. Ruth didn't want us any more than she wanted him. In that way I suppose Oliver and I are alike. Searching for that one thing we should all have from our parents. The only unconditional kind of care you can expect. No, there's no point pitying him.

'Madison hasn't tracked down Oliver yet either?' asks Dean.

I shake my head. 'I don't think so. He's married, you know.' I sigh. 'She's pregnant, his wife.'

'He's been getting on with his life, hasn't he?'

I shrug. 'I guess he was always going to. It was only in my stupid head that we would grow up, get married, and live happily ever after.' I feel the familiar wave of nausea again and an image of an awful incestuous monster of a child in my arms hits me before I can stop it.

Dean frowns at me. 'And you were nursing these thoughts for years?'

I laugh even though I know it's not funny.

He goes on, 'And you didn't think to tell me? So much for not keeping secrets.'

He's right. I have kept it from him. Because I knew somewhere deep down that the feelings I had for Oliver weren't right. 'I . . . I'm sorry, Dean. I didn't do it out of spite.'

He looks as though he's going to say something else but his phone rings. He checks and his face changes. 'It's a client. I'm so sorry, but I'm going to have to take this.'

I nod and get my things together. He is working. How stupid that I feel jealous of his client.

'Keep me updated,' he says as I go, closing the door quietly behind me.

I'm ashamed to say it but I now have the jitters walking around in broad daylight. I hurry back to my flat, taking a bus two stops to shorten the walking distance. I think about the awful feeling I had when I woke up. I'm quite sure that the night my door was unlocked someone had been in my flat. It had to be Oliver. My refuge, now not so safe. When I get in I shut the door and throw the bolt over it.

40.

Claudia Reynolds

One night I came to on my living room floor. My eyes opened and the pain hit me from every muscle, every digit, every bit of skin. My body was alive with it, the beating, the humiliation. I was in a wretched state – one of the times I couldn't think straight – where I wondered if I might have sustained serious damage. I cried for a while, lying there, prone, bleeding, sobbing like a fool. He was asleep, Bethany was asleep. I had an overwhelming desire to get out. I had to get out. The walls of my beautiful home were closing in on me. I managed to stand, to drag myself up, and to walk out the door. I had no destination in mind, though I vaguely thought of Mum and Dad's. My wonderful parents who I no longer saw. Who I communicated with via clipped messages.

Mum knew by then that something was up. She didn't know what, though, she still doesn't. But that was the idea I had in my head that night, to walk the twenty-odd miles to their house. I knew the way by car, I'd just follow the road. I was in my nightgown, I found wellies by the door and a coat. My purse was in the pocket of my coat. I had bank cards in there but it somehow didn't occur to me to call a taxi. I just had to go. I had to get out. It had to be over. I walked for seven miles before I passed out on the side of a main road. A passer-by called an ambulance. They found my purse in my coat pocket, my driving licence nestled within. When I came to this time it was in a hospital bed with my husband sitting beside me, concern etched into every line and his hand squeezing mine gently. I cried then, deep sobs. He held me tightly. Whispered my name into my hair, and then he said, 'Don't make me punish her for your mistakes,' and I knew then that there was no escape. Not for me. He would always win.

When he left to get my things from home, a nurse came in to see me. She said, 'It doesn't have to be this way, you know.'

'What are you talking about?' I asked, playing innocent.

She had sat on the edge of the bed and looked me directly in the eye. 'We see other women just like you, love.'

My voice had been a whisper, 'I don't know what you mean.'

'Whatever he's threatened, can it be much worse than where you are now?'

I wanted to talk to her, to tell her, to ask for help. Perhaps if Bethany had been anywhere but home with him I would have.

Instead I said, 'I must have been sleep-walking; I'm on tablets, you know. I'm sure my husband must have told you.'

'A lot of your bruises are old.'

'They make me clumsy.'

She had sighed. 'There's a refuge in Surbiton. They'd take you in, help you.'

'I think there's been a misunderstanding.'

She patted my hand and I had resisted the urge to grab it.

My one attempt at escape. We never discussed it. I came home, we carried on.

I'm sick to death of carrying on. Now I'm *literally* in a locked room. My husband and captor has put me here. It's time to be free.

I haven't let Bethany eat the food Martha brought in, even though she says she's starving and thirsty. I let her drink water from the bathroom tap and I do the same. Still, my tongue feels thick, fuzzy. Whatever we inhaled has left a residual hangover, but I don't feel like we've lost loads of time. Hours rather than days, I hope. There is a TV in the room which has been a godsend as Bethany is distracted by CBeebies. When I asked if she remembered getting here she says no and also that when I said we would be visiting her aunt she thought I meant Kate, not Martha. She doesn't look impressed, as though I had intentionally duped her. I smile and stroke her hair.

We need to get out of here. There is a window, but it's too high up for me to look out of and too narrow for us to fit through. Then there is the door. I don't know what's on the other side. This could be the upstairs of somewhere. We might get out, only to be greeted by more house. It doesn't matter, that's what we need to do. Get out. It's the only way we have any chance. Staying in here won't help us. I can probably overpower Martha if she comes back, but I can't overpower a fully grown man. Not that I ever tried with Marcus, but I felt it. The tipped scale, physical power always in his favour, never mine. A simple unchangeable biological fact.

Marcus. Poor me, poor Bethany. Maybe it's not going to be the devil I know though, maybe not this time; maybe I have a new enemy, but I can't think who. I guess I'm still stupid enough to think Marcus wouldn't stoop this low. I squelch the urge to cry hysterically. Bethany has drifted off watching TV. I cover her, glad that my legs are working again. I climb into bed with her because I'm cold and because I can't bear to be too far.

I make deals in my head. Please let us go. I'll do what I need to do and take better care of my daughter. I promise

I will. I'll leave and never look back and then I'll spend the rest of my life making it up to her. I need to get away from Marcus, to get Bethany away. The bits I love either aren't real or they're only a small irrelevant part of a much bigger, darker picture.

I keep stroking Bethany's hair and I hear her breathing get deeper, watch her small eyelids flutter and close. My daughter. My lovely daughter who I will not consign to a life of fear. If we can get through this, we will be fine. Somehow we will be fine.

We both snooze, though I don't think I am gone for long. I wake with a start, blood pumping around my veins, hot and full of purpose. I walk around the space, a plan formulating in my mind.

My little one's eyes flicker and open. She sits up stretching and I smile at her and pull her up to sit. I bend on my knees so that our eyes are level and I say, 'Bethany, I'm going to call for your aunt and I need you to be quiet while I do and be ready to run when I say. Okay?'

She nods, but looks worried. I go over the plan with her again and she starts crying. 'Why are we here, Mummy? Why do we have to run?'

'We'll talk about those things later, Bethany. Now, I need you to be strong and I need you to do what I'm saying. Can you do that?' She nods.

I put her behind me, pick up a small wooden chair and I start shouting. I've been calling for so long that I almost give up and then:

'Sssshhhhhh.'

'Martha, Bethany's not moving, her breathing isn't right. Whatever you gave us she's reacting to really badly.'

'I didn't give her anything. It should be safe. Please, Claudia, you just have to help her.'

'Martha, she's not right, she's going to die if you don't help us. She'll die and it will be your fault.'

It's quiet and then, 'He's not here . . . I have to call him . . .'

'Martha, now! You have to help me now. Oh my God, she's stopped breathing, Martha. Martha!'

There is silence from her side. I make panicked sounds, the door swings open and I do it before I have time to think, before I change my mind. Whack. I feel the wood land on her and the leg falls off the chair as she crumples to the floor, screaming. And Bethany is screaming and I'm sorry, I really am, but there's no time. I push Martha completely to the floor, pinning her by her shoulders with my knees.

'Key?'

'He'll kill me.'

'Key, Martha, now, or I'll kill you myself.'

Bethany screams again, loud, piercing.

'Bethany, be quiet.' Something in my voice stops her.

Martha hands me the key, sobbing. I walk out, dragging my daughter with me and I lock the door, ignoring the bangs coming from the other side. We are in a short hallway. It is a stand-alone purpose-built building made of breeze blocks. There is another room, one Martha must have come from. I'm tempted to look in it, see if the diary is still there at least, or anything else, but I don't have time to waste. I grab Bethany – she's too big for me to carry, but I half-drag, half-propel her and we are out. I don't know where we are. There isn't much else here, a big green expanse of grass. I can hear the river rushing by, but no sign of any people. I have no idea how long I've got, but we go quickly. Bethany is crying. I shush her but I don't stop. Outside are two large fields. I don't know where any of them go. There seems no point heading for the river, the other direction might lead to a road. That's the one we take. It's drizzling and soon enough we are wet through. Bethany

226

is keeping up, just about, and eventually we are rewarded and come to a road. A big main road. Lots of cars, lots of people. Safety. I am not going to fail this time. This time I'm going to keep putting one foot in front of the other and save us. Save myself and my daughter.

41.

Dear Ruth,

This letter won't get to you, you'll never read it. That makes me feel sad. I've enjoyed our correspondence, though I admit it's been a little one-sided. I was glad we got to meet again though. I asked you a few simple questions, didn't I? It's sad that you couldn't answer them, or wouldn't. Your final act of spite, I suspect.

I wanted to know if you had held me, before you said goodbye forever. I couldn't remember if we'd hugged. I wanted to know if you'd felt anything at all before you disposed of me from your life, like so much rubbish. You didn't give me a straight answer, blethering on and on about what good people the Horfields were, thinking I was unaware of who they were exactly to you.

They were pathetic people actually. Annoying do-gooders. They drove me mad with their incessant head-leaning sympathies, their constant quest to understand me and my fake brother. They couldn't crack me, though they thought they had.

I played my part well enough. You should have seen her face when she realised what I had in store for her. I like justice, Ruth. I did tell you that. If I had thought at any moment that you were sorry, even a little bit, for what you did to me then I might, might have been able to forgive you. You might still be alive, Ruth, my pathetic gaggle of siblings might still have had a mother, albeit a shit one!

*I think I'll probably keep writing to you. I sort of miss you, Ruth,
despite all your flaws.*

Love as always

42.

Madison Attallee

When I get back into the office Emma says I have a visitor. It's James Reynolds.

'I think it's about time we spoke,' he says.

'I think you're probably right.'

As soon as I shut the door he begins, and though I'm quite certain I already know what he's going to say I let him speak. 'You said you have children.'

I nod. 'One, a little girl.'

'What sort of child is she?'

I shrug. 'Just a normal little girl, I guess.'

'Right. Kate was like that, out of the three of mine, the most "normal". Doesn't say much in this family.' He wipes a hand over his brow and goes on, 'My wife, Ruth, was not a good mother. I knew it shortly after Martha was born. She seemed to start off okay with our son. We always had help, mind, but she played with Marcus, enjoyed dressing him up, taking him out. Didn't like pregnancy, was almost phobic about it, to be honest. Particularly the second time around, then the third.' He seems lost in that memory for a moment. 'She wouldn't let me be involved, which wasn't unusual for men then, mind. I think she was already depressed and, well, it was even worse with the hormones perhaps, and the children.

Their needs. Mine. You can imagine, I'm sure.'

'I can.'

He nods. 'Anyway, a few months after Martha was born Ruth became very withdrawn. Post-natal depression, or so I thought. She saw a doctor, he prescribed some pills, recommended exercise.'

'It didn't help?'

He shakes his head. 'No, though later I found out she hadn't been taking the tablets.' He waves a hand. 'It's by the by. I suspect they wouldn't have helped anyway. It wasn't just depression. Her behaviour was bizarre. As I said, she had been quite bonded with Marcus and then all of a sudden she turned on him.'

'Turned on him?'

'I can't think of a better way to put it than that. She wouldn't pick him up or cuddle him, sent him to the nanny. Poor little thing was devastated.' He looks at me intently. 'I know it's not an excuse . . . but perhaps you can see how he might have become the man he is?'

I shrug, thinking about Claudia's terrified voice on the phone.

James goes on, 'Anyway. She didn't bond with Martha, and then along came Kate. She cried when the test came back positive. She started ignoring me. She drank a lot, whilst pregnant and after Kate's birth. She'd lapse into silences that lasted days. Took herself off to bed. I'm ashamed to say I didn't manage well – I had an affair with the nanny.'

'Did Ruth find out?'

'Yes, but she didn't seem to care. Said she didn't blame me.'

'Kate mentioned that Ruth had no contact with her parents,' I say.

'No, none at all. She was living with them when we met, though she never introduced us and she didn't invite them to the wedding. All she would say on the matter was that they had treated her terribly and she could never forgive them. She had a therapist when I met her.'

'Can you remember the therapist's name?'

'Now you're really going back . . . Horton?'

'Could it have been Horfield?' I ask him.

'Yes. Yes, I think it was Dr Horfield! How did you know that?'

'I'll explain later. Please, carry on.'

He shrugs. 'There's not much more about Ruth, to be honest. I stopped the affair, threw myself into being the best dad I could while keeping money coming in. I tried to love the kids enough for both of us. I tried to love Ruth but she wouldn't let me, and then she died.'

'Suicide?'

He nods. His eyes shine with tears. 'I wasn't surprised.'

'It must have been awful.'

He nods. 'One of the worst things about it was that Martha found her, did you know that?'

'No.'

'No, why would you. She had been sitting with her body all day by the time we got home. She already had some difficulties.'

'What was wrong with her?' I ask, wondering if he knew that Oliver must have been causing chaos for his children. But I don't think so.

He shrugs. 'I don't know. I paid a fortune to the psychiatrists who couldn't seem to work it out either.'

He chokes for a moment, holding back a sob, I think. But I don't buy it. He told the nurses to stop treating her, after all. 'I have done many awful things in my life. I have felt inadequate so often.'

I don't say anything, but wait while he regains some composure. I don't know if I feel sorry for him. Parenting is probably the most important job we will ever do. This man has not got it right and he's had opportunities to change. But who am I to judge?

'Martha is not a normal little girl. She's not like her sister, Kate, who was always robust, able to manage even when faced with terrible adversity. I knew, just knew she would be okay, in some way.'

I don't even begin to point out all the ways in which this statement is not true. Kate is a nervous wreck. My guess is she was a nervous wreck back then. She just hid it under an agreeable smile. And then I realise what he is telling me. It isn't Marcus.

'You've been protecting Martha,' I say.

He looks at me, his eyes pleading. 'She'd never have managed.'

'You set Kate up?'

He's shaking his head. 'No, God no, of course not. It . . . it just somehow happened that way. If she hadn't walked into the room . . .'

'James, tell me what happened, from the beginning.'

A tear escapes then, making its way down his cheek. He seems oblivious. He tells me, 'I love Kate. Please, you must understand that. I love both of my girls, but I made a decision in a moment to save the one who was more fragile.'

'James . . .' I prompt him back to the night of Naomi's murder. Time is not on our side.

'I was . . . away that night.'

'Where were you?'

He pulls a tissue from his pocket and dabs his eyes gently. 'I had a . . . girlfriend I suppose you'd call her, nothing serious.'

'You were at her house?'

He nods. 'Yes, not far from home.'

'The children thought you were away working.'

'Yes. Kate planned the bloody party. I should have known.' He pauses. 'Anyway, I got a call from Marcus just before midnight. He was hysterical, absolutely beside himself, said I had to come home.' Marcus, again.

'And you did?'

'I did. I met him out in the back garden, he was a mess. I followed him up to Martha's room and there they were.'

'Naomi was already dead?'

He nods. 'And Martha was sitting there smiling and holding the knife.'

'You got her out?'

He's twisting the tissue now between his hands, turning it into a long thin line. 'It was instinct. I just picked her up and we left, the three of us. We went out the back. No one saw us; the kids were all in the living room, I suppose, or in other bedrooms. We went to one of the vacant properties – the flat Kate's in now, actually. I cleaned them up. Tried my best to calm Marcus. Martha was perfectly placid – seemed to have no idea what she'd done. Then the police rang to say they had Kate in custody.'

'You sent Martha to the hospital?'

'Yes, a day later, by which time she was pretty much comatose. Kate confessed and Marcus and I promised to do what we needed to protect Martha.'

He's crying openly now. Tears stream down his face.

'Why would Martha have killed Naomi?'

'I don't know. She never said. I'm not certain if she even remembers it.'

I think about what Denise had told me. 'That's why you didn't continue with her therapists – in case they uncovered it.'

'Yes.'

'What was in Naomi's diary?'

He shakes his head at that. 'I don't know, I had no idea Marcus had it.'

'It was Marcus who called you that night?'

He nods and his eyes widen as he takes in the implication.

'Martha has discharged herself from Sandcross,' I tell him.

'Oh no.' The blood seems to drain from his face.

'Do you remember Oliver?' I ask.

He frowns. 'Kate's boyfriend?'

'Yes. I have reason to believe he was Ruth's son.'

He looks at me as though I'm mad; I carry on. 'I think that her father, Raymond, was also Oliver's father.' I watch as that sinks in. He blinks. Looking at me wide-eyed.

'My God.' His face contorts. 'What the hell . . . Kate? What would he want with . . . his sister?'

'I don't know yet. Ruth gave him away for adoption, shortly after she met you.'

His face is crestfallen. 'That's terrible.' He shakes his head. 'Why didn't she tell me?'

I shrug. 'I don't know. Maybe she was ashamed.'

He looks appalled at that and says, 'Does Kate know this?'

I nod.

'She must be very upset,' he says.

'That's an understatement. Do you remember Ruth's mother, Margaret?'

'Yes. Well, vaguely. I waved at her a few times when I called to take Ruth out.'

'You didn't find it strange that you didn't know them?'

He shrugs. 'Yes, but Ruth had told me she didn't get on with her father and that her parents weren't people she wanted to know. I felt like a knight in shining armour, to be honest.'

I resist the urge to roll my eyes at him. Instead I tell him, 'I'm going to see Margaret. I've found her.'

And then I pass him the phone. 'You should speak to Kate.'

He's shaking his head and the little sympathy I felt for him wilts. He is a coward. A foolish, unquestioning coward. If he'd paid more attention to his family when they needed him he could have stopped all of this before it started. I look at him sternly. 'Call Kate. Say you'll explain later but make contact. She's your daughter, for God's sake.'

43.

Kate Reynolds

Madison's number flashes on my phone, but when I pick up it is my father's voice in my ear: 'Kate.'

I am hit again by just how much I've missed him.

'Daddy.'

There is a pause. A place in time where we must both be lost in thought. Something happens to my stomach, it clenches in on itself like a fist closing, taking with it all of my insides.

He's not speaking.

'Are you with Madison?' I ask.

'Yes.'

'Okay.'

'Are you all right?'

'I didn't kill Naomi, Dad.'

'I know, love, I already know.'

'What do you mean you already know?'

He pauses. 'I'll explain everything. Can I come round?'

I sit and wait and I am swamped by so many thoughts and feelings: anger at the years lost, confusion as to what I should do next, and sadness that he has kept things from me. The reality that whatever's he's been hiding, it looks like he sacrificed me.

I am trying to contain my rage, scared that I will attack him when I see him, but when he arrives at my door all I see is a man I have always loved, pale and old. His face is tear-stained. He whispers, 'I'm so sorry, Kate.'

I go to him and put my arms around him. I hear him sob as he holds me.

'Dad, what's going on?' I ask.

He is shaking as he releases me. He follows me through to the living room and says, 'How is the flat?'

I shrug. 'Nice. Thank you for letting me stay.'

He looks away. 'It's the least I could do.' We both sit down and he says, 'I . . . I did a terrible thing, Kate. I didn't know you would walk into that room. How would I have known?'

'Dad, what are you saying?'

'Your sister, Martha, she was at the party,' he goes on.

So Annie wasn't lying. 'I thought she was away.'

He looks forlorn. 'Oh, Kate, she was supposed to be. I'd dropped her at Sandcross myself that morning. She must have come back. Your Madison seems to think this Oliver might have had something to do with that?'

I blush. He says gently, 'None of that's your fault, love.' He pauses. 'I didn't know. About him, your mum.'

I don't say anything but there is some relief in his ignorance. He goes on, 'Marcus found her, your sister, with Naomi. He called me and . . . we panicked.'

I look at him, wide-eyed. 'I went to prison.'

He's nodding. 'I know, love, I know. I'm so sorry.'

I'm shaking from head to toe. I say, 'Do you have any idea what it was like?'

'I'm so sorry.'

His eyes are trained on his feet. I can't think what else to say. I look out of the window. Six years.

I almost laugh as I say, 'Out of all your children. I'm the best you've got.'

He half smiles. I try to return it. I say, 'I know about Marcus and Claudia.'

'I know . . . I know his faults, but he loves them underneath it all.'

I think about the awful bruises on Claudia's wrist and resist telling my dad to stop being so stupid. To stop being so weak. Until that moment I had thought perhaps he hadn't known. About Claudia. I've a good mind to shout abuse at him. Instead I take a deep breath and ask, 'Dad, why did Marcus have the diary?'

'I don't know.'

'I think it's time for some answers, Dad. We need to talk to him.'

He nods and I feel unbalanced in the world, like I am the parent and he is the child. I want him to look after me, to swoop in and rescue me. He's never been that man though. I used to think he was.

My phone rings. It's Madison.

'Hi.'

'Kate?' She sounds like she's driving. I hear a honking sound and she mutters. I make out several expletives. She barks, 'Are you there?' as though I might have hung up.

'Yes. My dad's here too. Where are you?'

'Claudia just rang. She's escaped – I'm going to pick her up.'

'Oh my God.' I hear more honking and then she says, 'Bethany's with her, I wanted to let you know they're safe. Get in a cab, meet me at the Oak, Kingston Road, yes?'

I agree and I'm halfway through goodbye when I realise she's gone.

44.

Claudia Reynolds

I am in a pub on the Kingston Road. It turns out we must have been somewhere on the way to Ham. The barman here has been kind. He let me use his phone and I called Madison's office. My voice was raspy. Every time I speak it hurts my throat. He got drinks for Bethany and me and gave her a chocolate bar. He also gave her a pen and paper which she's intently scribbling on now. He keeps throwing us curious glances and I don't blame him. Both of us smell bad. Bethany's hair is all over the place and she looks like she slept in her clothes, which she did. I don't suppose I look much better. I smile at the barman and take Bethany into the toilets. I put some water on her hair to smooth it down and do the same to mine. I also wash away black rings that have formed around my eyes. Yesterday's mascara has not held up well. I wash our hands and faces, which Bethany finds hysterically funny for some reason. I pause to watch her. Amazed at the resilience of young children. She's splashing about in a sink full of lukewarm water as though she hasn't a care in the world. By the time I return to the bar I feel like we both look slightly more presentable. Not that I suppose anyone will mind too much.

Madison walks in and shortly afterwards Kate arrives. Kate heads straight to us and we hug. She fusses over Bethany. Madison is straight down to business.

'I've called this in to the station, I had to.'

I nod, weary.

'Two of my ex-colleagues are on their way. They'll need to try and work out where you were, and then you both need to be seen by a doctor.'

I hate hospitals but I nod again.

She goes on, all business, and I try and keep up. 'You said Martha was there and you think you've hurt her, so that's our priority right now.' She looks at her watch. 'P—DCI Branning should be here any minute so let's hold off going through everything until then.'

I nod. 'Okay.'

Kate is holding Bethany in her arms. She says, 'James was with me when you called.'

I say quickly, 'Was he with Marcus?' Kate shakes her head but I hastily add, 'I don't want to see him.'

'Okay. But I don't think it was Marcus. Who took you.' I nod, more relieved than I should be. 'I still don't want to see him,' I say to Kate.

She says, 'Well, that's understandable. I'll message Dad, he can tell Marcus you're both okay but want him to leave you alone.'

I nod. 'Fine.'

'I'm hoping you'll both be happy to stay with me?'

'I would like to, but if it's an imposition I can call my mum.' Something I'm going to have to do at some point.

Kate frowns and puts a gentle hand on my arm. 'No, please, I'd like you to. There's no reason not to stick to the original plan, is there?'

'I don't have the diary, I'm so sorry.'

She squeezes my arm and I notice a long deep scar poking out the bottom of her jumper. She says, 'Hey, I'm just glad you're both okay.'

I nod weakly and realise she probably means it. Bethany

is starting to whine. The door opens again and a tall, good-looking man walks in with a short dumpy woman. Madison greets them with a nod. The man's eyes linger on her for a moment before he turns to me.

'Peter, Deanie,' she says, then she turns to us. 'This is DCI Peter Branning and DS Deanie Ockham.' She introduces everyone and the tall man sits in front of me with a recorder in his hand. He has a kind face and he says, 'Claudia, we are going to need to take a statement, but right now it's vital that you are both checked over for any injuries.'

'Okay.'

'I need you to try and tell me where you think you were being held. We have officers waiting outside and we'll try and get to Martha as soon as possible, then we'll come and take a statement later once you have the all-clear from the hospital. Is that all right?'

I nod and he fires questions at me which I answer as fast as I can. The woman makes notes at a furious pace and then he smiles reassuringly and they're gone.

We don't have to wait long at the hospital. Madison sees us in and then leaves. Kate entertains Bethany. I can't seem to muster the energy. I watch them, my giddy little daughter weaving in and out of Kate's legs as though nothing has happened. I suppose it's different for children. I think about calling Marcus. I have to exercise almost physical restraint not to. How pathetic is that. I go in with Bethany while she's poked and prodded then Kate takes her out. The doctor looks me over, my temperature is taken and blood, he asks a few questions and deems both of us fit and good to go.

Bethany falls asleep in the back of the cab. I carry her up and settle her into Kate's spare room and then I lie behind her and sob the way I have learned to. Silently.

45.

Kate Reynolds

Claudia has said I can call Marcus but that she wants it made clear she doesn't want to see or speak to him. Madison told me to mention police involvement 'in case he gets any stupid ideas'.

He picks up on the first ring.

'Kate?'

'They're here and they're okay,' I tell him.

'Oh, thank goodness. I'll be straight over.'

'No.'

There's a pause. 'What?'

'No, Marcus. She's going to stay here for now. She doesn't want to see you at the moment.'

Silence.

'Marcus . . . are you there?'

'Yes.'

'Are you crying?'

'Where were they?' He avoids the question.

'You mean you don't know?'

'Fuck, are you kidding? Is that what she thinks?'

I sigh. 'She doesn't know what to think.'

His voice breaks as he says, 'I just wanted a happy family, Kate.'

'You've destroyed your family, Marcus.'

'I know. Do you think I don't know?'

'She loved you.'

'I just wanted us to be perfect, ordered.'

I sigh. 'Martha was there.'

'What?'

'Martha was there when they were taken, and where they were held.'

'Oh, God.'

'I know what you and Dad did the night Naomi died.'

There is a silence that stretches. It isn't filled by an apology on his part.

'We thought we did the right thing.'

I ignore that and ask, 'Why did you have Naomi's diary, Marcus?'

He sighs. 'Honestly?'

'Yes.'

'I took it before . . .'

'Before she died?'

'Yes.'

I am incredulous. 'All of this trouble?' I ask him. I don't think he gets the gravity of the situation. 'Why?'

'I wanted to know.' I am appalled. I don't think he has made the connection that his wife and daughter were taken over that diary. Probably by Oliver, though how he found out is beyond me. My phone doesn't have a passcode so I'm wondering if he looked through my messages when he broke in. The thought makes me shudder. I sleep with the damn thing next to my bed.

'And did you find out?' I ask sarcastically.

'I found out plenty.'

'Why didn't you hand it in? After you'd read it?' I ask. 'You must have realised it would be evidence. It wouldn't have implicated Martha, would it?'

He is quiet for so long I think he might have gone, then he says, 'She made me look bad.'

'What?'

'In her diary, the things she said were humiliating.'

'Oh, Marcus.' My stupid, arrogant, fragile brother.

'I've got to go,' he says.

'Okay. You and Dad both have to speak to the police.'

I hang up the phone. I feel guilt, I feel actual guilt that Marcus is out in the cold, as though I have somehow caused the upset in his marriage. After what they did to me I somehow still manage to feel guilty. I call Dean. He doesn't pick up but sends a text shortly after saying he's tied up and can we talk later. I reply 'yes'. He sends a smiley face and, 'Do you need company?'

I reply 'Yes' with a sad face.

My phone rings and his voice is full of concern when he asks 'How about an out-of-hours session at mine?'

I am full of relief when I tell him, 'I need it after today.'

I make a note of his address and hang up.

46.

Madison Attallee

I listen in to Emma's call. Half hoping that they are not in, or that they flat out refuse. But no such luck. I've been dreading this visit. I guess that's why I've put it off for so long. Emma hands me a slip of paper with the address on and I smile my thanks.

I pull up in front of the Andrews' house and pause for a moment. I wish I'd had an extra fag on the way. Ah well. I knock on the door and an old woman answers. Then I realise that actually it's Anthea Andrews. She surveys me for a few seconds and her husband appears behind her, a firm hand on her shoulder.

He says, 'You must be Madison?'

'Yes. Thank you both for agreeing to see me.'

She scowls, but he nods and says, 'Come in, please.'

There are pictures of Naomi everywhere, at various stages of growth. Anthea and Damian are in a lot of them. He looks the same, she looks like a different person. I guess she was.

We sit down and she snaps, 'You're working for her.'

'I'm working for Kate Reynolds, yes.'

She half tuts, half hisses. I see her husband place a hand on her knee, she slaps it off. He sighs and says, 'You said new evidence had come to light. When we spoke to DCI Branning this morning he was of the mind that the investigation was likely to be reopened and that you might have something to tell us now?'

'I don't have anything concrete yet so I'm unable to divulge too much at this point. It does seem as though Kate isn't the responsible party though.'

'Then why was she found guilty? She pleaded guilty, for Christ's sake – who would do that?' Anthea's voice is high-pitched, angry. That's what's fuelling her. Simmering rage. I guess if she drops that and lets the grief in she might never get back up again.

I say, as gently as I can, 'Kate had memory loss on the evening in question. As you know, both she and Naomi had been drinking heavily as well as partaking in recreational drug use.'

Damian says, 'We know Naomi wasn't an angel.'

Anthea scowls at him.

'She wasn't,' he goes on. 'She was our daughter and I loved her, but she was off the rails.'

'You didn't tell us this at the time.'

Anthea is still shooting him daggers but Damian goes on anyway. 'No, and I guess we should have. We were in shock, as you can imagine. I'll admit we made mistakes with Naomi.' Anthea moves further away from him. He seems not to notice.

'What do you mean?' I ask.

'She was a miracle baby. We had been trying for years and had pretty much just accepted that we weren't meant to be parents, then there she was.'

Anthea's shoulders are shuddering and I realise she is crying.

Damian goes on, 'Children need boundaries, I think, and discipline, to be told no. We were so damn grateful to have her and so busy looking at her as a miracle that we didn't do that.'

'She was a miracle,' Anthea says.

'Is that why you think she rebelled?' I ask Damian.

He laughs then. 'She wasn't rebelling, there was nothing for her to rebel against. She was just doing what she wanted.'

'She was a good girl,' Anthea hisses.

'No.' He says it firmly but I can see in his eyes that he is trying to reason with his wife, that he doesn't want to hurt her. He tells her, 'She was our girl and we loved her and hopefully she would have turned around but she wasn't always good, Anthea.' Anthea stares daggers at him again. He sighs then says to me, 'I never thought Kate killed her.'

'Why?'

He shrugs, 'I don't know. She didn't have it in her. She was a lost little soul really. Way too eager to please, which Naomi took full advantage of, I'm sure.'

'But you didn't think to tell the police this?'

He frowns at me. 'Of course I did, I spoke to Malone, but he said the evidence doesn't lie.'

Jesus. 'I didn't realise.'

'Look, when Kate came back to Kingston I knew there'd be trouble. Anthea can't find any peace. We should have spoken to you sooner, but you can see how it is here.'

'I can imagine it must be awful.'

He nods. 'We need to let go and get on with our lives. I need to, anyway. Maybe this is the final thing we have to do.'

'Did you know Oliver Horfield?'

'Oh yes, I dragged him out of Naomi's bed a few times.'

'I thought he was Kate's boyfriend?' I glance at Anthea who is glaring at her husband. He seems to be carefully avoiding looking at her.

He shrugs. 'He probably was. Like I said, my daughter was no saint. I preferred him to the other lad, though, to be honest.'

'Marcus?'

'No, the older one, I think he introduced Oliver to Naomi.

We never really saw him properly – he always wore a ridiculous baseball cap and sunglasses.' I make a note of that, unsure who that might be.

'And you think this other guy was sleeping with Naomi?'

'No, actually, I think he was one of the few people who bossed my daughter around – I overheard him telling her off once in the kitchen.'

'What about?'

'Oliver.'

'What was his name?'

'I can't remember; he was only here maybe twice. Once with Oliver. He drove, I remember that – a maroon car. I was quite sure he'd picked Naomi up the night of the party. I told Malone that too and he said I was probably mistaken, since no one there remembered seeing him.'

For fuck's sake, Malone. I smile at Damian. 'This has been really useful. I'm sorry your concerns weren't taken seriously at the time.'

He half shrugs. 'Hey, I thought that Malone guy was a prick – but he was the police, right? And everything led to Kate.'

'I'm sorry you've had to go through this.'

As I leave I hear shouting and a door slamming. I light up in the car and put my phone on speaker. Ruth's mother is in a hospice out in Surrey. I think it's probably time I arranged for us to have a chat.

When I get back to the office Emma has the door open before I can get in.

'I found the clippings about Amelia Horfield.'

'Okay.'

'She wasn't driving.'

'What?'

'The day of the accident – she wasn't driving.'

'Who was?'

'Newspaper reports say "her son", who was being treated for shock afterwards.'

'Oliver.'

Emma nods. 'Disaster just seems to follow that boy everywhere, doesn't it?'

'Jesus.'

'Oh, and Denise called for you from Sandcross, by the way. She wanted to know if Martha had been found. I said yes, but didn't go into detail.'

I sigh. 'Looks like we spoke too soon on that one.'

'No sign of her?'

'No, not yet.'

Emma tuts. 'She has to be with Oliver.'

'The police are looking for her now.'

'Oh, yes, that lovely Deanie Ockham rang as well – the rooms where Claudia and Bethany were found belong to David and Amelia Horfield. They were her therapy rooms, apparently.'

'And you've still not managed to get hold of David Horfield?'

She shakes her head. Her sensible hair stays exactly in place as she does so. 'Not yet, no. I have his address, and he works at Sainsbury's in town. I've called there and he's on shift as we speak.'

'Right, I'll head out there now.'

I light up another cigarette in the car and dial Denise. She picks up on the first ring.

'Hi, Denise, it's Madison Attallee.'

'Thanks for returning my call,' she says.

'It's not great news, I'm afraid. Martha's currently missing and is also implicated in a kidnapping.'

'Dear God, you're kidding me?'

'I kid you not.'

'How awful.'

I start the engine and swerve out into the road. 'Denise, did anyone visit her, other than family?'

'Not really, not that I can think of.'

'So just family, doctors – no one else over the years?'

'Well, there was that criminal psychologist, I think he worked on her sister's case? He came a few times, lovely-looking chap.'

'Dean Hall?'

'That's the one. Wanted background on Kate's family.'

He hadn't mentioned it to me. I suppose I hadn't asked.

'Thanks, Denise, I'll let you know when we find Martha.'

'Appreciated.'

I ring off and pull up outside Sainsbury's. Inside, I ask a middle-aged woman with bleached-out hair if she knows where I might find David Horfield and she takes me over to him straight away. He's stacking shelves. I introduce myself and he doesn't bat an eyelid.

'I assume this is about my son?' He sounds resigned. I say it is and he nods but doesn't stop what he's doing. 'I can't talk to you now though, and I'm on a late. Come to mine tomorrow.'

'Mr Horfield, we have a missing woman who we think might be hurt. If there's anything you know that could assist I need to know now.'

'I don't have to talk to you,' he replies, 'but I do have to get paid – my wife's welfare depends on me earning every penny I can, so I'll be happy to help but I can't see you today.'

I notice bleached-out hovering at the end of the aisle. He nods when he sees me watching. 'The walls have ears here, miss.'

47.

Dear Ruth,

All this trouble for that bloody diary. What a disaster and nothing but pages and pages of nonsense. Why I expected anything else from her I don't know. It's your stupid son's fault. I thought there must be something more. Just amused line after amused line about his hurt feelings, scrawled in Naomi's acidic prose on every page. He deserved it. For being so stupid. I feel sort of sorry for him though. He's had to put up with you, his pathetic sisters, and then his stupid, vain wife.

Marcus should never have got involved with Naomi, that girl was trouble. But he seems to have learned from the experience I'll give him that, Claudia is in hand. She does what he tells her, like women ought to, although Kate may have put an end to that. See, Ruth, your daughters are just as much of a pain as you were. I suppose Naomi worked out well for me, for a while. I know how to deal with a child like that. I instilled a fear in her that no one had tried before and, usefully for me, she liked narcotics. She developed a nice little habit pretty fast. Do you know she tried to tell me that she loved me on the night she died, after threatening to tell Kate everything! I'd used her for access to the family. Nothing more and she was very easy. All it took was flattery, gifted drugs, and a feigned understanding of the pathetic things that bothered her idle mind. I wasn't going to have her making demands of me, or ruining what I had worked to achieve.

She found out about Martha. She had tried to tell me she felt sorry for her which wasn't the truth. She disliked my attention going elsewhere. Her vanity was her downfall in the end. And I certainly enjoyed it if I'm honest, killing her. I had thought Martha might take the fall, I was confident she wouldn't mention me. Too many shared secrets for that. But they got her out before the police arrived. No matter, silly Kate not only stumbled in but actually confessed too! I couldn't have planned it any better. There hadn't been any others since you, Ruth. But don't worry, even if there are more – and I think the next ones are likely to be your awful girl children – no one will ever match up to you. My first.

Maybe he's not quite as thick as your other children, Marcus. Not as clever as me, of course. Whatever else you might call me it wouldn't be stupid. I blame their father. And I blame you, of course I blame you.

The girls will be gone soon, as I've said. Martha's been on her way out for a while. I can't forgive her for seeing the awful, brash policewoman – sorry – PI. Martha apologised, but the damage had been done. I pretended to forgive her. She was grateful, of course. Pitiful as ever but still compliant. I might find a use for her yet but I'm undecided. As I am about Kate. It's all about to topple down on me either way, but since I'm different from the rest of you, I have a get-out plan. It's been in place for years and while it's rather sooner than I hoped I can honestly say I'm almost looking forward to it.

A fresh start is often just what we need, isn't it?

48.

Claudia Reynolds

The doctor calls and says both Bethany and I had Rohypnol in our system. It sounds shocking but he says it shouldn't do any long-term damage. I'm to keep an eye on her and call if there are any problems. Kate took me into the police station. I wasn't scared. I felt strong, and brave, and free. I answered all the questions they fired at me. I implicated Marcus and told the detective about his savage beatings and that we had been living in fear. I felt the weight lift from my shoulders just to say it aloud.

He keeps calling Kate's flat. I haven't got a phone any more and I'm in no hurry to replace my old one. Kate is fielding the calls – it's not a long-term solution but it will do for now. When we have everything more settled I'm going to start divorce proceedings and get a restraining order. The thought of it sends happy shivers up and down my spine.

Kate is sad. She's scared of Oliver turning up and scared that he won't. Everyone is looking for him but he seems to have disappeared into thin air. I'm doing what I can to help Kate and I think we have become sort of friends. It's been so long since I've had one I'd forgotten how it felt. I am worried for her now, but pleased it looks as though her name will be cleared eventually. The DCI, the one I get the feeling is soft on Madison, said as much. But things need to be tied up first. I would have thought the manhunt would be extensive and urgent but to be honest Madison is looking harder than the police. It seems they have other priorities.

Today, Bethany and I are on our way to go and see my mum and dad. Kate and Madison both offered to drive us there but we are on the train. It feels like something I have to do by myself. I've had so many years of things being done for me, even the things I wanted to do alone, that I think it has to stop. I'm going to live by myself – well, with my daughter, but I'll be the adult. I'll find a job, manage my own money. Maybe I'll use that law degree after all. The thought is terrifying and exciting. In my heart it seems that this trip to Mum and Dad's is the start of it all.

I am full of nerves, which increase at every stop. Bethany is excited, colouring and talking to herself on the journey. She claims to remember her grandma and grandpa but I know she doesn't – she was a babe-in-arms last time they met. I wrote them an email to let them know we're coming and to tell them what had happened. Not in detail, just enough. They'd written back and said they couldn't wait to see us.

I ring their bell and stand clutching my small daughter's hand. The door swings open and I'm pulled into familiar arms. It's as if no time at all has passed and relief floods through me. Letting me know I am safe.

49.

Madison Attallee

There are some things that people are better off not knowing. I guess that's the long and short of it. My mother used to pour out her childhood woes, her bitterness at her parent's desertion after I was born. She'd rage about my dad, later it was her boyfriends. Things I didn't need to know. I, on the other hand, probably didn't talk to Molly enough. I was always so eager to be away from her. Our relationship seemed to be a long series of goodbye hugs and hurried pick-ups before bed. Lots of 'good mornings' and 'night nights' with little in between.

Now I don't have the time with her, I savour every word we trade. I listen in a way I should have done before. If only I'd known. I felt trapped by motherhood, by marriage. Work felt more like home than they did. I was good at work, and so lacking domestically. In retrospect it was hardly surprising. I had no template of parenthood. Rob's capability made me seem unnecessary. He could get a smile and a giggle out of her when I couldn't. He'd stay up half the night singing to her, rocking her, whereas I'd be crying or shouting after half an hour. He'd come rushing in, quick to take her, giving me a sympathetic look, 'it is hard', and she'd shush and settle. I felt excluded, pointless. When I got to the station I knew what to do, people asked me questions and I had the answers.

I wonder if it would have been better for Kate if the truth about Oliver could have remained buried. Too late now. You can't un-know things. I can at least try and get her some answers. Help her to make some sense of it.

By the time I arrive at the home I'm late. When I head to reception to sign in I'm reminded of the fact by a dour-faced woman in a nurse's uniform. Then I am shown through to Margaret Hanover. She is old. Really old. Papery skin and hair so thin I can see pink scalp. She is also impeccably dressed and her back is ramrod straight. Despite her years you can see that she was a beauty in her day. Good scaffolding, high cheekbones, eyes wide apart. Like mother, like daughter, like granddaughter.

'Hello, Mrs Hanover. I think they told you I'd be coming.'

She looks at me and nods. 'You're here about Ruth?'

'Yes.'

'She's dead, you know.'

'I know. I'm working for her daughter, Kate.'

She makes a snorting sound which turns into a heavy, phlegmy cough. She reaches for a tissue but the box is just out of her reach; I pick it up and hand it to her. She snatches it and tells me, 'Getting old is a terrible thing, you know.' She wipes and I see thick snot layer the tissue. 'Unfortunately for me, I still have all my marbles. Most of them in here are as mad as hatters. Ignorance would certainly be bliss.'

I say, 'I think I'd rather still be sane.'

'You say that now, wait till you're wearing nappies. Everything has packed up, it's a life without dignity. No, I'm looking forward to it being over.' She leans over and slips the sodden tissue into a small metal bin by her feet.

She says, 'I haven't met Ruth's children. Well, I met the first boy. She gave him away, you know.'

'I heard.'

She smiles but it's a sad gesture. 'Ah, so you know all about our dirty family secret.'

'I do.'

She looks at me for a moment and then says, 'My husband was a bad man, Mrs Attallee.'

'Ms.'

'Lucky you.'

I smile and ask, 'Do you want to tell me about it?'

'Not really.' She coughs again. 'Why do you want to know?'

'You know Kate, your granddaughter, has been in prison?'

She nods. 'I do, yes.'

'She has hired me to prove her innocence.'

'And have you?'

'I'm close, though I'm afraid it looks like Ruth's first son is implicated.'

She laughs, which breaks down into phlegmy wheezes again. 'Considering how the poor bastard came about it's hardly any wonder, is it?'

'You said you met him?'

She wipes at her nose, tucking the tissue this time up a woolly sleeve. 'Oh yes. I used to take Ruth to visit him at his foster parents.'

'The Horfields?'

She nods. I am surprised at this; there is no mention of Margaret Hanover in the file I read. Finding her has been reasonably tricky. Ten years ago she had been in assisted living accommodation in Richmond.

'Was this when Ruth was still at home?'

'Yes.'

I ask her, 'What was he like?'

'He was a little boy. Needy in the way that children are. Loved Ruth.'

'Did she love him?'

Margaret sighs. 'As much as she could, I suppose.'

'But she stopped seeing him?'

'She stopped seeing all of us. She found a husband who loved her – at least I hope he did.'

I tell her, 'He did.' Though I'm not certain that James's cloying neediness and ability to brush over things is the sort of love Ruth needed.

'I'm glad.'

'That she married?'

She smiles. 'That she escaped.'

'Why didn't you leave, Mrs Hanover?'

'I really don't know. This is the first time I've ever been on my own. I've been here for ten years, you know, defying the odds, living on. I'm ninety-nine, nearly a hundred.'

I say, 'Very impressive.'

'It's not though, is it? It's as unimpressive as my life has been. I'm here waiting to die. I've spent my life waiting to die. I can't even get that right.'

I try to keep the outrage out of my voice when I ask her, 'You knew then?'

'That my husband was raping my daughter?'

I am shocked by her bluntness, but I nod.

She shakes her head and I'm a little relieved. I quite like this sharp, well-spoken old woman.

She says, 'No. No, I'm that stupid I'm afraid. I didn't know until afterwards. Until she came up pregnant. I should have. He was twenty years my senior, Raymond. I was barely sixteen when we met, didn't look a day over eleven. It was quite normal in those days.'

I try not to shudder. 'You didn't suspect anything?'

'Why would I?' She sighs. 'Looking back, the clues were there. He tired of me quite early on and I was relieved, if I'm honest. I was never very keen on him.'

'Why did you marry him?'

She laughs. 'He asked my father, my father agreed. Different times. I suspect money changed hands. Be grateful you were born now.'

'I am.'

She nods. 'Anyway, Ruth came along and he doted on her. Was happy to look after her when he got in from work, played with her, put her to bed. I was pleased, he was a good dad at least. Little did I know.'

I shake my head. 'Jesus.'

'Quite.'

'Were you close to Ruth?'

She pauses and I see her considering her answer. 'I loved my daughter, but no, you probably wouldn't have called us close. I referred to her as a "Daddy's Girl".' She flinches. 'Poor taste as it turns out.' She coughs again. 'After she fell pregnant and he admitted what had happened I tried. I tried to talk to her, I tried to say sorry.' She shrugs. 'But the damage was done. Mainly I kept them separate, and I got her a therapist, on the understanding that we didn't want to press charges.'

'Amelia Horfield?'

Her face breaks into a genuine smile then. 'Yes, she was very good. Not judgemental. Helped get Ruth some help afterwards. Spoke to me as though I were on my daughter's side, which I was. Didn't make any judgements when I chose to stay.'

'And then Ruth came home?'

'Yes, and Raymond spent most of his time out of the house. I had a lock put on Ruth's door and when he was in I watched him like a hawk.'

'You must have been sad when she left?'

'Only for myself. For her I was happy, and I told her to go, not look back, but also that she could contact me if she ever needed to.'

I say, 'And you never saw her again?'

She shakes her head, looking confused. 'Oh no, I saw her again.'

'When?'

Her eyes narrow. 'I saw her when the letters started arriving.'

'What letters?'

'You don't know? I assumed that's why you were here?'

'No, I don't know.'

Her voice rises slightly. 'Letters, from the boy.'

'Her son?'

She nods, coughing. She wipes again with the tissue, still nodding at me. 'Yes.'

'Saying what?'

'Threatening her, saying he was angry. He was upset she had another family. That he didn't see her.'

'Threatening what?'

'Firstly threatening to tell James, which was her biggest fear. I thought she ought to have just told him. She was convinced he would see her as ruined goods, abandon her.'

'But she wouldn't?'

She shakes her head. 'No. She was quite adamant and it wasn't my place. But I was worried. I called Amelia.'

'You told her?'

'Oh yes, I told her it was out of hand. She said she'd speak to him.'

'When was this?'

She thinks about it. 'Christmas 2004. Amelia was in a terrible accident shortly after. Apparently she hasn't been the same since.'

'No, I believe it shattered the whole family. Her husband had a breakdown.'

'David?'

'Yes.'

'I'm sad to hear that, I saw him when we went to visit the boy. A lovely man. Not keen on taking the lad in but utterly devoted to Amelia from what I can tell.'

I ask her, 'Did the letters stop?'

Her eyes fill. 'I don't know. She was gone three months later. The last time I saw her I had been badgering her to tell James.'

'I'm so sorry.'

She shrugs. 'It's as it is, isn't it? You can't change the past, can you? It should be her alive and in the world, not me. I wish that I'd been a better mother sooner but I like to think in the end I was able to show up, even if it was too little too late.'

I say, 'I'm sure she was glad to have someone to talk to about it, especially when the letters started.'

'You think it's him.' It's not a question.

'Who killed Naomi?'

'Yes. That's why you're here, isn't it?'

I nod and tell her, 'I do, yes. He started a . . . friendship of sorts with Kate and I think he may have used Ruth's other daughter to make it happen, I'm not entirely sure how yet.'

She pauses. 'Martha?'

'Yes.'

'Ruth said she was unwell. I'm sure all of the children suffered. That was what the letters were about, you know.'

I ask, 'The children?'

'Yes. He didn't want her to love them.'

I am incredulous. 'What do you mean?'

'That's what he asked of her, he wanted her to show them the same lack of love she showed him.'

I think about what Kate has told me, about Ruth sitting around unconnected. Unable to love them. I say, 'Oh God.'

'Yes, awful, isn't it.'

'James said she suffered some kind of depression and then became distant . . . is that why?'

She nods her frail head. 'Yes, I would suspect so. She sobbed to me about it. About not being able to hold them, but she said he spied on them. He always seemed to know what she'd been up to. She was quite certain that James could love them enough for them both. I didn't agree.'

'What did he threaten her with?'

'Exposure.'

I say, 'But none of it was her fault.'

She shrugs. 'That's what I told her. Over and over, but she wouldn't hear it. I begged her to go the police, she begged me not to. I felt it wasn't my place to force her.'

'How did she know he was watching her?'

'She saw him.'

'In the house?'

She nods. 'Once, more usually when she was out and about. Though he'd never speak to her. He'd include details of her life in the letters. Things that had happened at home so she knew he'd been watching somehow. She lived in fear, I'm afraid, Ms Attallee, again – as if Raymond's destruction of her hadn't been complete enough.' She purses thin lips and asks me, 'Do you have enough to arrest him?'

'I think we will. He's missing at the moment, even his wife doesn't know where he is.'

'His wife?'

'Yes, they've been married for five years. She's expecting her first child. You didn't know?'

She shakes her head. 'No, I didn't.'

'Have you any idea where he might have gone?'

'I don't think I do, no.'

'Mrs Hanover, if you think of anywhere significant that

Oliver might head to it would really help.'

Her eyes widen and she says, 'Oliver?'

'Yes.'

She's shaking her head. 'Oliver was the Horfields' biological boy, not Ruth's son.'

And something clicks in my mind. Little things have suddenly started adding up: the visit to Martha, not mentioning it to me, the fact that he had been up to date on everything as it unfolded. At that very second I know the answer even as I ask, 'Mrs Hanover, what was Ruth's son called?'

'Dean. The name she gave him was Dean.'

50.

Dear Ruth,

*It's all happening, isn't it? I'm writing this in a hurry, so you'll
have to excuse my cursive. She's on her way over here now. Kate.
Martha is with me as I write but she's really only here in body.
Don't worry, she's still breathing. For now. I'll leave them both here.
That meddling, tarty bitch Madison has likely found my bastard
grandmother, Margaret, and my fake family by now, so it won't be
long until they work out I'm here. If they haven't already. Tick tock,
tick tock.*

*I'm most sad about losing this place, I must admit. The house
you grew up in. The house you made me in. The one I didn't get
to spend my childhood in. I've made it my own. The décor was a
bit dated – not to my taste at all. I was surprised when I found out
Margaret had kept it, to be honest, after he died. I used to visit her
as well as visiting you, you know. Not when she was in, mind. She
never guessed. I even took a few knick-knacks over the years. When
she sold it I waited and then made an offer the new owners could
hardly refuse. I had a feeling she might want rid of it eventually but
she shouldn't have. It was her husband's house after all. Seems she
was as unsentimental as you, eh? I can't really remember her, though
apparently we've met. Amelia said she used to accompany you on
visits. She stressed over and over again that you both loved me.*

I think I would have preferred to have met him. Raymond. My father. The man you both despised. I can see why you'd have been cross but my guess is, Ruth, that you encouraged it. I bet you were like Kate. She hugs and squeezes, bats her eyelids and makes all the right 'poor little girl' noises. They'd be hard to resist for a different kind of man. I'm immune. But I can see how it might test a man who wasn't.

I don't delight in women. Not at all.

I've got to go. I can hear your daughter knocking.

51.

Madison Attallee

As soon as I get outside I break into a run. I need to call Emma. My efficient helper picks up on the second ring and is halfway through hello when I butt in, struggling to breathe and wishing not for the first time that I didn't have a thirty-a-day fucking habit.

'Peter, you need to call Peter,' I say, breathlessly.

She asks, 'DCI Branning?'

'Yes. If you can't get him, Deanie Ockham.' I rush her through what I've just discovered. 'We need to find out where Dean lives ASAP. They'll do it quicker than we will, but I want you to stress to Deanie that I want in on it, okay?'

'Of course. Where are you going to be?'

'I'm going to go and get Kate.'

'Okay, got it.'

I hang up and swing clumsily into my car. I dial Kate as I go. It rings and then goes to voicemail. Fuck. I call the landline and back out, almost hitting a car heading towards me. She picks up just as I shout an obscenity at the other driver. Shit.

'Pardon me?'

'Fuck, sorry, not you, Claudia.'

'Madison?'

I say, 'Claudia, is Kate there?'

'No, you've just missed her.'

Oh God. 'Where did she go?'

'She went to meet Dean for dinner.'

Fuck. 'Claudia, I don't suppose you know where she's gone to meet him?'

'His house.'

'Do you know where that is?'

'No, I'm afraid I don't. Madison, what's going on?'

'I'll explain later. I need to keep calling her.'

She says, 'There's no point.'

'What?'

'Her phone's here. I just heard it ringing in the kitchen.'

'Oh, shit.'

She says, 'Madison, what can I do?'

'Nothing. Stay there. If she comes back, call me.'

Emma's on call waiting. I let Claudia go and pick up Emma's call, narrowly swerving to avoid a stupidly large SUV.

'Emma.'

'We have an address for Dean in North Kingston. Deanie says they are sending officers over there straight away. I got the address, though I must say she was a bit sniffy about sharing it.' A PI solving their case probably isn't going to look good. I wonder if Malone's had a go. Oh well.

'Okay, text it to me. I need to call David Horfield. I'm not going to make it to him today.'

'Okay. Are you driving?'

I sigh like a naughty child, caught out. She tuts. 'Be careful.'

'Fine.'

I suddenly realise I have no idea where I'm supposed to go. I pull over to the side of the road to put the address into my phone's satnav and light a cigarette with a shaking hand. Just as I am fumbling trying to put in the postcode my phone rings. 'Peter, I'm on my way,' I snap, annoyed that he's delaying me

268

while I'm trying to get my damn map to work.

He says, 'Don't bother, that's what I'm calling to say.'

'They're not there?'

'No, but Dean's tenant is.'

I let it sink in and say to Peter, 'He doesn't live there?'

'No and isn't registered anywhere else either, nowhere we can find anyway. Deanie's doing her best.'

'Shit.' I tell him about Kate.

He says, 'We need to find him.'

'I know,' I almost shout.

I hang up and sit for a moment. Feeling impotent. Emma messages me with the same information I've just got from Peter. Fuck it, I need to do something. I floor the accelerator. The tyres squeal as I U-turn out and cross lanes. I get to David's at almost the same time as he does. I half expect him to turn and run or at least tell me to get stuffed but he doesn't. He stands looking at me. Hands in pockets.

52.

Anthea Andrews

I am still fuming from Damian's outlandish behaviour around the PI. I hate it when he talks about Naomi like that. He thinks it's because I have a skewed view of who our daughter really was. It's not that at all. I of all people knew that girl's failings, which were legion. I know that, on some level at least, we must have been at fault, or perhaps it was just me. I had been so happy to have my little girl. I was so overwhelmed with the pleasure of motherhood. I didn't mind the two a.m. nursing and rocking. So grateful was I to be permitted into the Mummy Club.

I had jumped every time the baby had whimpered. I'd run in, guns blazing, to fix every problem before it erupted. That was a mistake. I know that. Damian had chastised me along the way and I'd rolled my eyes at him playfully and carried on letting our princess child do whatever she wanted. And she'd turned into a young adult who did exactly the same. Damian thinks I don't know it but I do. By the time the weight of it had sunk in it felt too late to fix. And besides, it never stopped me loving the girl. Not even a little bit.

The funny thing is, Damian doesn't even know the half of it. There were plenty of things that I had kept away from him: finding her in bed with various boys, watching her pick on Kate, knowing she was sleeping with Kate's boyfriend – though it turns out he knew about that. Naomi never had an ounce of shame either. I'd walked in on her and Marcus right in the middle once. Poor lad had nearly died, jumping up, grabbing at covers. My daughter had stood up naked, stretched, and breezed past me with a smile. I'd threatened to tell her father and Naomi had shrugged 'upset him if you like'. And I hadn't. It was just another thing I'd kept to myself.

This morning I feel jittery and panicky. Tailing Kate has led me to a bad place, a place of doubt where I had been so sure. Because coming out of that office I had suddenly realised why that psychologist had seemed familiar at the trial. He was a man I'd encountered before. One I'd found holding my daughter against the kitchen wall by her throat, not long before Naomi died. We'd come home early and heard our daughter sobbing in the kitchen. We'd walked in and seen a grown man pinning her to the kitchen wall. I'd only seen him briefly, from behind, which is how I'd just seen him coming out of the office. It had jogged my memory. His face had been covered with glasses then and he'd dropped Naomi when he saw me. Pulled a large baseball cap down over his eyes and hurried out the back door, hunching his shoulders exactly as he'd been doing coming out of the glass building. I had run to my daughter, trying to comfort her as she sobbed, asking if I should call the police. I'd gained a slap around the face for being stupid and had been left, dazed. Damian had chased Naomi up the stairs, fuming, the man forgotten.

Now I'd seen that man again. I'd followed him for long enough to be certain it was the same one. He'd headed into that office shortly after Kate, and I'd googled him later to make sure. Dean Hall. The man I'd seen with my child two days before she died.

53.

Dean Hall

I can see the look of surprise on her face when I open the door. And why wouldn't she be surprised. The house doesn't match me. Not from the outside anyway. I know how I present and this small terraced two-up two-down isn't fitting of a man who wears handmade suits. She lets out a low whistle once she's in though. As well she might. I have a flair for aesthetics and I've made the most of the small space. Everything is knocked through, the kitchen is cordoned off but the rest of it is one big open space. White, simple and beautiful. I'm looking at it now, trying to take it in through her eyes. It really is nice. I'm broken from my thoughts by the vile sound of Kate snivelling. I turn and try to look at her sympathetically as she sobs. I lead her to the sofa and gently help her sit. She sinks down immediately and I ask if she wants tea. She nods and I go and prepare her a cup and one myself, careful not to mix them up. I sit down opposite her and tilt my head to one side, a look I've practised often enough in the mirror, along with smiling, looking sad, and other things that don't come naturally to me. I ask her, 'What's happening?'

'My dad and Marcus were covering for Martha.'

I make my eyes widen and find myself having to push aside a genuine laugh. 'She killed Naomi?'

She's shaking her head. 'No. Oliver did.'

'Bloody hell. I'm so sorry.'

She laughs, but it's a hollow sound. She sips at the tea, evidently savouring a moment of relaxation.

'Why did they think it was Martha?' I ask.

'She was in the room. She must have stumbled on Naomi before I did.'

I shake my head, the perfect portrayal of outrage, and mutter, 'Goodness me.'

'She helped Oliver take Claudia and Bethany as well. At least, she helped him keep them captive. Stupid girl.'

I say, 'He must have been manipulating her.'

Kate snaps back, 'We all have choices, Dean.'

'You're angry with her?'

'Of course I'm bloody angry. Sorry. It's not your fault.'

'Who else are you angry with?'

We've done this dance before and she replies exactly as I've pushed her to. 'Myself.'

'Why?'

'I brought Oliver into our lives.'

'Because you just had to have him?'

She shakes her head, I suspect she's starting to feel dizzy. 'I was so lonely, Dean.'

'And so needy. There he was served up on a plate.' She looks suitably chastised.

'Naomi introduced us,' she stammers. I smile at that. I remember sending Oliver in. He'd been reluctant at first, whining that it wasn't right. He'd taken a shine to Naomi after he'd seen her, though. I had had to have strong words with my foolish fake brother about that. It was Kate I'd wanted access to. Not Naomi. Oliver had nearly wrecked everything with his pathetic lust. I had had to come in, start afresh with Naomi and make it all like a mysterious game.

One where Kate would end up being the victim. Nasty girl that Naomi was she hadn't even questioned it. Just laughed at the thought of setting up her new, older boyfriend with her best friend and keeping it all shtum. I shudder at the memory of the stupid girl. So full of herself but ultimately so pathetic. I'd been so very glad when I saw the last scrap of life drain out of her eyes. Some people were just asking for it.

I say to Kate, 'So you went for the first interested bloke that came along?' It's spiteful but she doesn't pick up on it.

I suspect she feels sick now, as well as dizzy. She's only drunk half the cup but it will have been enough. 'Could I have some water?' she asks me.

'Not feeling well?'

'No.'

I pour her a glass of water in the kitchen. By the time I get back to her she looks awful, damp and blotchy. She grasps at it but struggles. In the end I hold it to her lips. She glugs gratefully. 'Thanks.'

She slumps backwards mumbling, 'Sorry.'

'Maybe it's everything catching up on you?'

'Yes.'

'The realisation that it's all your fault.'

She shakes her head, trying to clear it and asks, 'What?'

'I said worrying that it's all your fault.'

She wipes a hand over her forehead. 'It is. No one would have known Oliver. Or Naomi, for that matter.'

There is a crash. Bugger. I stand quickly. 'Let me just go and check that out.'

When I come back down the stairs I see her fumbling in her bag.

She nearly jumps out of her skin when I speak. She hadn't realised I'd come back into the room. I'm so close to her I can see sweat glisten on her stupid face. I ask, 'Are you okay?' My face is screwed up in concern.

She nods and mumbles, 'I forgot my phone.' God she's an absolute blessing. This saves me the job of taking it. I feel almost fond of her. She says, 'Bathroom?'

'Upstairs, door straight ahead.'

She lurches as she stands and I am by her side, holding her elbow. I can smell her.

I say, 'Do you need help?' She shakes her head. I let go of her and she manages to get to the stairs. I watch as she leans against the wall, hand gripping the banister as she goes. It seems to take her forever. Which is fair enough. The drugs will be making her feet feel as though they are embedded in concrete blocks. I wait and then I follow her up. She's left the door open and I watch as she runs cold water, pushing her wrists under its spray, splashing it on her face. She leans forward, grasping the edge of the sink. I hope she doesn't puke.

Kate, Kate, Kate. Her idiot sister makes that banging sound again. I slide myself behind the door and watch Kate stagger out into the hallway, making her way towards the sound. Breathing heavily. Martha sees me before Kate does and even attempts to call out. It makes me laugh. I can't help it and I can't keep it in any more. Kate turns, startled, and I laugh even harder.

Kate manages, 'Dean.' And I can almost see it as things start flicking through her fuzzy head. She is leaning against the doorframe for support. When I walk up to her she almost falls. It wouldn't take much. I say 'Dean' at her, imitating her whiny tone of voice. She whimpers and I smile.

Kate just stares at me, trying to add up what she must now know to be the truth. Ruth is in my face and I put my features now into the expression that makes me most like my mother. Hoping her vile daughter can see it. I am the best-looking of her children. I have inherited her beauty in a way Kate, Martha and Marcus have not. And I'm the cleverest.

I say, 'Hello, sis.'

'Oliver . . .?' and she actually looks a little relieved.

'No relation of ours, my dear, so whilst your romantic choices may be poor at least they are not incestuous, eh?'

She springs at me then, pushing herself off against the wall. Using all of the strength she can muster, but it's feeble. Martha makes a gurgling sound.

'What have you done to her?' Kate asks as she tries to hit at me.

I sidestep her and say, 'Nothing yet. Why, do you think I should?' I arch an eyebrow and find I'm laughing again. I push Kate's arms down, moving her deftly away. She sinks to the floor. She reaches out a hand for her sister and Martha's eyes open again. Kate works her fingers around her sister's and Martha whispers, 'I'm sorry.' I bend down and smile at them both in turn. I say, 'Well, isn't this nice,' and I find a little buzz start to build up as I sense it in them. Fear. So cloying and so obvious it's like a palpable thing. It seems so solid, like I could reach out and touch it if I wanted. Good.

I lean down and pick up Martha as though she weighs nothing. Her small hand is wrenched out of Kate's who cries out. I plonk Martha on the bed. Then I stand watching them both, letting a little moment pass to savour it all.

'Be careful,' Kate shouts.

I'm annoyed she's broken my enjoyment and I tell her, 'Oh, shut up. She won't be making it out of here any more than you will.'

Kate lets out a cry then. Of frustration, of anger, too late in coming. People-pleasing, stupid, stupid Kate. I stand over her and then bend down, lifting her up. She struggles, I feel her spindly little bones wriggling under her skin. She's tiny so it's pointless and I clasp my arms more tightly, hearing her gasp as I push air out. Maybe I should take her now. Suffocate her, death by hugging. I'm humming as we go downstairs. I don't crush her, instead I lay her flat across the couch. She shouts and I laugh. 'No one can hear you, dear – neighbours are all at work.'

She hears my helper come into the room and moves her head frantically. She looks like a fish on the shore, out of water and gasping for air. Oliver sits in the chair opposite her and I can see her trying to implore him with her eyes. She says, 'Oliver?'

He shrugs at her. He is limp-looking, sagging into the chair. Head down, hands dangling, a sad sack of a man, just like he was a sad sack of a boy. He is filled with guilt, I know that, though of course I can't relate. I watch it on his face as he keeps his eyes on the floor, unable to meet her gaze. He says, 'I tried to warn you.' I roll my eyes. His face is tear-stained and dirty. He looks forlorn, beaten. They probably would have made quite a good couple after all. She says, 'You have to help me.'

'What can I do?' He shrugs.

She starts to lose consciousness then. And I watch her chest rising and falling. She makes a small moaning sound. Oliver looks at me and says, 'Why don't you just go? Leave them to it.'

I smile and ask him, 'What, and ruin all the fun?'

He sighs. It's the closest he'll come to disapproval. I sit in the armchair watching Kate. She won't be out for long. She looks almost like our mother. A cheap imitation though.

I watched her like this, Ruth, all those years ago. As the life drained out of her. She was the first person I killed. Which seemed right. Her back was pressed against the wall. Her hands dangled next to her open legs, she was leaning, almost com- ically, to one side. I'd paused for a moment to take it in. She could have been resting if the brutality of her death wasn't everywhere; in the sticky vomit trailing down her chin, in the stained puddle that she sat in. She was disgusting and I was pleased. She finally looked like what she was. There was no more hiding behind a pretty face. She had made a mess of the kitchen. Her fluids were busily staining everything they touched. I had wondered if the family would ever use that room again. If they would stay in the house. I was surprised when they did. The house on the hill.

I had been enjoying my silent communion with Ruth when Martha walked in. I'd already started feeding her with lies. The girl was unstable and I had used it to my advantage. She'd even given me a set of keys. As always I'd had to resist the urge to laugh, particularly that day – the look of shock on her face was so cartoonish. Everyone else would believe Ruth had done this to herself but Martha would know. I hadn't planned it but actually I hadn't minded. I'd suspected it would eat her up inside and so it did. People. Silly people and their pathetic debilitating feelings. Stupid cow had dropped her bag with a clatter and was screaming before I could stop her. She'd looked from me to the prone body of her mother.

I'd taken this as my cue to go, annoyed when I put my coat on that some of Ruth's filth had transferred to me.

It had been too hot for a coat that day but obviously I couldn't take it off. It hadn't been sunny but muggy and close. English weather. I've never liked it, perhaps it's good that it's time to go.

I had wanted Ruth to love me, accept me, and welcome me into her home. She'd made it clear this wouldn't happen, so I'd settled for the next best thing. The last words I'd said to her were 'I'm going to ruin your children's lives' and then I'd hummed her a lullaby familiar to us both. I guess it's right that things have turned out the way they have. I watch Kate's eyes flicker and grin at her. I'm keeping my promise to Ruth all right.

54.

Madison Attallee

'David, I need your help and I need it now.'

He nods. 'I figured you might. You'd better come in. I'll grab my coat.'

The flat reminds me of a hotel suite. There is nothing personal anywhere except a framed photo of David and a smiling woman with a small child. 'Is this Amelia?'

He nods. 'And Oliver.'

'Didn't want to include Dean?'

I see him shudder.

I tell him, 'Dean has Kate.'

He says, 'He has Oliver too.'

I ask him, 'Can you think where they might be?'

'He'll be at the house in Richmond.'

'What house?'

He's getting his coat on now and heading for the door, 'Margaret and Raymond's. He bought it about nine years ago. That's where he'll take them, of course it is. Come on.'

I shouldn't be letting him come too but time is running out. I get in, start the car and dial Emma. I put her on speaker and David relays the address. Emma agrees to call Peter, though I think we'll get there first. We hit traffic on the Kingston Road. I swear under my breath.

He tells me, 'He near enough killed Amelia, you know.'

'They were in an accident?'

He snorts. 'It was no bloody accident. There are no accidents with Dean. He plans everything far too well for that.'

A single tear brims in the corner of his eye as he looks at me. 'I should have been focusing on Oli. But I wasn't. I've just been biding time. Amelia would be so cross with me.'

I know the answer, but ask anyway, 'Why did he want to hurt Amelia?'

'He was sending letters. Stalking, I suppose you'd call it, his mother Ruth.'

'I met Margaret.'

'So, you'll know she came to us for help?'

'What did you do?'

He sighs. 'I'm ashamed to say I huffed and puffed about how I'd been right all along.'

'About Dean?'

He nods. 'I'd been saying for years that there was something wrong with him.'

'Amelia didn't agree?'

'She doesn't believe in evil, and that's what that boy was.' And then David says sadly, 'He's going to kill them.'

'What?'

He says it again. 'He's going to kill them.'

'What makes you so sure?'

'They've served their purpose, I would have thought.'

'What purpose?'

David sighs. 'I'm not sure even Dean knew, to start with. He just wanted to harass Ruth. Terrorise her is more apt. He would have found messing with the children some sort of payback.'

'Messing' is such an understatement. Dean is clever, he graduated from a top university with a first-class degree in psychology. Brainwashing Martha, a nervous kid, must have been child's play for him. I say to David, 'You really think he meant to kill Amelia?'

'I do, yes. Though I think he's probably happier with the way things turned out.'

'Why?'

He shrugs. 'She'd be better off dead.'

I look at him sharply and try and weave around a large black sedan. The driver gives me the finger. I give it right on back.

I ask David, 'Her quality of life isn't good?'

'No, she's just a shell. Watching her has been hell. Dean would enjoy that.'

'Jesus.'

I see him nod. 'I've played right into his hands. I should have been watching out for Oliver. It's what Amelia would have wanted.'

'You lost your wife.'

'But I still had my son.' His voice is so desperate I almost flinch. I recognise the bitter regret. When we don't put our energies where we're supposed to. One life. We only get one life.

'Everyone makes mistakes. You can make up for it now,' I tell him.

He sighs again. 'If I get the chance.'

55.

Anthea Andrews

I have followed Kate. I'd had to scramble onto the bus, three people behind her, cap down. Anonymous, invisible. I'd almost lost her on the walk, but luckily Kate didn't seem to know exactly where she was going and had to double back. I nearly ran when I saw her heading towards me. I hadn't though, I'd carried on walking, eyes ahead, and then turned around just in time to see Kate go into a little mews house. I'd found a side gate and opened it quietly, squirrelling in and putting myself behind oversized bins in the garden. A large set of French windows exposed the back of the house and I had a good view. I'd watched the therapist faff about. I'd seen Kate arrive and then I'd seen that man Oliver go in through the back. He'd passed within inches of me and I'd held my breath, certain that he'd be able to hear me. He hadn't though, but he had left the door open and I'd followed him in.

Now I'm in the kitchen, a galley affair, newly decorated. No amount of fresh paint can make it any better though; it's pokey. What an estate agent would call 'cosy', no doubt. The rest of the downstairs looks good, all opened up. No good for hiding though. If anyone comes in here they will see me standing behind the shutter door, but I don't care any more. I'm here to finish this once and for all. I squeeze my hand around the handle of my large kitchen knife. I carried it here. Feeling it in my bag. The knife had thumped between my shoulder blades and I'd wondered if I'd be able to use it when the time came. I grip harder. I will use it. I will avenge Naomi's death. But for now I'm listening and I can feel the anger grow even more. I want to hear him say it. That he killed my beloved child. Just to be certain. My breathing is getting more shallow as I take it all in, that she was just an afterthought. Not even particularly important to this maniac.

I sent an email to Damian before I left. I told him that I was sorry, that I loved him and would be ending this today.

I hear Dean laughing at Kate. Kate makes small muttering sounds interspersed with words that are getting more slurred. I saw him add something to her drink. I wonder if he'd forced drugs upon Naomi. Probably not. Naomi never needed much cajoling on that front. Oliver sounds defeated. I think about stabbing him too, but there'd be no reason other than spite. It's Dean I need to get to. Dean who has to pay. And he will. But I want to hear him say it first.

56.

Kate

'What have you given me?'

'Rohypnol,' Oliver says.

Dean grins. 'Ah, my fake brother knows me so well.'

Oliver goes on, 'He's been drip-feeding it to Martha for years.' Dean scowls at him. Oliver looks at his feet.

I say, 'Oli, you have to help me.' I lean forward, attempting to stand but instead I flop off the sofa onto the floor. Oliver is at my side quickly but Dean gently pushes him back.

'If she prefers the floor let her have it. Go and get Martha, would you. I am more disappointed in these stupid girls than I thought possible.' He smiles down at me and I feel bile rise into my throat. 'I was going to leave you both alone. I've bought a natty little villa in Tenerife and a load of paperwork with a name change.' He sighs. 'I'm finally ready to give up "Dean", and it's all she left me, you know. A poxy name.' He glares down at me as though this is also my fault somehow. Who knows, maybe in his sick head it is. I swallow thickly, feeling the acid slide back down. He says, 'I would have been happy enough to let you live, Kate, but you've pissed me off now.'

'Oliver?' I'm trying to scream but it comes out small, raspy.

Oliver looks at me without meeting my eyes and sadly tells me, 'You can't do anything, Kate.'

Dean repeats, 'Get Martha. Now.' Then he turns his attention back to me. 'No, you'll have to go and you may as well take that whiny Martha with you. Besides, I've been forced to get her to undertake some admin for me of late, and if I'm not around to remind her what not to say the silly cow will probably slip up.' He shrugs as though this is all an unfortunate mistake which can't be helped.

Once Oliver is gone Dean leans down and puts his face next to mine. He's so close I can see his pores, some of them wide and open, a small flaw on an otherwise perfect face. He hisses, 'Years I've listened to you and your crap and this is the thanks I get. It needn't have ended this way, you know.'

I'm crying now and I hate myself for it. I say, 'I thought we were friends.' It comes out as a long slur.

He snorts. 'I probably would have let you live, a favour for taking the fall, even if it was unintentional. But not now, Kate. Now I have to leave this house, my career, all before I'm ready because you couldn't keep quiet about Naomi.'

'Please.'

'Oh, begging, are we? Bit bloody late for that, and disappointing. She begged too. Ruth.'

'What?' Even through the fuzzy drug haze his words reach me and I'm desperately trying to untangle them.

He smiles. It makes his face even prettier but it doesn't quite make it to his eyes – they are crazy, blazing. How had I not noticed? He says, 'Oh yes, Mummy pleaded with me. Not for herself, mind, for you brats.' He spits out the words. 'The kids that mattered.'

I shut my eyes. I'm thinking about listening to Ruth sing. My mother sweeping me up into her arms. That feeling of being loved. She loved me. I'm surprised to feel a joy sweep through me.

I smile at Dean then and I tell him, 'She loved me.'

His face twists and I'm pleased even when he slaps me quickly

285

and hard across my face. I say it again and he hisses, 'Shut up.'

I glare at him, using my hate to focus, to fight the drugs, to pin him in my sights. I ask, 'What did you do to her?'

His face contorts and he pushes it close to mine. I feel his hot breath roll across my cheek, fear shatters in my bowels but I keep the terror off my face. I don't flinch, I don't move, and I don't look away. 'I gave her chances,' he shouts and the sound reverberates in my ears.

'Gave her chances to do what?' I ask him and suddenly it's important. I'm going to die but I want to know. I want to die knowing as much about her as I can.

'To be a better person. The bitch. Like all you fucking women. You plunge us out into the world, unasked for, and then fucking abandon us.'

'I don't understand.'

'Why would you? She kept you.'

'Did Dad know?'

He laughs. 'No. The stupid man. I said I'd tell him though. I should have told him. I felt sorry for the poor sod. And Marcus, but at least Marcus grew a bit of backbone. His wife is in far better order than Ruth ever was.'

'You were in contact with Ruth?' My voice is sludgy again, slow. I'm having a hard time getting words out. A hard time staying awake. But I must.

He smiles again now and somehow it's worse than the twisted look of anger. He's low on the floor, his face near mine once more. 'Oh, yes. I used to write her letters. I gave her many chances but she wouldn't play.'

'Oh God.'

He laughs and I wonder how I failed so completely to see that he is insane.

Oliver comes back into the room with Martha in his arms. 'Where do you want her?'

Dean stands. 'She can go on the sofa, since sis here has made space.'

He puts her down gently. She's half asleep. Dean slaps her face and her eyes spring open. 'Look who's still visiting.'

Martha looks down at me, tears escaping silently down her cheeks. I try to stretch a hand to her but it doesn't work. My poor sister. Who knows what she's been through. My anger towards her evaporates.

Dean heads to the garden. 'Oliver, come.' And he goes off obediently. Everyone so obedient.

I am overwhelmed. Thinking about Ruth. My mother. Thinking about Martha who I watch lying on the sofa staring blankly out of glassy eyes. It's all too much. I'm trapped again. There's no point fighting and I think about shutting my eyes and letting go, accepting my fate, when a thin figure slides in from the kitchen. It's Anthea Andrews. She has a large knife in her hand. She puts a finger to her lips. I try to struggle into a sitting position; I look at Martha who has shut her eyes again. Anthea shakes her head at me and I lean back down. It's not me she's after. The room spins. I struggle to stay awake. I try saying song lyrics, 'Amazing Grace', and I try hard to picture Ruth singing it. My voice is a slurry whisper but it's there, I can hear it: '. . . how sweet the sound, that saved a wretch like me . . .'.

Anthea is waiting behind the open living room door now. The two men head back into the room, carrying large garden sacks. I don't let my head think about what they will put in them. Suddenly everything explodes – Anthea is there and her arms are flailing madly; Oli steps back open-mouthed. I watch from the floor as Dean raises his arms but the knife has already struck him more than once. Dean shouts, 'Oliver!' And to my utter dismay Oliver picks up the little woman, who may have rage on her side but is still barely nine stone.

I keep going: '. . . I once was lost, but now I am found . . .'

Dean is wounded but still laughs, it's an awful sound. '. . . was blind but now I see . . .'

He drags himself to me and puts his face near mine. 'Oh, sister. Did you think that oafish Horfield boy would come to your rescue? He has a wife to protect from the truth. He found some sad cow willing to marry him.' My eyes close and open again. I reach out a hand to strike him but it falls before it rises. Dean is laughing. 'Oliver is as pathetic as his bitch mother.' And suddenly Dean stops speaking. He jerks forward and I wonder if he is going to body slam me and why he'd bother. Then I realise that a hand has swiped across his neck. A hand holding a large knife and the hand is not his. Anthea's calm face peeks out from behind his head as a wave of red pours from Dean's throat. It spills onto me and drips down to Martha. Anthea holds him firmly in place, moving closer to him, gently wrapping her legs around his waist, one hand gripping his face. I see a small twitch at the corner of her mouth.

Dean gurgles: 'Oliver.'

My voice continues, '. . . twas grace that taught my heart to fear, and grace my fears relieved . . .'

Oliver is just standing, watching, horrified. The hands that held Anthea, that must finally have had enough and let her go, are now hanging limply by his sides. Dean sinks to the floor and Anthea keeps her grip on him. They are both red and covered. Her legs stay astride him and she leans down. It gives the odd effect of lovers, of intimacy. Dean makes a sound like a sigh and then he is silent. Anthea slides backwards, dropping the knife. Kneeling beside him now, resting a hand on his wrist, and she smiles slightly.

Then Madison is there with the policeman. He rushes to Oliver who promptly bursts into tears. Then there are police and people. I am pulled up from the floor and I wonder if I am dying. Either way I'm so very, very tired.

57.

Anthea Andrews

I am talkative today. I feel light and floaty. I even laugh when Damian does an impression of his boss, and he looks surprised. I reach out a hand to him; *I'm back*, I hope it says. *I'm here*. We are clearing out Naomi's room, boxing things up. They will go in the loft – getting rid of them would be too much. Damian agreed with me on that.

I know that my husband is wary of me but he'll come round. He has his wife back after all and that is what he wanted. Me smiling again, laughing and doing. And I've got away with murder, well, attempted murder anyway. Everyone agrees that I was justified. Self-defence. Both witnesses have testified as much. I don't think Damian buys it though. To be honest I don't care one way or another whether he does. When he asked me how I felt I told him I'm just sorry Dean lived and that I'd checked his pulse and was quite sure I'd felt nothing.

Dean has stuck to his story that I attacked him in cold blood. Said I was deranged, which would be more convincing coming from someone else. Damian has found out that I had been following Kate for days. I confessed to him that I'd worked out who Dean was. I'd also realised that Kate didn't know he was linked to Naomi and nor did the police or he wouldn't have been allowed to counsel Kate. This had made me quite certain he had had something to do with my daughter's death. The day I hid in his kitchen had confirmed it.

Damian is looking at me sideways again, he is uncomfortable and I am sorry for that. He thinks I'm a vigilante though he won't say it. I keep pointing out that I saved Kate's life, actually, and probably Martha's. I think it's the only thing that will bring him back to me. I come up behind him and circle him with my arms. He squeezes back, then untangles himself, glancing at his watch. 'I'm off to see Marilyn then.'

'Okay.' I smile.

'Sure you won't come?'

I smile wider, head leaning to one side. 'Darling, I've explained to you that I can't see the point of a therapist any more. It's done and dusted, isn't it?'

'Dean will be out one day.'

'He's criminally insane. I doubt he'll ever be free.'

'But what if he is?'

I shrug. 'Then we'll deal with it.' The thought almost gives me something to look forward to.

58.

Kate Reynolds

I steal glances at Martha. She has put on weight. Not much, she'll never be fat, but she looks healthy. So do I. I think it every time I catch sight of myself in a shop window, or in the bathroom. I still don't look in the mirror much but it's not because I can't meet my own eyes any more. I just have so many other, important things to do. Martha and I are sitting at Heathrow and soon we will board a plane to take us to Australia. We are going to travel the world. She is as desperate to see everything as I am. As keen to make up for lost time. Our father has given us our inheritance from Ruth and said there's always more if we need it. He's tried to instigate some kind of relationship with us both but his efforts are half-hearted and I don't know about my sister but I doubt I will ever fully trust him. Or forgive him. I forgave Martha that day at Dean's when I suddenly felt with force all that she had been through.

Dad should have protected us both and he didn't. We were denied a mother and while I'm sad about Ruth I can see how damaged she must have been, how confused. She genuinely thought she was protecting us. Dad was just after a quiet life. He and Marcus are at the house we grew up in now, and as far as I'm concerned they are welcome to each other.

Martha is almost jumping out of her seat and grinning.

'Flights been called.' She's like a new person. No longer under a chemical cosh. No longer living in fear. She looks different, sounds different.

She takes my hand and we almost run towards the boarding gate. Eventually I make her slow down or we're going to knock someone over. When we arrive at the gate the plane isn't ready to board, but she's too excited to sit down and I find so am I. I take out my new fancy smartphone. I've got used to the million things it does and I quite like it now. I put my arm around Martha and take a picture of us both. I send it to Claudia via WhatsApp and seconds later my phone pings with a picture of her at her new desk. I say how brilliant it looks and it does. She says get pictures for Bethany and I know I will. She won't be a Reynolds soon and I don't blame her but she'll always be family to me.

The plane is finally ready and we climb aboard. Martha looks out of the window, pulls at the tray and grins at everyone. As we start to take off I feel the weight of the past drop away. We lift into the air and I know that the future looks different, better, real, and I can hardly contain my excitement.

59.

Madison Attallee

Emma is tapping away at her keyboard. Claudia is filing. I've taken her on temporarily. We've been swamped since the Reynolds case hit all the front pages and her legal knowledge is proving to be very useful already. She and Emma make an unlikely couple. Claudia, beautiful and glamorous without any effort. Emma, matronly and sensible with her short hair and brogues, and yet they've hit it off well. Claudia is in Kate's old flat, which is in Marcus's name but it will be Claudia's soon enough. It's all she's asked for from the divorce and since Kate has said she doesn't want it I suspect she'll get it. She could get plenty more too, but I think she's just glad to be free. I answer the phone to the reporter from the *Comet* again. Kate's already given them a few comments. They are suddenly her biggest champions, as though years of inflammatory reporting never happened. It's not just them either, all the nationals are in on it. I'm pleased she's not here to see it. Kate seemed optimistic when I saw her last and I'm glad that Martha also seems to have a new zest for life. She sent me a 'thank you' card. Written in shaky silver letters, it just said, 'for helping free the Reynolds girls'. It had a picture of an aeroplane on the front.

The focus of the press now is Dean. A maniac working within our legal system. His testimony has been key in many convictions over the years. An investigation has begun into how he had been missed. No one can prove that he killed Ruth. No charges can be brought on Martha's behalf, but he has been convicted of killing Naomi. Anthea Andrews has pretty much got away with a charge of self-defence. Dubious at best, since it turns out had she not been stalking Kate she wouldn't have been at the scene at all. But Oliver's backed her up and so has Kate. Martha has said she was drugged and out of it and refused to comment either way. I wonder if this has been at Claudia's advice but I haven't asked. Marcus is living with James. They see Bethany every other weekend.

When the girls leave I pack up the office and for once I'm out of there at six on the dot. This is a new thing but something I do happily now. Because tomorrow Molly will arrive in the morning and we will have forty-eight blissful hours together.

The doorbell rings. Before I have the chance to open it Peter does and sweeps Molly up. She squeals in delight and immediately starts up with stories of the morning so far. They go in search of the cat. Both are equally delighted with my feline nemesis and I have to admit she's cuteness and light around both of them. But she still tries to kill me when it's just the two of us. Peter says she's after attention. I take this as meaning I don't give her enough and try and lavish strokes on the little bugger whenever Peter is around to see it, which is becoming increasingly more often.

We head to the playground. Molly runs around like a lunatic. Peter and I chase her. Then I get bored and stand smiling and waving. I say I need to nip to the car, and smoke two cigarettes in the car park and then head back. We eat a disgusting, overpriced meal in Bill's and then go home and watch a loud film about a little girl and a secret society of monsters. Molly passes out on the sofa at seven o'clock and I tuck her up in her bedroom. (Her bedroom!) I must doze off shortly afterwards. Peter covers me over before he leaves and I wake up the following morning to Mimi gently scratching my face. It's only fucking five a.m. I smoke a cigarette on the balcony and down coffee before Molly gets up at six. She starts talking as soon as her eyes open and pauses only when she's eating. I hug her too close and she laughs and says I'm needy like the cat. I don't let go though I tell her I love her and when she says it back everything feels a little bit brighter.

Acknowledgements

Firstly, thanks to my agent Jo Hayes at The Blair Partnership, my editor at Orion, Francesca Pathak, and assistant editor, Bethan Jones, for making this book better than I could alone. Thanks to Orion for publishing me and all that entails.

I have always read a lot, a laughable understatement. I don't suppose I would do this if I didn't. So a massive thanks to all the writers who can tell a good tale, and the readers who keep them going.

Thanks also to my mum, Kathy, and Diane for keeping a well-stocked bookshelf during my formative years. Mum, also thanks for reading me not just the classics, but some weirder stuff too. To my dad, Tom, for endless trips to Dillons and Waterstones, and a library card.

To my sons, Elliot and Eddie, who make me a better person in all kinds of ways.

Rachel for being there always. Madison for being the fiercest girl I know and letting me nick your name.

Kay for reading, support, pep-talks, encouragement and just being, great, and lovely you.

Gemma for taking me through a different kind of book, one that changed my life. I'm glad we trudge together.

Wise-women, Gillian, Val and Edel for the support, advice

and all the many chats. Val, Edel, Shan, Brenda, and Sharon, also a huge thanks for reading this in its early version.

Graham for Wednesday morning musings and coffee. My weeks suffer when these are missed.

Another great woman, who doesn't wish to be named, for giving me valuable info on the police and how investigations work, and for bearing with me when I forgot to bring a pad. Thanks to Grant Parker for some advice on family law.

A huge gratitude to all friends of Bill W. We must be in the millions and I'd be screwed without you.

When I started to write Madison (a grumpy metaller who swears incessantly), I realised the person she is most like in temperament is my husband, Andrew. So as well as the pedantic editing, the support, the laughs, and the love, thanks for the inspiration too, my mew.